FACING DEATH

THE HERO OF THE VAUGHAN PIT

A Tale Of The Coal Mines

By

G. A. Henty

About G. A. Henty

George Alfred Hent was born in Trumpington, near Cambridge but spent some of his childhood in Canterbury. He was a sickly child who had to spend long periods in bed. During his frequent illnesses he became an avid reader and developed a wide range of interests which he carried into adulthood. He attended Westminster School, London, as a half-boarder when he was fourteen, :2 and later Gonville and Caius College, Cambridge, where he was a keen sportsman.

He left the university early without completing his degree to volunteer for the (Army) Hospital Commissariat of the Purveyors Department when the Crimean War began. He was sent to the Crimea and while there he witnessed the appalling conditions under which the British soldier had to fight. His letters home were filled with vivid descriptions of what he saw. His father was impressed by his letters and sent them to the Morning Advertiser newspaper which printed them. This initial writing success was a factor in Henty's later decision to accept the offer to become a special correspondent, the early name for journalists now better known as war correspondents.

Facing death

Shortly before resigning from the army as a captain in 1859 he married Elizabeth Finucane. The couple had four children. Elizabeth died in 1865 after a long illness and shortly after her death Henty began writing articles for the Standard newspaper. In 1866 the newspaper sent him as their special correspondent to report on the Austro-Italian War where he met Giuseppe Garibaldi. He went on to cover the 1868 British punitive expedition to Abyssinia, the Franco-Prussian War, the Ashanti War, the Carlist Rebellion in Spain and the Turco-Serbian War. He also witnessed the opening of the Suez Canal and travelled to Palestine, Russia and India.

Henty was a strong supporter of the British Empire all his life; according to literary critic Kathryn Castle: "Henty ... exemplified the ethos of the [British Empire], and glorified in its successes". Henty's ideas about politics were influenced by writers such as Sir Charles Dilke and Thomas Carlyle.

Henty once related in an interview how his storytelling skills grew out of tales told after dinner to his children. He wrote his first children's book, Out on the Pampas in 1868, naming the book's main characters after his children. The book was published by Griffith and Farran in November 1870 with a title page date of 1871. While most of the 122 books he wrote were for children and published by Blackie and Son of London, he also wrote adult novels, non-fiction such as The March to Magdala and Those Other Animals, short stories for the likes of The Boy's Own Paper and edited the Union Jack, a weekly boy's magazine.

Henty was "the most popular Boy's author of his day." Blackie, who published his children's fiction in the UK, and W. G. Blackie estimated in February 1952 that they were producing about 150,000 Henty books a year at the height of his popularity, and stated that their records showed they had produced over three and a half million Henty books. He further estimated that considering the US and other overseas authorised and pirated editions, a total of 25 million was not impossible. Arnold notes this estimate and that there have been further editions since that estimate was made.

Facing death

His children's novels typically revolved around a boy or young man living in troubled times. These ranged from the Punic War to more recent conflicts such as the Napoleonic Wars or the American Civil War. Henty's heroes – which occasionally included young ladies – are uniformly intelligent, courageous, honest and resourceful with plenty of 'pluck' yet are also modest. These themes have made Henty's novels popular today among many conservative Christians and homeschoolers.

Henty usually researched his novels by ordering several books on the subject he was writing on from libraries, and consulting them before beginning writing. Some of his books were written about events (such as the Crimean War) that he witnessed himself; hence, these books are written with greater detail as Henty drew upon his first-hand experiences of people, places, and events.

On 16 November 1902, Henty died aboard his yacht in Weymouth Harbour, Dorset, leaving unfinished his last novel, By Conduct and Courage, which was completed by his son Captain C.G. Henty.

Henty is buried in Brompton Cemetery, London.

Henty wrote 122 works of historical fiction and all first editions had the date printed at the foot of the title page.[15] Several short stories published in book form are included in this total, with the stories taken from previously published full-length novels. The dates given below are those printed at the foot of the title page of the very first editions in the United Kingdom. It is a common misconception that American Henty titles were published before those of the UK. All Henty titles bar one were published in the UK before those of America.

The simple explanation for this error of judgement is that Charles Scribner's Sons of New York dated their Henty first editions for the current year. The first UK editions published by Blackie were always dated for the coming year, to have them looking fresh for Christmas. The only Henty title published in book form in America before the UK book was In the Hands of the Cave-Dwellers dated 1900 and published by Harper of New York. This title was published in book form in the UK in 1903, although the story itself had already been published in England prior to the first American edition, in The Boy's Own Annual.

LITERARY CRITIQUES

George Alfred Henty (1832–1902) was a British novelist and writer known for his historical adventure stories for children and young adults. His works often combined fictional characters with real historical events, aiming to educate young readers about history while also providing entertaining narratives. Henty's writing style and themes have been the subject of various literary critiques over the years. Here are some common points made by critics:

Formulaic Structure: One common critique of Henty's works is that they tend to follow a formulaic structure. Many of his novels share similar plotlines, where a young British protagonist overcomes challenges, exhibits moral values, and plays a significant role in historical events. Critics argue that this predictable structure might make his stories less engaging for older or more experienced readers.

Simplistic Characterization: Some critics have noted that Henty's characters can be rather one-dimensional, often falling into stereotypical roles. The heroes are typically brave, resourceful, and morally upright, while the villains are often portrayed as scheming and unscrupulous. This lack of complexity in character development can limit the emotional depth of the stories.

Colonial and Imperialist Views: Henty's works are reflective of the time period in which he lived, which saw the height of the British Empire's power and influence. Some critics argue that his novels promote colonial and imperialist viewpoints, as they often depict British characters as heroic figures bringing civilization to "uncivilized" regions. This portrayal can be seen as ethnocentric and insensitive to the experiences and perspectives of other cultures.

Educational Value: Henty's novels have been praised for their educational value, as they introduce readers to historical events and periods that might not be covered in traditional history textbooks. However, critics have pointed out that his narratives sometimes prioritize historical accuracy at the expense of engaging storytelling, resulting in passages that read more like history lessons than compelling fiction.

Language and Style: Henty's writing style can be considered somewhat dated by modern standards. His prose tends to be formal and descriptive, which might not resonate with contemporary readers, especially younger ones. Some critics argue that the language could create a barrier for readers seeking fast-paced and accessible narratives.

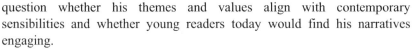

Relevance to Modern Readers: Another point of critique is the relevance of Henty's works to modern readers. While his stories offer insights into historical contexts, some critics question whether his themes and values align with contemporary sensibilities and whether young readers today would find his narratives engaging.

Limited Diversity: Henty's works often lack diverse representation, both in terms of characters and perspectives. Critics have noted that his novels predominantly focus on white, male British protagonists, which can limit the inclusivity and relatability of his stories for a broader readership.

In summary, while George Alfred Henty's historical adventure novels have been cherished by many readers over the years for their educational content and engaging narratives, they have also faced criticism for their formulaic structure, simplistic characterization, colonial viewpoints, and limited relevance to modern audiences. It's important to approach his works with an understanding of the historical context in which they were written and to consider these critiques alongside their literary merits.

CONTENTS

Facing death

CHAPTER I.

EVIL TIDINGS.

Arow of brick-built houses with slate roofs, at the edge of a large mining village in Staffordshire. The houses are dingy and colourless, and without relief of any kind. So are those in the next row, so in the street beyond, and throughout the whole village. There is a dreary monotony about the place; and if some giant could come and pick up all the rows of houses, and change their places one with another, it is a question whether the men, now away at work, would notice any difference whatever until they entered the houses standing in the place of those which they had left in the morning. There is a church, and a vicarage half hidden away in the trees in its pretty old-fashioned garden; there are two or three small red-bricked dissenting chapels, and the doctor's house, with a bright brass knocker and plate on the door. There are no other buildings above the common average of mining villages; and it needs not the high chimneys, and engine-houses with winding gear, dotting the surrounding country, to notify the fact that Stokebridge is a mining village.

It is a little past noon, and many of the women come to their doors and look curiously after a miner, who, in his working clothes, and black with coal-dust, walks rapidly towards his house, with his head bent down, and his thick felt hat slouched over his eyes.

"It's Bill Haden; he works at the 'Vaughan.'"

"What brings he up at this hour?"

"Summat wrong, I'll be bound."

Bill Haden stopped at the door of his house in the row first spoken of, lifted the latch, and went in. He walked along a narrow passage into the back-room. His wife, who was standing at the washing-tub, turned round with a surprised exclamation, and a bull-dog with half-a-dozen round tumbling puppies scrambled out of a basket by the fire, and rushed to greet him.

"What is it, Bill? what's brought thee home before time?"

Facing death

For a moment Bill Haden did not answer, but stooped, and, as it were mechanically, lifted the dog and stroked its head.

"There's blood on thy hands, Bill. What be wrong with 'ee?"

"It bain't none of mine, lass," the man said in an unsteady voice. "It be Jack's. He be gone."

"Not Jack Simpson?"

"Ay, Jack Simpson; the mate I ha' worked with ever since we were butties together. A fall just came as we worked side by side in the stall, and it broke his neck, and he's dead."

The woman dropped into a chair, threw her apron over her head, and cried aloud, partly at the loss of her husband's mate, partly at the thought of the narrow escape he had himself had.

"Now, lass," her husband said, "there be no time to lose. It be for thee to go and break it to his wife. I ha' come straight on, a purpose. I thawt to do it, but I feel like a gal myself, and it had best be told her by another woman."

Jane Haden took her apron from her face.

"Oh, Bill, how can I do it, and she ill, and with a two-month baby? I misdoubt me it will kill her."

"Thou'st got to do it," Bill said doggedly, "and thou'd best be quick about it; it won't be many minutes afore they bring him in."

When Bill spoke in that way his wife knew, as he said, that she'd got to do it, and without a word she rose and went out, while her husband stood staring into the fire, and still patting the bull-dog in his arms. A tear falling on his hand startled him. He dropped the dog and gave it a kick, passed his sleeve across his eyes, and said angrily:

"Blest if I bain't a crying like a gal. Who'd a thawt it? Well, well, poor old Jack! he was a good mate too"—and Bill Haden proceeded to light his pipe.

Slowly and reluctantly Mrs. Haden passed along the row. The sad errand on which she was going was one that has often to be discharged in a large colliery village. The women who had seen Bill go in were still at their doors, and had been joined by others. The news that he had come in at this unusual hour had passed about quickly, and there was a general feeling of uneasiness among the women, all of whom had husbands or relatives below ground. When, therefore, Jane Haden came out with signs of tears on her cheeks, her neighbours on either side at once assailed her with questions.

"Jack Simpson's killed by a fall," she said, "and I ha' got to break it to his wife."

Rapidly the news spread along the row, from door to door, and from group to group. The first feeling was everywhere one of relief that it was not their turn this time; then there was a chorus of pity for the widow. "It will go hard with her," was the general verdict. Then the little groups broke up, and went back to their work of getting ready for the return of their husbands from the pit at two o'clock. One or two only, of those most intimate with the Simpsons, followed Jane Haden slowly down the street to the door of their house, and took up a position a short distance off, talking quietly together, in case they might be wanted, and with the intention of going in after the news was broken, to help comfort the widow, and to make what preparations were needed for the last incoming of the late master of the house. It was but a minute or two that they had to pause, for the door opened again, and Jane Haden beckoned them to come in.

It had, as the gossips had predicted, gone hard with the young widow. She was sitting before the fire when Jane entered, working, and rocking the cradle beside with her foot. At the sight of her visitor's pale face, and tear-stained cheeks, and quivering lips, she had dropped her work and stood up, with a terrible presentiment of evil—with that dread which is never altogether absent from the mind of a collier's wife. She did not speak, but stood with wide-open eyes staring at her visitor.

"Mary, my poor girl," Mrs. Haden began.

That was enough, the whole truth burst upon her.

"He is killed?" she gasped.

Mrs. Haden gave no answer in words, but her face was sufficient as she made a step forward towards the slight figure which swayed unsteadily before her. Mary Simpson made no sound save a gasping sob, her hand went to her heart, and then she fell in a heap on the ground, before Mrs. Haden, prepared as she was, had time to clasp her.

"Thank God," Jane Haden said, as she went to the front door and beckoned the others in, "she has fainted."

"Ay, I thawt as much," one of the women said, "and a good job too. It's always best so till he is brought home, and things are straightened up."

11

Facing death

Between them Mary Simpson was tenderly lifted, and carried upstairs and laid on the bed of a lodger's room there. The cradle was brought up and put beside it, and then Jane Haden took her seat by the bed, one woman went for the doctor, while the others prepared the room below. In a short time all that remained of Jack Simpson was borne home on a stretcher, on the shoulders of six of his fellow-workmen, and laid in the darkened room. The doctor came and went for the next two days, and then his visits ceased.

It had gone hard with Mary Simpson. She had passed from one long fainting fit into another, until at last she lay as quiet as did Jack below; and the doctor, murmuring "A weak heart, poor little woman; the shock was too much for her," took his departure for the last time from the house. Then Jane Haden, who had not left her friend's side ever since she was carried upstairs, wrapped the baby in a shawl and went home, a neighbour carrying the cradle.

When Bill Haden returned from work he found the room done up, the table laid for tea, and the kettle on the fire. His wife was sitting by it with the baby on her lap.

"Well, lass," he said, as he entered the room, "so the poor gal's gone. I heard it as I came along. Thou'st's had a hard two days on't. Hulloa! what's that?"

"It's the baby, Bill," his wife said.

"What hast brought un here for?" he asked roughly.

Jane Haden did not answer directly, but standing in front of her husband, removed the handkerchief which covered the baby's face as he lay on her arm.

"Look at him, Bill; he's something like Jack, don't thou see it?"

"Not a bit of it," he said gruffly. "Kids don't take after their father, as pups do."

"I can see the likeness quite plain, Bill. Now," she went on, laying her hand on his shoulder, "I want to keep him. We ain't got none of our own, Bill, and I can't abear the thought of his going to the House."

Bill Haden stood irresolute.

"I shouldn't like to think of Jack's kid in the House; still he'll be a heap of trouble—worse nor a dozen pups, and no chance of winning a prize with him nohow, or of selling him, or swopping him if his points don't turn out right. Still, lass, the trouble will be thine, and by the time he's ten he'll begin to earn his grub in the pit; so if thy mind be set on't, there's 'n end o' the matter. Now let's have tea; I ain't had a meal fit for a dog for the last two days, and Juno ain't got her milk regular."

So little Jack Simpson became a member of the Haden family, and his father and mother were laid to rest in the burying-ground on the hillside above the village.

CHAPTER II.

BULL-DOG.

Acurious group as they sit staring into the fire. Juno and Juno's daughter Bess, brindles both, with their underhanging lower jaws, and their black noses and wrinkled faces, and Jack Simpson, now six years old, sitting between them, as grave and as immovable as his supporters. One dog is on either side of him and his arms are thrown round their broad backs. Mrs. Haden is laying the table for her husband's return; she glances occasionally at the quiet group in front of the fire, and mutters to herself: "I never did see such a child in all my born days."

Presently a sudden and simultaneous pricking of the closely-cropped ears of Juno and Bess proclaim that among the many footsteps outside they have detected the tread of their master.

Jack accepts the intimation and struggles up to his feet just as Bill Haden lifts the latch and enters.

"It's a fine day, Bill," his wife said.

"Be it?" the collier replied in return. "I took no note o't. However it doant rain, and that's all I cares for. And how's the dogs? Did you give Juno that physic ball I got for her?"

"It's no manner of use, Bill, leaving they messes wi' me. I ha' tould you so scores o' times. She woant take it from me. She sets her jaws that fast that horses could na pull 'em apart, and all the while I'm trying she keeps oop a growl like t' organ at the church. She's a' right wi'out the physic, and well nigh pinned Mrs. Brice when she came in to-day to borrow a flatiron. She was that frighted she skirled out and well nigh fainted off. I had to send Jack round to the "Chequers" for two o' gin before she came round."

"Mrs. Brice is a fool and you're another," Bill said. "Now, ooman, just take off my boots for oim main tired. What be you staring at, Jack? Were you nearly pinning Mother Brice too?"

"I doant pin folk, I doant," Jack said sturdily. "I kicks 'em, I do, but I caught hold o' Juno's tail, and held on. And look 'ee here, dad, I've been a thinking, doant 'ee lift I oop by my ears no more, not yet. They are boath main sore. I doant believe neither Juno nor Bess would stand bein lifted oop by their ears, not if they were sore. I be game enough, I be, but till my ears be well you must try some other part. I expect the cheek would hurt just as bad, so you can try that."

"I do wish, Bill, you would not try these tricks on the boy. He's game enough, and if you'd ha' seen him fighting to-day with Mrs. Jackson's Bill, nigh twice as big as himself, you'd ha' said so too; but it ain't Christian-like to try children the same way as pups, and really his ears are sore, awful sore. I chanced t' notice 'em when I washed his face afore he went to school, and they be main bad, I tell 'ee."

"Coom here," the miner said to Jack. "Aye, they be sore surely; why didn't 'ee speak afore, Jack? I doant want to hurt 'ee, lad."

"I wa'n't going to speak," Jack said. "Mother found it out, and said she'd tell 'ee o't; but the last two nights I were well nigh yelping when 'ee took me up."

"You're a good plucked 'un, Jack," Bill Haden said, "and I owt not t' ha done it, but I didn't think it hurt 'ee, leastways not more nor a boy owt to be hurt, to try if 'ee be game!"

"And what's you and t' dogs been doing to-day, Jack?" the miner asked, as he began at his dinner.

"We went for a walk, dad, after school, out in the lanes; we saw a big black cat, and t' dogs chased her into a tree, then we got 't a pond, and d'ye know, dad, Bess went in and swam about, she did!"

"She did?" the miner said sharply. "Coom here, Bess;" and leaving his meal, he began anxiously to examine the bull-dog's eyes and listened attentively to her breathing. "That were a rum start for a bull too, Jack. She doant seem to ha' taken no harm, but maybe it ain't showed itself. Mother, you give her some hot grub t' night. Doant you let her go in t' water again, Jack. What on airth made her tak it into her head to go into t' water noo, I wonder?"

"I can't help it if she wants to," Jack said; "she doant mind I, not when she doant want to mind. I welted her t'other day when she wanted to go a't parson's coo, but she got hold o' t' stick and pulled it out o' my hand."

"And quite raight too," Bill Haden said; "don't 'ee try to welt they dogs, or I'll welt thee!"

Facing death

"I doant care," the child said sturdily; "if I goes out in charge o' they dogs, theys got to mind me, and how can I make 'em mind me if I doant welt 'em? What would 'ee say to I if Bess got had up afore the court for pinning t' parson's coo?"

As no ready reply occurred to Bill Haden to this question he returned to his meal. Juno and Bess watched him gravely till he had finished, and then, having each received a lump of meat put carefully aside for them, returned to the fire. Jack, curling himself up beside them, lay with his head on Juno's body and slept till Mrs. Haden, having cleared the table and washed up the things, sent him out to play, her husband having at the conclusion of his meal lighted his pipe and strolled over to the "Chequers."

Bill Haden had, according to his lights, been a good father to the child of his old mate Simpson. He treated him just as if he had been his own. He spent twopence a day less in beer than before, and gave his wife fourteen pence in addition to her weekly money for household expenses, for milk for the kid, just as he allowed twopence a day each for bones for Juno and Bess. He also when requested by his wife handed over what sum was required for clothing and shoes, not without grumbling, however, and comparisons as to the wants of dorgs and boys, eminently unfavourable to the latter. The weekly twopence for schooling Mrs. Haden had, during the year that Jack had been at school, paid out of her housekeeping money, knowing that the expenses of the dogs afforded no precedent whatever for such a charge.

Bill Haden was, however, liberal to the boy in many ways, and when in a good temper would often bestow such halfpence as he might have in his pocket upon him, and now and then taking him with him into town, returned with such clothes and shoes that "mother" held up her hands at the extravagance.

Among his young companions Jack was liked but feared. When he had money he would purchase bull's-eyes, and collecting all his acquaintances, distribute them among them; but he was somewhat sedate and old-fashioned in his ways, from his close friendships with such thoughtful and meditative animals as Juno and Bess, and when his wrath was excited he was terrible. Never uttering a cry, however much hurt, he would fight with an obstinacy and determination which generally ended by giving him the victory, for if he once got hold of an antagonist's hair—pinning coming to him naturally—no amount of blows or ill-treatment could force him to leave go until his agonized opponent confessed himself vanquished.

It was not often, however, that Jack came in contact with the children of his own age. His duties as guardian of the "dorgs" absorbed the greater part of his time, and as one or both of these animals generally accompanied him when he went beyond the door, few cared about having anything to say to him when so attended; for the guardianship was by no means entirely on his side, and however excellent their qualities and pure their breed, neither Juno nor Bess were animals with whom strangers would have ventured upon familiarity.

Jack's reports to his "dad" of Bess's inclination to attack t' parson's coo was not without effect, although Bill Haden had made no remark at the time. That night, however, he observed to his wife: "I've been a thinking it over, Jane, and I be come to the opinion that it's better t' boy should not go out any more wi' t' dorgs. Let 'em bide at home, I'll take 'em oot when they need it. If Bess takes it into her head to pin a coo there might be trouble, an I doan't want trouble. Her last litter o' pups brought me a ten pun note, and if they had her oop at 'a court and swore her life away as a savage brute, which she ain't no way, it would pretty nigh break my heart."

The execution of this, as of many other good intentions, however, was postponed until an event happened which led to Jack's being definitely relieved of the care of his canine friends.

Two years had passed, when one morning Jack was calmly strolling along the road accompanied by Juno and Bess. A gig came rapidly along containing two young bagmen, as commercial travellers were still called in Stokebridge. The driver, seeing a child with two dogs, conceived that this was a favourable opportunity for a display of that sense of playful humour whose point lies in the infliction of pain on others, without any danger of personal consequences to the inflictor.

With a sharp sweep he brought down his whip across Jack's back, managing to include Bess in the stroke.

Jack set up a shout of mingled pain and indignation, and stooping for a stone, hurled it after the man who had struck him. Bess's response to the assault upon her was silent, but as prompt and far more effectual. With two springs she was beside the horse, and leaping up caught it by the nostrils and dragged it to the ground.

Juno at once joined in the fray, and made desperate attempts to climb into the gig and seize its inmates, who had nearly been thrown out as the horse fell.

Recovering himself, the driver, pale with terror, clubbed his whip, and struck at Juno with the butt-end.

"Don't 'ee hit her," Jack cried as he arrived on the spot; "if thou dost she'll tear 'ee limb from limb."

Facing death

"Call the brute off, you little rascal," cried the other, "it's killing the horse."

"Thou'd best keep a civil tongue in thy head," the child said coolly, "or it will be bad for 'ee. What did 'ee hit I and Bess for? It would serve 'ee roight if she had pinned 'ee instead o' t' horse."

"Call them off," the fellow shouted as Juno's teeth met in close proximity to his leg.

"It be all very well to say call 'em orf," Jack said, "but they doan't moind I much. Have 'ee got a strap?"

The man hastily threw down a strap, and this Jack passed through Juno's collar, she being too absorbed in her efforts to climb into the gig to heed what the child was doing; then he buckled it to the wheel.

"Noo," he said, "ye can light down t' other side. She caan't reach 'ee there."

The young men leapt down, and ran to the head of the horse; the poor brute was making frantic efforts to rise, but the bull-dog held him down with her whole might.

Jack shouted and pulled, but in vain; Bess paid no attention to his voice.

"Can you bite his tail?" one of the frightened men said; "I've heard that is good."

"Boite her tail!" Jack said in contempt; "doan't yer see she's a full-bred un; ye moight boite her tail off, and she would care nowt about 't. I've got summat here that may do."

He drew out a twisted paper from his pocket.

"This is snuff," he said; "if owt will make her loose, this will. Now one o' yer take holt by her collar on each side, and hoult tight, yer know, or she'll pin ye when she leaves go o' the horse. Then when she sneezes you pull her orf, and hoult fast."

The fear of the men that the horse would be killed overpowered their dread of the dog, and each took a firm grip upon its collar. Then Jack placed a large pinch of snuff to its nostrils. A minute later it took effect, the iron jaws unclosed with a snap, and in an instant Bess was snatched away from the horse, which, delivered from its terrible foe, sank back groaning on the road. Bess made the most furious attempts to free herself from her captors, but in vain, and Juno strained desperately at the strap to come to the assistance of her offspring.

"Ha' ye got another strap?" Jack asked.

"There's a chain in the box under the seat."

Jack with some difficulty and an amount of deliberation for which the men could gladly have slain him, climbed up into the gig, and presently came back with the chain.

"Noo tak' her round to t' other side o' gig," he said; "we'll fasten her just as Juno is."

When Bess was securely chained to the wheel the men ran to raise the horse, who lay with its head in a pool of blood.

"There's a pond in yon field," Jack said, "if 'ee wants water."

After Bess was secured Jack had slipped round to Juno, and kept his hand upon the buckle in readiness to loose her should any attempt be made upon his personal safety. The men, however, were for the moment too scared to think of him. It was some time before the horse was got on to its legs, with a wet cloth wrapped round its bleeding wound. Fortunately Bess's grip had included the bit-strap as well as the nostrils, and this had somewhat lessened the serious nature of the hurt.

Jack had by this time pacified the dogs, and when the men looked round, after getting the horse on to its legs, they were alarmed to see him standing by quietly holding the dogs by a strap passing through their collar.

"Doan't 'ee try to get into that ere cart," he said; "you've got to go wi' me back to Stokebridge to t' lock-oop for hitting I and Bess. Now do you walk quietly back and lead t' horse, and oi'll walk beside 'ee, and if thou mov'st, or tries to get away, oi'll slip t' dogs, you see if I doan't."

"You little villain," began one of the men furiously, but a deep growl from Bess in reply to the angry tone at once silenced him; and burning with rage they turned the horse's head back towards the village and walked on, accompanied by Jack and his dogs on guard.

The arrival of this procession created much excitement, and a crowd of women and children soon gathered. Jack, however, serenely indifferent to questions and shouts, proceeded coolly on his way until he arrived at the residence of the local constable, who, hearing the din, appeared at his door.

Facing death

"Maister Johnson," the child says, "I give them chaps in charge for saulting I and Bess."

"And we give this little ruffian in charge," shouted the men, secure that, in face of the constable and crowd, Jack could not loose his terrible bull-dogs, "for setting his dogs at us, to the risk of our lives and the injury of our horse, which is so much hurt that we believe it will have to be killed."

Just at this moment Bill Haden—who had returned from work at the moment that a boy running in reported that there was a row, that a horse was covered wi' blood, and two chaps all bluidy over t' hands and clothes, were agoing along wi' Jack and t' dorgs oop street to lock-oop—arrived upon the spot.

"What's oop, lad?" he asked as he came up.

"They chaps hit I and Bess, dad, and Bess pinned t' horse, and Juno would ha' pinned 'em boath hadn't I strapped she oop, and then we got Bess orf, and I brought 'em back to t' lock-oop."

"How dar 'ee hit my lad?" Bill Haden said angrily, stepping forward threateningly.

"Look oot, dad, or t' dogs will be at 'em again," Jack shouted.

Bill seized the strap from the child's hand, and with a stern word silenced the dogs.

"Well," the constable said, "I can't do nowt but bring both parties afore Mr. Brook i' the morning. I suppose I needn't lock 'ee all oop. Bill, will you bind yourself to produce Jack Simpson t'morrow?"

"Ay," said Bill, "oi'll produce him, and he'll produce hisself, I'm thinking; seems to me as Jack be able to take 's own part."

This sally was received with laughter and applause, for local feeling was very strong in Stokebridge, and a storm of jeers and rough chaff were poured upon the bagmen for having been brought in prisoners by a child.

"Thee'd best get away to th' inn," the constable said, "else they'll be a stoaning thee next. There be only two on us here, and if they takes to 't we sha'n't be able to do much."

So the men, leading their horse, went off to the Inn, groaned and hooted at by the crowd on the way. On their arrival a messenger was at once sent off for a veterinary surgeon who resided some four miles away.

Facing death

On the following morning the parties to the quarrel, the two bagmen and the injured horse on the one hand, and Jack Simpson with the two bulldogs under charge of Bill Haden on the other, appeared before Mr. Brook, owner of the Vaughan pit and a county magistrate.

Jack first gave his account of the transaction, clearly and with much decision.

"I war a walking along quiet wi' t' dogs," he said, "when I hears a cart a coming from Stokebridge. I looks round and seed they two chaps, but didn't mind no further about it till as they came oop that sandy-haired chap as was a driving lets me and Bess ha' one which made me joomp, I can tell 'ee. Bess she pinned the horse, and Juno she tried to get into t' cart at 'em. They were joost frighted, they hollers, and yawps, and looks as white as may be. I fastens Juno oop wi' a strap and they houlds Bess while I poot some snoof t' her nose."

"Put what?" Mr. Brook asked.

"Joost a pinch of snoof, sir. I heard feyther say as snoof would make dogs loose, and so I bought a haporth and carried it in my pocket, for th' dogs don't moind oi when they are put oot. And then they gets horse oop and I makes 'em come back to t' lock-oop, but maister Johnson," he said, looking reproachfully at the constable, "wouldn't lock 'em oop as I wanted him."

There was some laughter among the audience, and even the magistrate smiled. The young men then gave their story. They denied point blank that either of them had struck Jack, and described him as having set his dog purposely on the horse. Jack had loudly contradicted them, shouting, 'That's a lee;' but had been ordered to silence. Then drawing back he slipped off his jacket and shirt, and when the evidence was closed he marched forward up to the magistrate bare to the waist.

"Look at moi back," he said; "that 'ull speak for itself."

It did; there was a red weal across the shoulder, and an angry hiss ran through the court at the prisoners, which was with difficulty suppressed.

"After what I have seen," Mr. Brook said, "there is no doubt whatever in my mind that the version given by this child is the correct one, and that you committed a cowardly and unprovoked assault upon him. For this you," he said to the man who had driven the horse, "are fined £5 or a month's imprisonment. It is a good thing that cowardly fellows like you should be punished occasionally, and had it not been that your horse had been severely injured I should have committed you to prison without option of a fine.

Facing death

Against you," he said to the other, "there is no evidence of assault. The charge against the child is dismissed, but it is for the father to consider whether he will prosecute you for perjury. At the same time I think that dogs of this powerful and ferocious kind ought not to be allowed to go out under the charge of a child like this."

The man paid the fine; but so great was the indignation of the crowd that the constable had to escort them to the railway-station; in spite of this they were so pelted and hustled on the way that they were miserable figures indeed when they arrived there.

And so Jack was released from all charge of the "dorgs," and benefited by the change. New friendships for children of his own age took the place of that for the dogs, and he soon took part in their games, and, from the energy and violence with which, when once excited, he threw himself into them, became quite a popular leader. Mrs. Haden rejoiced over the change; for he was now far more lively and more like other children than he had been, although still generally silent except when addressed by her and drawn into talk. He was as fond as ever of the dogs, but that fondness was now a part only instead of the dominating passion of his existence. And so months after months went on and no event of importance occurred to alter the current of Jack Simpson's life.

CHAPTER III.

THE RESOLUTION.

An artist sitting in the shade under a tree, painting a bit of rustic gate and a lane bright with many honeysuckles. Presently he is conscious of a movement behind him, and looking round, sees a sturdily built boy of some ten years of age, with an old bull-dog lying at his feet, and another standing by his side, watching him.

"Well, lad, what are you doing?"

"Nowt!" said the boy promptly.

"I mean," the artist said with a smile, "have you anything to do? if not, I will give you sixpence to sit still on that gate for a quarter of an hour. I want a figure."

The boy nodded, took his seat without a word, and remained perfectly quiet while the artist sketched him in.

"That will do for the present," the artist said. "You can come and sit down here and look at me at work if you like; but if you have nothing to do for an hour, don't go away, as I shall want you again presently. Here is the sixpence; you will have another if you'll wait. What's your name?" he went on, as the boy threw himself down on the grass, with his head propped up on his elbows.

"Bull-dog," the lad said promptly; and then colouring up, added "at least they call me Bull-dog, but my right name be Jack Simpson."

"And why do they call you Bull-dog, Jack?"

The artist had a sympathetic voice and spoke in tones of interest, and the lad answered frankly:

"Mother—that is, my real mother—she died when I were a little kid, and Juno here, she had pups at the time—not that one, she's Flora, three years old she be—and they used to pretend she suckled me. It bain't likely, be it?" he asked, as if after all he was not quite sure about it himself.

Facing death

"Schoolmaster says as how it's writ that there was once two little rum'uns, suckled by a wolf, but he can't say for sure that it's true. Mother says it's all a lie, she fed me from a bottle. But they called me Bull-dog from that, and because Juno and me always went about together; and now they call me so because," and he laughed, "I take a good lot of licking before I gives in."

"You've been to school, I suppose, Jack?"

"Yes, I've had five years schooling," the boy said carelessly.

"And do you like it?"

"I liked it well enough; I learnt pretty easy, and so 'scaped many hidings. Dad says it was cos my mother were a schoolmaster's daughter afore she married my father, and so learning's in the blood, and comes natural. But I'm done with school now, and am going down the pit next week."

"What are you going to do there? You are too young for work."

"Oh, I sha'n't have no work to do int' pit, not hard work—just to open and shut a door when the tubs go through."

"You mean the coal-waggons?"

"Ay, the tubs," the boy said. "Then in a year or two I shall get to be a butty, that ull be better pay; then I shall help dad in his stall, and at last I shall be on full wages."

"And after that?" the artist asked.

The lad looked puzzled.

"What will you look forward to after that?"

"I don't know that there's nowt else," the boy said, "except perhaps some day I might, perhaps—but it ain't likely—but I might get to be a viewer."

"But why don't you make up your mind to be something better still, Jack—a manager?"

"What!" exclaimed the boy incredulously; "a manager, like Fenton, who lives in that big house on the hill! Why, he's a gentleman."

"Jack," the artist said, stopping in his work now, and speaking very earnestly, "there is not a lad of your age in the land, brought up as a miner, or a mechanic, or an artisan, who may not, if he sets it before him, and gives his whole mind to it, end by being a rich man and a gentleman. If a lad from the first makes up his mind to three things—to work, to save, and to learn—he can rise in the world. You won't be able to save out of what you get at first, but you can learn when your work is done. You can read and study of an evening. Then when you get better wages, save something; when, at twenty-one or so, you get man's wages, live on less than half, and lay by the rest. Don't marry till you're thirty; keep away from the public-house; work, study steadily and intelligently; and by the time you are thirty you will have a thousand pounds laid by, and be fit to take a manager's place."

"Do'st mean that, sir?" the boy asked quickly.

"I do, Jack. My case is something like it. My father was a village schoolmaster. I went when about twelve years old to a pottery at Burslem. My father told me pretty well what I have told you. I determined to try hard at any rate. I worked in every spare hour to improve myself generally, and I went three evenings a week to the art school. I liked it, and the master told me if I stuck to it I might be a painter some day. I did stick to it, and at twenty could paint well enough to go into that branch of pottery. I stuck to it, and at five-and-twenty was getting as high pay as any one in Burslem, except one or two foreign artists. I am thirty now. I still paint at times on china, but I am now getting well known as an artist, and am, I hope, a gentleman."

"I'll do it," the boy said, rising slowly to his feet and coming close to the artist. "I'll do it, sir. They call me Bull-dog, and I'll stick to it."

"Very well," the artist said, holding out his hand; "that's a bargain, Jack. Now, give me your name and address; here are mine. It's the 1st of June to-day. Now perhaps it will help you a little if I write to you on the 1st of June every year; and you shall answer me, telling me how you are getting on, and whether I can in any way give you help or advice. If I don't get an answer from you, I shall suppose that you have got tired of it and have given it up."

"Don't you never go to suppose that, sir," the boy said earnestly. "If thou doesn't get an answer thou'llt know that I've been killed, as father was, in a fall or an explosion. Thank you, sir." And the boy walked quietly off, with the old bull-dog lazily waddling behind him.

"There are the makings of a man in that boy," the artist said to himself. "I wish though I had finished his figure before we began to talk about his plans for the future. I shall be very proud of that boy if he ever makes a name for himself."

That evening Jack sat on a low stool and gazed into the fire so steadily and silently that Bill Haden, albeit not given to observe his moods, asked:

Facing death

"What ail'st, lad? What be'st thinkin' o'?"

Jack's thoughts were so deep that it took him some time to shake them off and to turn upon his stool.

"Oi'm thinking o' getting larning."

"Thinking o' getting larning!" the miner repeated in astonishment, "why, 'ee be just a dun o' getting larning. 'Ee ha' been at it for the last foive year, lad, and noo thou'st going to be done wi' it and to work in the pit."

"Oi'm a going to work in the pit, dad, and oi'm a gwine to get larning too. Oi've made oop my mind, and oi'm gwine to do it."

"But bain't 'ee got larning?" the miner said. "Thou canst read and write foine, which is more nor I can do and what dost want more?"

"Oi'm a going to get larning," Jack said again, steadily repeating the formula, "and oi'm gwine soom day to be a manager."

Bill Haden stared at the boy and then burst into a fit of laughter. "Well, this bangs a'."

Mrs. Haden was as surprised but more sympathetic.

"Bless the boy, what hast got in your head now?"

Jack showed not the slightest sign of discomfiture at his father's laughter.

"I met a chap to-day," he said in answer to Mrs. Haden, "as told I that if I made up my moind to work and joost stuck to 't, I could surely make a man o' myself, and might even roise soom day to be a manager; and I'm a going to do it."

"Doant 'ee say a word to check the boy, Bill," Mrs. Haden said to her husband, as he was about to burst out into jeering remarks. "I tell 'ee, what Jack says he sticks to, and you oughter know that by this time. What the man, whos'ever he might be, said, was right, Jack," she went on, turning to the boy. "Larning is a great thing. So far you ain't showed any turn for larning, Jack, as I ever see'd, but if you get it you may raise yourself to be an overman or a viewer, though I doan't say a manager; that seems too far away altogether. If you stick to what you say you may do it, Jack. I can't help you in larning, for I ain't got none myself, but if I can help you in any other way I 'ull, and so 'ull feyther, though he does laugh a bit."

Facing death

"He be roight enough to laugh," Jack said, "for I hain't had any turn that way, I doant know as I ha' now, but I'm a going to try, and if trying can do it," he said in his steady tones, "oi'll do it. I think I ha' got some o' the bull-dog strain in me, and I'll hoult on to it as Bess would hoult on to a man's throat if she pinned him."

"I know you will, my lad," Mrs. Haden said, while her husband, lighting his pipe and turning to go out, said:

"It matters nowt to me one way or t'other, but moind, lad, larning or no larning, thou'st got to go into the pit next week and arn your living."

"Jack," Mrs. Haden said presently, "dost know, I wouldn't do nowt wi' this new fancy o' thine, not till arter thou'st a been to work i' the pit for a while; a week or two will make no differ to 'ee, and thou doan't know yet how tired ye'll be when ye coom oop nor how thou'lt long for the air and play wi' lads o' thy own age. I believe, Jack, quite believe that thou be'st in arnest on it, and I know well that when thou dost begin thou'lt stick to 't. But it were better to wait till thou know'st what 'tis thou art undertaking."

Jack felt that there was a good deal in what his mother said. "Very well, mother. 'Twant make no differ to me, but oi'll do as th' asks me."

CHAPTER IV.

THE VAUGHAN PIT.

Among the group of men and boys assembled round the mouth of the Vaughan pit on the 7th of June were two little lads, Jack Simpson and Harry Shepherd, who were to make the descent for the first time. The boys were fast friends. Harry was the taller but was slighter than Jack, and far less sturdy and strong. Both were glad that they were to go into the pit, for although the life of a gate-boy is dull and monotonous, yet in the pit villages the boys look forward to it as marking the first step in a man's life, as putting school and lessons behind, and as raising them to a position far in advance of their former associates.

Nowadays the law has stepped in, and the employment of such mere children in the mines is forbidden, but at that time it had not been changed, and if a boy was big enough to shut a door he was big enough to go into a mine.

"Dost feel skeary, Jack?" Harry asked.

"Noa," Jack said; "what be there to be skeary aboot? I bean't afeard of the dark, and they say in time 'ee get used to it, and can see pretty nigh loike a cat. There be dad a calling. Good-bye, Harry, I'll see thee to-night."

The yard of the Vaughan resembled that of other large collieries. It was a large space, black and grimy, on which lines of rails were laid down in all directions; on these stood trains of waggons, while here and there were great piles of coal. In the centre rose up a lofty scaffolding of massive beams. At the top of this was the wheel over which a strong wire rope or band ran to the winding engine close by, while from the other end hung the cage, a wooden box some six feet square. At the corner of this box were clips or runners which fitted on to the guides in the shaft and so prevented any motion of swinging or swaying. So smoothly do these cages work that, standing in one as it is lowered or drawn up, only a very slight vibration or tremor tells that you are in motion. Near the square house in which stood the winding engine was another precisely similar occupied by the pumping engine.

28

Facing death

The Vaughan was worked by a single shaft divided by a strong wooden partition into two, one of these known as the downcast shaft, that is, the shaft through which the air descends into the mine, the other the upcast, through which the current, having made its way through all the windings and turnings of the roadways below, again ascends to the surface. This system of working by a single shaft, however, is very dangerous, as, in the event of an explosion, both shafts may become involved in the disaster and there will be no means of getting at the imprisoned miners. Nowadays all well-regulated mines have two shafts, one at a distance from the other, but this was less common thirty years back, and the Vaughan, like most of its neighbours, was worked with a single shaft.

Each miner before descending went to the lamp-room and received a lighted "Davy." As almost every one is aware, the principle of this lamp, and indeed of all that have since been invented, is that flame will not pass through a close wire-gauze. The lamp is surrounded with this gauze, and although, should the air be filled with gas to an explosive point, it will ignite if it comes in contact with flame, the gauze prevents the light of the lamp from exploding the gas-charged air outside. When the air is of a very explosive character even the Davy-lamps have to be extinguished, as the heat caused by the frequent ignitions within the lamp raises the gauze to a red heat, and the gas beyond will take fire.

Jack took his place in the cage with Bill Haden and as many others as it could contain. He gave a little start as he felt a sudden sinking; the sides of the shaft seemed to shoot up all round him, wet, shining, and black. A few seconds and the light of day had vanished, and they were in darkness, save that overhead was a square blue patch of sky every moment diminishing in size.

"Be'st afeard, Jack?" Bill Haden asked, raising his lamp so as to get a sight of the boy's face.

"Noa, why should I?" Jack said; "I heard 'ee say that the ropes were new last month, so there ain't nothin to be afeard on!"

"That is the young un they call Bull-dog, ain't it, Bill?"

"Ay!" Bill Haden answered; "he's game, he is; you can't make him yelp. I've licked him till I was tired, but he never whimpered. Now then, out you go;" and as the cage stopped the men all stepped out and started for the places in which they were working.

"Coom along, Jack; the viewer told me to put you at No. 10 gate."

Facing death

It was ten minutes fast—and as Jack thought very unpleasant—walking. The sleepers on which the rails for the corves, or little waggons, were laid, were very slippery. Pools of water stood between them and often covered them, and blocks of coal of all sizes, which had shaken from the corves, lay in the road. When it was not water it was black mud. Sometimes a line of waggons full or empty stood on the rails, and to pass these they had to squeeze against the damp walls. Before he reached his post the gloss of Jack's new mining clothes had departed for ever. The white jumper was covered with black smears, and two or three falls on the slippery wooden sleepers had effectively blackened his canvas trousers.

"There, lad," Bill Haden said at length, holding his lamp high to afford a general view of the situation; "that's your place."

"The place" was a hollow like a cupboard, some five feet high, two deep, and a little wider. There was a wooden seat in it, a peg or two had been driven into the rock to hang things from, and a handful or so of hay upon the ground showed that Jack's predecessor had an idea of comfort.

"There you are, and not a bad place either, Jack. You see this cord? Now when thou hearst a team of corves coming along, pull yon end and open the door. When they have passed let go the cord and the door shuts o' 'tself, for it's got a weight and pulley. It's thy business to see that it has shut, for if a chunk of coal has happened to fall and stops the door from shutting, the ventilation goes wrong and we all goes to kingdom come in no time. That's all thou'st got to do 'cept to keep awake. Of course you woan't do that; no boy does. So that you larn to wake up when the corves come along, that ull do foine."

"But if I doan't?" Jack asked.

"Well, if thou doan't thou'lt get waked with a cuff o' th' ear by the driver, and it depends on what sort o' chap he be how hard the cuff thou'lt get. I doan't think thou'lt feel lonely here, for along that side road they bring down other corves and the horse comes and takes 'em on. On this main road the horses go through to the upper end of the mine, half a mile farther."

"How do it make a differ whether this door be open or shut, father?"

"Well, lad, the air comes up the road we ha come by. Now it's wanted to go round about by the workings on that side road. This door be put to stop it from going by the straight road, so there's nothing for it but for to go round by the workings, maybe for a mile, maybe three miles, till it gets back into the main road again. So when the door is open the ventilation is checked right round the workings; so mind doan't 'ee open the door till the horse is close to it, and shut it directly it's past."

Facing death

When the door closed behind his foster-father, and Jack Simpson remained alone in the dense darkness, a feeling of utter loneliness and desertion stole over him. The blackness was intense and absolute; a low confused murmur, the reverberation of far-off noises in the pit, sounded in his ears. He spoke, and his voice sounded muffled and dull.

"This be worse nor I looked for," the boy said to himself; "I suppose I'll get used to it, but I doan't wonder that some young uns who ain't strong as I be are badly frighted at first."

Presently the confused noise seemed to get louder, then a distinct rumble was heard, and Jack felt with delight that a train of waggons was approaching. Then he saw far along the gallery a light swinging, as the man who bore it walked ahead of the horse. The water in the little pools between the sleepers reflected it in a score of little lines of light. Now he could hear the hollow splashing sound of the horses' hoofs, and prepared to answer to the shout of "door" by pulling at the string beside him. When the light came within twenty yards it changed its direction; he heard the grating of the wheels against the points, and saw that the waggons were going up the other road. There upon a siding they came to a stop, and a minute or two later a number of full waggons were brought down by another horse. A few words were exchanged by the drivers, but Jack's ear, unaccustomed to the echoes of a mine, could not catch what they said; then the first man hitched his horse on to the full waggons, and started for the shaft, while the other with the empties went up the road to the workings.

The incident, slight as it had been, had altogether dissipated the feeling of uneasiness of which Jack had been conscious. Before, he had seemed shut out from the world, as if within a living tomb, but the sight of men engaged at their ordinary work close by him completely restored the balance of his mind, and henceforth he never felt the slightest discomfort at being alone in the dark.

A few minutes after the rumbling of the departing train of "tubs" had died in his ear, he again heard it. Again he watched the slowly approaching light, and when it came within a few yards of him he heard the expected shout of "Gate!" He replied by a shout of "All right!" and as the driver came level with him pulled the cord and the door opened.

"G'long, Smiler," the driver said, and the horse went forward. The man leaned forward and raised his lamp to Jack's face.

"I thawt 'twasn't Jim Brown's voice. Who be'st thou?"

"Jack Simpson; I live along wi' Bill Haden."

Facing death

"Ay, ay, I know'st, I knew thy father, a good sort he was too. Be'st thy first day doon the pit?"

"Ay," Jack said.

"Foind it dark and lonesome, eh? Thou'lt get used to it soon."

"How often do the corves come along?" Jack asked as the man prepared to run on after the waggons, the last of which had just passed.

"There be a set goes out every ten minutes, maybe, on this road, and every twenty minutes on the other, two o' ours to one o' theirs;" and he moved forward.

Jack let the door slam after him, went out and felt that it had shut firmly, and then resumed his seat in his niche. He whistled for a bit, and then his thoughts turned to the learning which he had determined firmly to acquire.

"I wish I'd ha' took to it afore," he said to himself. "What a sight o' time I ha' lost! I'll go over in my head all the lessons I can remember; and them as I doant know, and that's the best part, I reckon I'll look up when I get hoame. Every day what I learns fresh I'll go over down here. I shall get it perfect then, and it will pass the time away finely. I'll begin at oncet. Twice two is four;" and so Jack passed the hours of his first day in the pit, recalling his lessons, reproaching himself continually and bitterly with the time he had wasted, breaking off every ten minutes from his rehearsals to open the door for the train of corves going in empty and going out full, exchanging a few words each time with the drivers, all of whom were good-naturedly anxious to cheer up the new boy, who must, as they supposed, be feeling the loneliness of his first day in the pit keenly. Such was by no means the case with Jack, and he was quite taken by surprise when a driver said to him, "This be the last train this shift."

"Why, it bean't nigh two o'clock, surely?" he said.

"It be," the driver said; "wants ten minutes, that's all."

Soon the miners began to come along.

"Hullo, Jack!" Bill Haden's voice said. "Be'st still here. Come along of me. Why didst stop, lad? Thou canst always quit thy post when the first man comes through on his way out. Hast felt it lonely, lad?"

"Not a bit, dad."

Facing death

"That's strange too," Bill said. "Most young boys finds it awful lonely o' first. I know I thowt that first day were never coming to an end. Weren't frighted at t' dark?"

"I thought it was onnatural dark and still the first ten minutes," Jack admitted honestly; "but arter the first set o' corves came along I never thawt no more about the dark."

"Here we are at the shaft, joomp in, there's just room for you and me."

CHAPTER V.

.

SETTING TO WORK.

Aweek after Jack Simpson had gone to work in the "Vaughan" there was a knock one evening at the door of the schoolmaster of the Stokebridge National School.

"Please, Mr. Merton, can I speak to 'ee?"

"What, is that you, Jack Simpson!" the schoolmaster said, holding the candle so that its light fell upon the boy before him. "Yes, come in, my boy." The lad followed him into the parlour. "Sit down, Jack. Now what is it? Nothing the matter at home, I hope?"

"Noa, sir. I wanted to ask 'ee what books I orter read, so that I may grow up a clever man?"

"Bless me, Jack," Mr. Merton said, "why, I never expected this from you."

"Noa, sir, but I ha' made up my mind to get on, and I means to work hard. I ha' been told, sir, that if I studies at books in all my spare time, and saves my money, and works well, I may get up high some day;" and the boy looked wistfully up in the master's face for a confirmation of what had been told him.

"That's quite right, Jack, whoever told you. Hard work, study, thrift, and intelligence will take any lad from the bottom of the tree to the top. And you are quite in earnest, Jack?"

"Quite, sir."

The schoolmaster sat in silence for a little time.

"Well, my boy, for a bit you must work at ordinary school-books, and get a fair general knowledge, and be careful to observe the way things are expressed—the grammar, I mean; read aloud when you are alone, and try in speaking to get rid of "thees" and "thous," and other mistakes of speech. I can lend you ordinary school-books, fit for you for the next four or five years, and will always explain any difficulties you may meet with. The books you will want afterwards you can buy second-hand at Wolverhampton or Birmingham. But there will be time to talk about that hereafter. What time have you to study? You have gone into the Vaughan pit, have you not?"

"Yes, sir. I ha' time enough all day, for I ha' nowt to do but just to open and shut a door when the tubs come along; but I ha' no light."

"The time must seem very long in the dark all day."

"It do seem long, sir; and it will be wuss when I want to read, and know I am just wasting time. But I can read at home after work, when dad goes out. It's light now, and I could read out o' doors till nine o'clock. Mother would give me a candle now and again; and I should get on first rate in the pit, but the Vaughan is a fiery vein, and they ha' nowt but Daveys."

"Well, my boy, here are a few books, which will suit you for a time. Let me know how you are getting on; and when you have mastered the books, let me know. Remember you want to learn them thoroughly, and not just well enough to rub through without getting the strap. But don't overdo it. You are a very small boy yet, and it is of as much importance for your future life that you should grow strong in body as well as in brain. So you must not give up play. If you were to do nothing but sit in the dark, and to study at all other times, you would soon become a fool. So you must give time to play as well as to work. Remember, do not be cast down with difficulties; they will pass by if you face them. There is an old saying, 'God helps those who help themselves.' And look here, Jack, I can tell you the best way to make the time pass quickly while you are in the dark. Set yourself sums to do in your head. You will find it difficult at first, but it will come easier with practice, and as you get on I will give you a book on 'mental arithmetic,' and you will find that there is nothing more useful than being able to make complicated calculations in your head."

The next six months passed quickly with Jack Simpson. He started early with his father for the pit, and the hours there, which at first had seemed so long, slipped by rapidly as he multiplied, and added, and subtracted, finding that he could daily master longer lines of figures. Of an afternoon he played with the other pit boys, and after that worked steadily at his books till eleven o'clock, two hours after Bill Haden and his wife had gone to bed. Once a week he went in the evening to Mr. Merton, who was astonished at the progress that the boy was making, and willingly devoted an hour to explaining difficulties and helping him on with his work.

Satisfied now that the boy was in earnest, Mr. Merton a few days afterwards took occasion, when Mr. Brook, the owner of the Vaughan mine, called in on school business, to tell him how one of the pit boys was striving to educate himself.

"He is really in earnest, Merton; it is not a mere freak?"

"No, Mr. Brook, the lad will stick to it, I'm sure. He goes by the nickname of Bull-dog, and I don't think he is badly named; he has both the pluck and the tenacity of one."

"Very well, Merton; I am glad you spoke to me about it. I wish a few more boys would try and educate themselves for viewers and underground managers; it is difficult indeed to get men who are anything but working miners. I'll make a note of his name."

A few days afterwards Mr. Brook, after going through the books, went over the mine with the underground manager.

"Do the waggons often get off the metals along this road, Evans?" he asked, stopping at one of the doors which regulate the ventilation.

"Pretty often, sir; the rails are not very true, and the sleepers want renewing."

"It would be as well if there were an extra light somewhere here; it would be handy. This is Number Ten door, is it not?"

"Yes sir."

"Who is this? a new hand, is he not?" raising his lamp so as to have a full look at the lad, who was standing respectfully in the niche in the rock cut for him.

"Yes, sir; he is the son of a hand who was killed in the pit some ten years ago—Simpson."

"Ah! I remember," Mr. Brooks said. "Well, serve the boy a lamp out when he goes down of a day. You'll be careful with it, lad, and not let it fall?"

"Oh yes, sir," Jack said, in a tone of delight; "and, please, sir, may I read when I am not wanted?"

"Certainly you may," his master said; "only you must not neglect your work;" and then Mr. Brook went on, leaving Jack so overjoyed that for that afternoon at least his attempts at mental arithmetic were egregious failures.

CHAPTER VI.

"THE OLD SHAFT."

In the corner of a rough piece of ground near the "Vaughan" was situated what was known as the old shaft. It had been made many years before, with a view to working coal there. The owners of the Vaughan, which at the time was just commencing work, had, however, bought up the ground, and as it adjoined their own and could be worked in connection with it, they stopped the sinking here. This was so long ago that the rubbish which had formed a mound round the mouth of the shaft had been long covered with vegetation, and a fence placed round the pit had fallen into decay.

The shaft had been sunk some fifty fathoms, but was now full of water, to within forty feet of the surface. Some boards covered the top, and the adventurous spirits among the boys would drop stones through the openings between them, and listen to the splash as they struck the water below, or would light pieces of paper and watch them falling into the darkness, until they disappeared suddenly as they touched the water.

The winch used in the process of excavation remained, and round it was a portion of the chain so old and rusty as to be worthless for any purpose whatever. Lengths had from time to time been broken off by boys, who would unwind a portion, and then, three or four pull together until the rust-eaten links gave way; and the boys came to the ground with a crash. It was a dirty game, however, dirty even for pit boys, for the yellow rust would stick to hands and clothes and be very difficult to remove.

One Saturday afternoon a group of boys and girls of from ten to fourteen were playing in the field. Presently it was proposed to play king of the castle, or a game akin thereto, half a dozen holding the circular mound round the old pit, while the rest attacked them and endeavoured to storm the position. For some time the game went on with much shouting on the part of the boys and shrill shrieks from the girls, as they were pulled or pushed down the steep bank.

"Let us make a charge a' together," said Jack Simpson, who although not thirteen was the leader of the attacking party.

Facing death

Then heading the rush he went at full speed at the castle. Harry Shepherd, who was one of the defenders, was at the top, but Jack had so much impetus that he gained his footing and thrust Harry violently backwards.

The top of the bank was but three feet wide, and within sloped down to the mouth of the old pit shaft, fifteen feet below. Harry tottered, and to avoid falling backwards turned and with great strides ran down the bank. He was unable to arrest his course, but went through the rotten fence and on to the boarding of the shaft. There was a crash, a wild cry, and Harry disappeared from the sight of his horror-stricken companions. The rotten wood-work had given way and the boy had fallen into the old shaft.

A panic seized the players, some rushed away at the top of their speed shouting, "Harry Shepherd has fallen down the old shaft!" others stood paralysed on the top of the mound; girls screamed and cried. Two only appeared to have possession of their wits. The one was Jack Simpson, the other was a girl of about twelve, Nelly Hardy. Jack did not hesitate an instant, but quickly ran down to the shaft, Nelly more quietly, but with an earnest set face, followed him. Jack threw himself down by the edge and peered down the shaft.

"Harry, Harry," he shouted, "bee'st killed?" A sort of low cry came up.

"He be alive, he be drowning," Jack exclaimed, "quick, get off them boords."

Nelly at once attempted to aid Jack to lift the boards aside.

"Coom," Jack shouted to the boys on the top, "what bee'st feared of? Thou art shamed by this lass here. Coom along and help us."

Several of the boys hurried down, stung by Jack's taunt, and half the boards were soon pulled off.

"What bee'st goin' to do, Jack?"

"Go down, to be sure," Jack said. "Catch hold o' th' windlass."

"The chain woan't hold you, Jack."

"It maun hold me," Jack said.

"It woan't hold two, Jack."

"Lower away and hold thee jaw," Jack said; "I am going to send him up first if he be alive; lower away, I say."

Facing death

Jack caught hold of the end of the rusty chain, and the boys lowered away as rapidly as they could.

Jack held on stoutly, and continued to shout, "Hold on, Harry, I be a-coming; another minute and I'll be with 'ee."

The chain held firmly, and Jack swung downward safely.

The shaft was of considerable size, and the openings in the planks had enabled the air to circulate freely, consequently there was no bad air. As Jack reached the water he looked eagerly round, and then gave a cry of joy. Above the water he saw a hand grasping a projecting piece of rock.

Harry could not swim, but he had grasped the edge of a projecting stone near which he had fallen, and when his strength had failed, and he had sunk below the surface, his hand still retained its grasp.

"Lower away," Jack shouted, and the chain was slackened.

Jack could swim a little, just enough to cross the Stokebridge Canal where the water was only out of his depth for some fifteen feet in the middle. First he took off his handkerchief from his neck, a strong cotton birdseye, and keeping hold of the chain before him swam to the spot where the hand was above water. He had a terrible fear of its slipping and disappearing below the dark pool, and was careful to make a firm grasp at it. He was surprised to find the body was of no weight. Without a moment's delay he managed to bind the wrist fast to the chain with his handkerchief.

"Above there," he shouted.

"Ay," came down.

"Wind up very steadily, don't jerk it now." Slowly the winch revolved and the body began to rise from the water.

Jack clung to the stone which Harry had grasped and looked upwards. He wondered vaguely whether it would ever reach the top; he wondered whether the arm would pull out of the socket, and the body plump down into the water; he wondered how long he could hold on, and why his clothes seemed so heavy. He wondered whether, if his strength went before the chain came down again, his hand would hold on as Harry's had done, or whether he should go down to the bottom of the shaft. How far was it! Fifty fathoms, three hundred feet; he was fifty below the mouth, two hundred and fifty to sink; how long would his body be getting to the bottom? What would his mother and Bill Haden say? Would they ever try to get his body up?

IN THE OLD SHAFT—WILL HE BE SAVED?

He was growing very weak. As from another world he had heard the shout from above when the body of Harry Shepherd reached the brink, and afterwards some vague murmurs. Presently his fingers slipped and he went down in the black pool. The chill of the water to his face, the sudden choking sensation, brought his senses back for a moment and he struck to the surface.

There, touching the water, he saw the chain, and as he grasped it, heard the shouts of his comrades above calling to him. He was himself again now. The chain being some feet below the surface he managed to pass it round him, and to twist it in front. He was too exhausted to shout.

He saw a great piece of paper on fire fluttering down, and heard a shout as its light showed him on the end of the chain; then he felt a jar and felt himself rising from the water; after that he knew nothing more until he opened his eyes and found himself lying on the bank.

Nelly Hardy was kneeling by him and his head was in her lap. He felt various hands rubbing him and slapping the palms of his hands; his animation was quickly restored. He had swallowed but little water, and it was the close air of the shaft which had overpowered him.

"Hallo!" he said, shaking himself, "let me up, I be all right; how's Harry?"

Harry had not yet come round, though some of them, trying to restore him to consciousness, said that they had heard him breathe once. Jack as usual took the command, ordered all but two or three to stand back, told Nelly Hardy to lift Harry's head and undo his shirt, stripped him to the waist, and then set the boys to work to rub vigorously on his chest. Whether the efforts would have been successful is doubtful, but at this moment there was a sound of hurrying feet and of rapid wheels.

Those who had started at the first alarm had reached the village and told the news, and most fortunately had met the doctor as he drove in from his rounds. A man with a rope had leaped into the gig, and the doctor as he drove off had shouted that hot blankets were to be prepared.

When he reached the spot and heard that Harry had been brought to bank, he leapt out, climbed the mound, wrapped him in his coat, carried him down to his gig, and then drove back at full speed to Stokebridge, where with the aid of hot blankets and stimulants the lad was brought back to consciousness.

Jack Simpson was the hero of the hour, and the pitmen, accustomed to face death as they were, yet marvelled at a boy trusting himself to a chain which looked unfit to bear its own weight only, and into the depth of a well where the air might have been unfit to breathe.

Jack strenuously, and indeed angrily, disclaimed all credit whatever.

"I didn't think nowt about the chain, nor the air, nor the water neither. I thought only o' Harry. It was me as had pushed him down, and I'd got to bring him oop. If I hadn't a gone down Nelly Hardy would ha' gone, though she be a lass and doan't know how to swim or to hold on by a chain, or nowt; but she'd ha' gone, I tell e'e, if I hadn't; I saw it in her face. She didn't say nowt, but she was ready to go. If she hadn't gone down to th' shaft none of them would ha gone. She's a rare plucked 'un, she is, I tell e'e."

But in spite of Jack's indignant repudiation of any credit, the brave action was the talk of Stokebridge and of the neighbouring pit villages for some time. There are no men appreciate bravery more keenly than pitmen, for they themselves are ever ready to risk their lives to save those of others. Consequently a subscription, the limit of which was sixpence and the minimum a penny, was set on foot, and a fortnight later Jack was presented with a gold watch with an inscription.

This was presented in the school-room, and Mr. Brook, who presided at the meeting, added on his own account a chain to match. It needed almost force on the part of Bill Haden to compel Jack to be present on this occasion. When he was led up, flushed with confusion, to Mr. Brook, amid the cheers of the crowd of those in the room, he listened with head hung down to the remarks of his employer.

When that gentleman finished and held out the watch and chain, Jack drew back and held up his head.

"I doan't loike it, sir; I pushed Harry in, and in course I went down to pick him out; besides, Harry's my chum, he be; was it loikely I should stand by and he drowning? I tell 'ee, sir, that you ain't said a word about the lass Nelly Hardy; she had pluck, she had. The boys ran away or stood and stared, but she came down as quiet as may be. I tell 'ee, sir, her face was pale, but she was as steady and as still as a man could ha' been, and did as I told her wi'out stopping for a moment and wi'out as much as saying a word. She'd ha' gone down if I'd told her to. Where be ye, Nelly Hardy? coom oot and let me show ye to Mr. Brook."

But Nelly, who was indeed in the building, had shrunk away when Jack began to speak, and having gained the door, was on the point of flying, when she was seized and brought forward, looking shamefaced and sullen.

"That be her, sir," Jack said triumphantly, "and I say this watch and chain ought to be hers, for she did much more for a lass than I did for a boy, and had no call to do't as I had."

"I cannot give them to her, Jack," Mr. Brook said, "for the watch has been subscribed for you; but as a token of my appreciation of the bravery and presence of mind she has shown, I will myself present her with a silver watch and chain, with an inscription saying why it was given to her, and this she will, I am sure, value all her life."

Perhaps she would, but at present her only thought was to get away. Her hair was all rough, she had on a tattered dress, and had only slipped in when those in charge of the door were intent upon hearing Mr. Brook's address. Without a word of thanks, the instant the hands restraining her were loosed she dived into the crowd and escaped like a bird from a snare. Satisfied that justice had been done, Jack now said a few words of thanks to his employer and the subscribers to his present, and the meeting then broke up, Jack returning with Bill Haden and his mother, both beaming with delight.

"I be roight down glad, lad, I doan't know as I've been so glad since Juno's dam won the first prize for pure-bred bull-dogs at the Birmingham show. It seems joost the same sort o' thing, doan't it, Jane?"

CHAPTER VII.

FRIENDSHIP.

Nelly Hardy had been unfortunate in her parents, for both drank, and she had grown up without care or supervision. She had neither brother nor sister. At school she was always either at the top or bottom of her class according as a fit of diligence or idleness seized her. She was a wild passionate child, feeling bitterly the neglect with which she was treated, her ragged clothes, her unkempt appearance. She was feared and yet liked by the girls of her own age, for she was generous, always ready to do a service, and good-tempered except when excited to passion. She was fonder of joining with the boys, when they would let her, in their games, and, when angered, was ready to hold her own against them with tooth and nail.

So wild were her bursts of passion that they were sources of amusement to some of the boys, until Jack upon one occasion took her part, and fought and conquered the boy who had excited her. This was on the Saturday before the accident had taken place.

For some days after the presentation no one saw her; she kept herself shut up in the house or wandered far away.

Then she appeared suddenly before Jack Simpson and Harry Shepherd as they were out together.

"I hate you, Jack Simpson," she said, "I hate you, I hate you;" and then dashed through the gap in the hedge by which she had come.

"Well," Harry exclaimed in astonishment, "only to think!"

"It be nat'ral enough," Jack said, "and I bain't surprised one bit. I orter ha' known better. I had only to ha' joodged her by myself and I should ha' seen it. I hated being dragged forward and talked at; it was bad enough though I had been made decent and clean scrubbed all over, and got my Soonday clothes on, but of course it would be worse for a lass anyway, and she was all anyhow, not expecting it. I ought to ha' known better; I thawt only o' my own feelings and not o' hers, and I'd beg her pardon a hundred times, but 'taint likely she'd forgive me. What is she a doing now?"

44

Facing death

The lads peered through the hedge. Far across the field, on the bank, the other side, lay what looked like a bundle of clothes.

"She be a crying, I expect," Jack said remorsefully. "I do wish some big chap would a come along and give I a hiding; I wouldn't fight, or kick, or do nowt, I would just take it, it would serve me roight. I wonder whether it would do her any good to let her thrash me. If it would she'd be welcome. Look here, Harry, she bain't angry wi' you. Do thou go across to her and tell her how main sorry I be, and that I know I am a selfish brute and thought o' myself and not o' her, and say that if she likes I will cut her a stick any size she likes and let her welt me just as long as she likes wi'out saying a word."

Harry was rather loath to go on such an errand, but being imperatively ordered by Jack he, as usual, did as his comrade wished. When he approached Nelly Hardy he saw that the girl was crying bitterly, her sobs shaking her whole body.

"I be coom wi' a message," he began in a tone of apprehension, for he regarded Nelly as resembling a wild cat in her dangerous and unexpected attacks.

The girl leapt to her feet and turned her flushed tear-stained cheeks and eyes, flashing with anger through the tears, upon him.

"What dost want, Harry Shepherd? Get thee gone, or I'll tear the eyes from thy head."

"I doan't coom o' my own accord," Harry said steadily, though he recoiled a little before her fierce outburst. "I came on the part o' Jack Simpson, and I've got to gi' you his message even if you do fly at me. I've got to tell you that he be main sorry, and that he feels he were a selfish brute in a thinking o' his own feelings instead o' thine. He says he be so sorry that if 'ee like he'll cut a stick o' any size you choose and ull let you welt him as long as you like wi'out saying a word. And when Jack says a thing he means it, so if you wants to wop him, come on."

To Harry's intense surprise the girl's mood changed. She dropped on the ground again, and again began to cry.

After standing still for some time and seeing no abatement in her sobs, or any sign of her carrying out the invitation of which he had been the bearer, Jack's emissary returned to him.

"I guv her your message, Jack, and she said nowt, but there she be a crying still."

"Perhaps she didn't believe you," Jack said; "I'd best go myself."

Facing death

First, with great deliberation, Jack chose a hazel stick from the hedge and tried it critically. When fully assured that it was at once lissom and tough, and admirably adapted for his purpose, he told Harry to go on home.

"Maybe," Jack said, "she mayn't loike to use it and you a looking on. Doan't 'ee say a word to no un. If she likes to boast as she ha' welted me she ha' a roight to do so, but doan't you say nowt."

Jack walked slowly across the field till he was close to the figure on the ground. Then he quietly removed his jacket and waistcoat and laid them down. Then he said:

"Now, Nelly, I be ready for a welting, I ha' deserved it if ever a chap did, and I'll take it. Here's the stick, and he's a good un and will sting rare, I warrant."

The girl sat up and looked at him through her tears.

"Oh, Jack, and didst really think I wanted to welt thee?"

"I didn't know whether thou didst or no, Nelly, but thou said thou hate'st me, and wi' good reason, so if thou likest to welt me here's the stick."

The girl laughed through her tears. "Ah! Jack, thou must think that I am a wild cat, as John Dobson called me t'other day. Throw away that stick, Jack. I would rather a thousand times that thou laidst it on my shoulders than I on thine."

Jack threw away the stick, put on his coat and waistcoat, and sat down on the bank.

"What is it then, lass? I know I were cruel to have thee called forward, but I didn't think o't; but I had rather that thou beat me as I orter be beaten, than that thou should go on hating me."

"I doan't hate thee, Jack, though I said so; I hate myself; but I like thee better nor all, thou art so brave and good."

"No braver than thou, Nelly," Jack said earnestly; "I doan't understand why thou should first say thou hates me and then that thou doan't; but if thou are in earnest, that thou likest me, we'll be friends. I don't mean that we go for walks together, and such like, as some boys and girls do, for I ha' no time for such things, and I shouldn't like it even if I had; but I'll take thy part if anyone says owt to thee, and thou shalt tell me when thou art very bad at hoam"—for the failings of Nelly's parents were public property. "Thou shalt be a friend to me, not as a lass would be, but as Harry is, and thou woan't mind if I blow thee up, and tells 'ee of things. Thou stook to me by the side o' the shaft, and I'll stick to thee."

"I'll do that," the girl said, laying her hand in his. "I'll be thy friend if thou'lt let me, not as lasses are, but as lads."

And so the friendship was ratified, and they walked back together to the village. When he came to think it over, Jack was inclined to repent his bargain, for he feared that she would attach herself to him, and that he would have much laughter to endure, and many battles to fight. To his surprise Nelly did nothing of the sort. She would be at her door every morning as he went by to the pit and give him a nod, and again as he returned. Whenever other girls and boys were playing or sitting together, Nelly would make one of the group. If he said, as he often did say, "You, Nell Hardy come and sit by me," she came gladly, but she never claimed the place. She was ready to come or to go, to run messages and to do him good in any way.

Jack had promised she should be his friend as Harry was, and as he got to like her more he would ask her or tell her to accompany them in their walks, or to sit on a low wall in some quiet corner and talk. Harry, stirred by his friend's example, had begun to spend half an hour a day over his old school-books.

"Why dost like larning so much, Jack?" Nelly asked, as Jack was severely reproaching his friend with not having looked at a book for some days; "what good do it do?"

"It raises folk in the world, Nell, helps 'em make their way up."

"And dost thou mean to get oop i' the world?"

"Ay, lass," Jack said, "if hard work can do it, I will; but it does more nor that. If a man knows things and loves reading it makes him different like, he's got summat to think about and talk about and care for beside public-houses and dorgs. Canst read, Nell?"

"No, Jack," she said, colouring. "It bain't my fault; mother never had the pence to spare for schooling, and I was kept at hoam to help."

Jack sat thoughtful for some time.

"Wouldst like to learn?"

"Ay."

"Well, I'll teach thee."

"Oh, Jack!" and she leapt up with flashing eyes; "how good thou be'est!"

"Doan't," Jack said crossly; "what be there good in teaching a lass to spell? There's twopence, run down to the corner shop and buy a spelling-book; we'll begin at once."

And so Nelly had her first lesson.

NELLY'S FIRST LESSON.

After that, every afternoon, as Jack came home from work, the girl would meet him in a quiet corner off the general line, and for five minutes he would teach her, not hearing her say what she had learned, but telling her fresh sounds and combinations of letters. Five or six times he would go over

49

them, and expected—for Jack was tyrannical in his ways—that she would carry them away with her and learn them by heart, and go through them again and again, so that when he questioned her during their longer talks she would be perfect.

Then, the five minutes over, Jack would run on to make up for lost time, and be in as soon as Bill Haden.

But however accurately Jack expected his pupil to learn, his expectations were surpassed. The girl beyond clearing up the room had nothing to do, and she devoted herself with enthusiasm to this work. Once she had mastered simple words and felt her own progress, her shyness as to her ignorance left her. She always carried her book in her pocket, and took to asking girls the pronunciation of larger words, and begging them to read a few lines to her; and sitting on the door-step poring over her book, she would salute any passer-by with: "Please tell us what is that word." When she could read easily, which she learned to do in two or three months, she borrowed left-off school-books from the girls, and worked slowly on, and two years later had made up for all her early deficiencies, and knew as much as any of those who had passed through the school.

From the day of her compact of friendship with Jack her appearance and demeanour had been gradually changing. From the first her wild unkempt hair had been smoothly combed and braided, though none but herself knew what hours of pain and trouble it took her with a bit of a comb with three teeth alone remaining, to reduce the tangled mass of hair to order.

Her companions stared indeed with wonder on the first afternoon, when, thus transformed and with clean face, she came among them, with a new feeling of shyness.

"Why, it be Nelly Hardy!" "Why, Nell, what ha' done to t'yself? I shouldn't ha' known ye." "Well, ye be cleaned up surely."

The girl was half inclined to flame out at their greetings, but she knew that the surprise was natural, and laughed good-humouredly. She was rewarded for her pains when Jack and some other boys, passing on their way to play, Jack stopped a moment and said to her quietly, "Well done, lass, thou lookst rarely, who'd ha' thought thou wert so comely!"

As time went on Nelly Hardy grew altogether out of her old self. Sometimes, indeed, bursts of temper, such as those which had gained her the name of the "Wild Cat," would flare out, but these were very rare now. She was still very poorly dressed, for her house was as wretched as of old, but there was an attempt at tidiness. Her manner, too, was softer, and it became more and more quiet as things went on, and her playmates wondered again and again what had come over Nell Hardy; she had got to be as quiet as a mouse.

The boys at first were disposed to joke Jack upon this strange friendship, but Jack soon let it be understood that upon that subject joking was unacceptable.

"She stood by me," he said, "and I'm a-going to stand by her. She ain't got no friends, and I'm going to be her friend. She's quiet enough and doan't bother, no more nor if she were a dorg. She doan't get in no one's way, she doan't want to play, and sits quiet and looks on, so if any of you doan't like her near ye, you can go away to t' other side o' field. I wish she'd been a boy, 'twould ha' been fitter all ways, but she can't help that. She's got the sense o' one. and the pluck, and I like her. There!"

CHAPTER VIII.

PROGRESS.

"Bless me, lad, another poond o' candles! I never did hear o' sich waste," Mrs. Haden exclaimed as Jack entered the cottage on a winter's afternoon, two years and a half after he had gone into the pit. "Another poond o' candles, and it was only last Monday as you bought the last—nigh two candles a night. Thou wilt kill thyself sitting up reading o' nights, and thy eyes will sink i' thy head, and thou'lt be as blind as a bat afore thou'rt forty."

"I only read up to eleven, mother, that gives me six hours abed, and as thou know, six for a man, seven for a woman, is all that is needful; and as to the expense, as dad lets me keep all my earnings save five bob a week—and very good o' him it is; I doan't know no man in the pit as does as much— why, I ha' plenty o' money for my candles and books, and to lay by summat for a rainy day."

"Aye, aye, lad, I know thou be'st not wasteful save in candles; it's thy health I thinks o'."

"Health!" Jack laughed; "why, there ain't a lad in the pit as strong as I am of my age, and I ha' never ailed a day yet, and doan't mean to."

"What ha' ye been doing all the arternoon, Jack?"

"I ha' been sliding in the big pond wi' Harry Shepherd and a lot o' others. Then Dick Somers, he knocked down Harry's little sister Fan, as she came running across th' ice, and larfed out when she cried—a great brute— so I licked he till he couldn't see out o' his eyes."

"He's bigger nor thee, too," Mrs. Haden said admiringly.

"Aye, he's bigger," Jack said carelessly, "but he ain't game, Dick ain't; loses his temper, he does, and a chap as does that when he's fighting ain't o' no account. But I must not stand a clappeting here; it's past six, and six is my time."

Facing death

"Have your tea first, Jack, it's a' ready; but I do believe thou'dst go wi'out eating wi'out noticing it, when thou'st got thy books in thy head."

Jack sat down and drank the tea his mother poured out for him, and devoured bread and butter with a zest that showed that his appetite was unimpaired by study. As soon as he had finished he caught up his candle, and with a nod to Mrs. Haden ran upstairs to his room.

Jack Simpson's craze for learning, as it was regarded by the other lads of Stokebridge, was the subject of much joking and chaff among them. Had he been a shy and retiring boy, holding himself aloof from the sports of his mates, ridicule would have taken the place of joking, and persecution of chaff. But Jack was so much one of themselves, a leader in their games, a good fellow all round, equally ready to play or to fight, that the fact that after six o'clock he shut himself up in his room and studied, was regarded as something in the nature of a humorous joke.

When he had first begun, his comrades all predicted that the fit would not last, and that a few weeks would see the end of it; but weeks and months and years had gone by, and Jack kept on steadily at the work he had set himself to do. Amusement had long died away, and there grew up an unspoken respect for their comrade.

"He be a rum 'un, be Jack," they would say; "he looves games, and can lick any chap his age anywhere round, and yet he shoots himself oop and reads and reads hours and hours every day, and he knows a heap, Bull-dog does." Not that Jack was in the habit of parading his acquirements; indeed he took the greatest pains to conceal them and to show that in no respect did he differ from his playfellows.

The two hours which he now spent twice a week with Mr. Merton, and his extensive reading, had modified his rough Staffordshire dialect, and when with his master he spoke correct English almost free of provincialisms, although with his comrades of the pit he spoke as they spoke, and never introduced any allusion to his studies. All questions as to his object in spending his evenings with his books were turned aside with joking answers, but his comrades had accidentally discovered that he possessed extraordinary powers of calculation. One of the lads had vaguely said that he wondered how many buckets of water there were in the canal between Stokebridge and Birmingham, a distance of eighteen miles, and Jack, without seeming to think of what he was doing, almost instantaneously gave the answer to the question. For a moment all were silent with surprise.

"I suppose that be a guess, Jack, eh?" Fred Orme asked.

"Noa," Jack said, "that's aboot roight, though I be sorry I said it; I joost reckoned it in my head."

"But how didst do that, Jack?" his questioner asked, astonished, while the boys standing round stared in silent wonder.

"Oh! in my head," Jack said carelessly; "it be easy enough to reckon in your head if you practise a little."

"And canst do any sum in thy head, Jack, as quick as that?"

"Not any sum, but anything easy, say up to the multiplication or division by eight figures."

"Let's try him," one boy said.

"All right, try away," Jack said. "Do it first on a bit of paper, and then ask me."

The boys drew off in a body, and a sum was fixed upon and worked out with a great deal of discussion.

At last, after a quarter of an hour's work, when all had gone through it and agreed that it was correct, they returned and said to him, "Multiply 324,683 by 459,852." Jack thought for a few seconds and then taking the pencil and paper wrote down the answer: 149,306,126,916.

"Why, Jack, thou be'est a conjurer," one exclaimed, while the others broke out into a shout of astonishment.

From that time it became an acknowledged fact that Jack Simpson was a wonder, and that there was some use in studying after all; and after their games were over they would sit round and ask him questions which they had laboriously prepared, and the speed and accuracy of his answers were a never-failing source of wonder to them.

As to his other studies they never inquired; it was enough for them that he could do this, and the fact that he could do it made them proud of him in a way, and when put upon by the pitmen it became a common retort among them, "Don't thou talk, there's Jack Simpson, he knows as much as thee and thy mates put together. Why, he can do a soom as long as a slaate as quick as thou'd ask it."

Jack himself laughed at his calculating powers, and told the boys that they could do the same if they would practise, believing what he said; but in point of fact this was not so, for the lad had an extraordinary natural faculty for calculation, and his schoolmaster was often astonished by the rapidity with which he could prepare in his brain long and complex calculations, and that in a space of time little beyond that which it would take to write the question upon paper.

So abnormal altogether was his power in this respect that Mr. Merton begged him to discontinue the practice of difficult calculation when at work.

"It is a bad thing, Jack, to give undue prominence to one description of mental labour, and I fear that you will injure your brain if you are always exercising it in one direction. Therefore when in the pit think over other subjects, history, geography, what you will, but leave calculations alone except when you have your books before you."

CHAPTER IX.

THE GREAT STRIKE.

It was Saturday afternoon, a time at which Stokebridge was generally lively. The men, (dinner over, and the great weekly wash done,) usually crowded the public-houses, or played bowls and quoits on a piece of waste land known as "the common," or set off upon a spree to Birmingham or Wolverhampton, or sat on low walls or other handy seats, and smoked and talked. But upon this special Saturday afternoon no one settled down to his ordinary pursuits, for the men stood talking in groups in the street, until, as the hour of four approached, there was a general move towards the common. Hither, too, came numbers of men from the colliery villages round, until some four or five thousand were gathered in front of an old "waste tip" at one corner of the common. Presently a group of some five or six men came up together, made their way through the throng, and took their stand on the edge of the tip, some twenty feet above the crowd. These were the delegates, the men sent by the union to persuade the colliers of Stokebridge and its neighbourhood to join in a general strike for a rise of wages.

The women of the village stand at their doors, and watch the men go off to the meeting, and then comment to each other concerning it.

"I ain't no patience wi' 'em, Mrs. Haden," said one of a group of neighbours who had gathered in front of her house; "I don't hold by strikes. I have gone through three of 'em, bad un's, besides a score of small un's, and I never knowed good come on 'em. I lost my little Peg in the last—low fever, the doctor called it, but it was starvation and nothing more."

"If I had my way," said Mrs. Haden, "I'd just wring the heads off they delegates. They come here and 'suades our men to go out and clem rather than take a shilling a week less, just a glass o' beer a day, and they gets their pay and lives in comfort, and dunna care nowt if us and th' childer all dies off together."

"Talk o' woman's rights, as one hears about, and woman's having a vote; we ought to have a vote as to strikes. It's us as bears the worse o't, and we ought to have a say on't; if we did there wouldn't be another strike in the country."

"It's a burning shame," another chimed in; "here us and the childer will have to starve for weeks, months may be, and all the homes will be broke up, and the furniture, which has took so long to get together, put away, just because the men won't do with one glass of beer less a day."

"The union's the curse of us a'," Mrs. Haden said. "I know what it'll be —fifteen bob a week for the first fortnight, and then twelve for a week, and then ten, and then eight, and then six, and then after we've clemmed on that for a month or two, the union'll say as the funds is dry, and the men had best go to work on the reduction. I knows their ways, and they're a cuss to us women."

"Here be'st thy Jack. He grows a proper lad that."

"Ay," Jane Haden agreed, "he's a good lad, none better; and as for learning, the books that boy knows is awesome; there's shelves upon shelves on 'em upstairs, and I do believe he's read 'em all a dozen times. Well, Jack, have ee cum from meeting?"

"Ay, mother; I heard them talk nonsense till I was nigh sick, and then I comed away."

"And will they go for the strike, Jack?"

"Ay, they'll go, like sheep through a gate. There's half a dozen or so would go t'other way, but the rest won't listen to them. So for the sake of a shilling a week we're going to lose thirty shillings a week for perhaps twenty weeks; so if we win we sha'n't get the money we've throw'd away for twenty times thirty weeks, mother, and that makes eleven years and twenty-eight weeks."

Jack Simpson was now sixteen years old, not very tall for his age, but square and set. His face was a pleasant one, in spite of his closely cropped hair. He had a bright fearless eye and a pleasant smile; but the square chin, and the firm determined lines of the mouth when in rest, showed that his old appellation of Bull-dog still suited him well. After working for four years as a gate-boy and two years with the waggons, he had just gone in to work with his adopted father in the stall, filling the coal in the waggon as it was got down, helping to drive the wedges, and at times to use the pick. As the getters—as the colliers working at bringing down the coal are called—are paid by the ton, many of the men have a strong lad working with them as assistant.

Facing death

"Is t' dad like to be at home soon, Jack?" Mrs. Haden asked, as she followed him into the house.

"Not he, mother. They pretty well all will be getting themselves in order for earning nothing by getting drunk to-night, and dad's not slack at that. Have you got tea ready, mother?"

"Ay, lad."

"I've made up my mind, mother," the boy said, as he ate his slice of bacon and bread, "that I shall go over to Birmingham to-morrow, and try to get work there. John Ratcliffe, the engineman, is going to write a letter for me to some mates of his there. The last two years, when I've been on the night-shift, I have gone in and helped him a bit pretty often in the day, so as to get to know something about an engine, and to be able to do a job of smith's work; anyhow, he thinks I can get a berth as a striker or something of that sort. I'd rather go at once, for there will be plenty of hands looking out for a job before long, when the pinch begins, and I don't want to be idle here at home."

"They've promised to give some sort o' allowance to non-unionists, Jack."

"Yes, mother, but I'd rather earn it honestly. I'm too young to join the union yet, but I have made up my mind long ago never to do it. I mean to be my own master, and I ain't going to be told by a pack of fellows at Stafford or Birmingham whether I am to work or not, and how much I am to do, and how many tubs I am to fill. No, mother, I wasn't born a slave that I know of, and certainly don't mean to become one voluntarily."

"Lor, how thou dost talk, Jack! Who'd take 'ee to be a pitman?"

"I don't want to be taken for anything that I am not, mother. What with reading and with going two hours twice a week of an evening for six years, to talk and work with Mr. Merton, I hope I can express myself properly when I choose. As you know, when I'm away from you I talk as others do, for I hate any one to make remarks. If the time ever comes when I am to take a step up, it will be time enough for them to talk; at present, all that the other lads think of me is, that I am fond of reading, and that I can lick any fellow of my own age in the mine," and he laughed lightly. "And now, mother, I shall go in and tell Mr. Merton what I have made up my mind to do."

Mr. Merton listened to Jack's report of his plans in silence, and then after a long pause said:

Facing death

"I have been for some time intending to talk seriously to you, Jack, about your future, and the present is a good time for broaching the subject. You see, my boy, you have worked very hard, and have thrown your whole strength into it for six years. You have given no time to the classics or modern languages, but have put your whole heart into mathematics; you have a natural talent for it, and you have had the advantage of a good teacher. I may say so," he said, "for I was third wrangler at Cambridge."

"You, sir!" Jack exclaimed in astonishment.

"Yes, lad, you may well be surprised at seeing a third wrangler a village schoolmaster, but you might find, if you searched, many men who took as high a degree, in even more humble positions. I took a fellowship, and lived for many years quietly upon it; then I married, and forfeited my fellowship. I thought, like many other men, that because I had taken a good degree I could earn my living. There is no greater mistake. I had absolutely no knowledge that was useful that way. I tried to write; I tried to get pupils: I failed all round. Thirteen years ago, after two years of marriage, my wife died; and in despair of otherwise earning my bread, and sick of the struggle I had gone through, I applied for this little mastership, obtained it, and came down with Alice, then a baby of a year old. I chafed at first, but I am contented now, and no one knows that Mr. Merton is an ex-fellow of St. John's. I had still a little property remaining, just enough to have kept Alice always at a good school. I do not think I shall stay here much longer. I shall try to get a larger school, in some town where I may find a few young men to teach of an evening. I am content for myself; but Alice is growing up, and I should wish, for her sake, to get a step up in the world again. I need not say, my lad, that I don't want this mentioned. Alice and you alone know my story. So you see," he went on more lightly, "I may say you have had a good teacher. Now, Jack, you are very high up in mathematics. Far higher than I was at your age; and I have not the slightest doubt that you will in a couple of years be able to take the best open scholarship of the year at Cambridge, if you try for it. That would keep you at college, and you might hope confidently to come out at least as high as I did, and to secure a fellowship, which means three or four hundred a year, till you marry. But to go through the university you must have a certain amount of Latin and Greek. You have a good two years, before you have to go up, and if you devote yourself as steadily to classics as you have to mathematics, you could get up enough to scrape through with. Don't give me any answer now, Jack. The idea is, of course, new to you. Think it very quietly over, and we can talk about it next time you come over from Birmingham."

"Yes, sir, thank you very much," Jack said, quietly; "only, please tell me, do you yourself recommend it?"

The schoolmaster was silent for a while.

Facing death

"I do not recommend one way or the other, Jack. I would rather leave it entirely to you. You would be certain to do well in one way there. You are, I believe, equally certain to do well here, but your advance may be very much slower. And now, Jack, let us lay it aside for to-night. I am just going to have tea, I hope you will take a cup with us."

Jack coloured with pleasure. It was the first time that such an invitation had been given to him, and he felt it as the first recognition yet made that he was something more than an ordinary pit-boy; but for all that he felt, when he followed his master into the next room, that he would have rather been anywhere else.

It was a tiny room, but daintily furnished—a room such as Jack had never seen before; and by the fire sat a girl reading. She put down her book as her father entered with a bright smile; but her eyes opened a little wider in surprise as Jack followed him in.

"My dear Alice, this is my pupil, Jack Simpson, who is going to do me great credit, and make a figure in the world some day. Jack, this is my daughter, Miss Merton."

Alice held out her hand.

"I have heard papa speak of you so often," she said, "and of course I have seen you come in and out sometimes when I have been home for the holidays."

"I have seen you in church," Jack said, making a tremendous effort to shake off his awkwardness.

Jack Simpson will to the end of his life look back upon that hour as the most uncomfortable he ever spent. Then for the first time he discovered that his boots were very heavy and thick; then for the first time did his hands and feet seem to get in his way, and to require thought as to what was to be done with them; and at the time he concluded that white lace curtains, and a pretty carpet, and tea poured out by a chatty and decidedly pretty young lady, were by no means such comfortable institutions as might have been expected.

It was two months from the commencement of the strike before Jack Simpson returned from Birmingham, coming home to stay from Saturday till Monday. Nothing can be more discouraging than the appearance of a colliery village where the hands are on strike. For the first week or two there is much bravado, and anticipation of early victory; and as money is still plentiful, the public-houses do a great trade. But as the stern reality of the struggle becomes felt, a gloom falls over the place. The men hang about listlessly, and from time to time straggle down to the committee-room, to hear the last news from the other places to which the strike extends, and to try to gather a little confidence therefrom. At first things always look well. Meetings are held in other centres, and promises of support flow in. For a time money arrives freely, and the union committee make an allowance to each member, which, far below his regular pay as it is, is still amply sufficient for his absolute wants. But by the end of two months the enthusiasm which the strike excited elsewhere dies out, the levies fall off, and the weekly money scarce enables life to be kept together.

It is distinctive of almost all strikes, that the women, beforehand averse to the movement, when it has once begun, throw themselves heartily into the struggle. From the time it is fairly entered upon until its termination it is rare indeed to hear a collier's wife speak a word against it. When the hardest pinch comes, and the children's faces grow thin and white, and the rooms are stripped of furniture, much as the women may long for an end of it, they never grumble, never pray their husbands to give in. This patient submission to their husbands' wills—this silent bearing of the greatest of suffering, namely, to see children suffer and to be unable to relieve them—is one of the most marked features of all great strikes in the coal districts.

"Well, mother, and how goes it?" Jack asked cheerfully after the first greetings.

"We be all right, Jack; if we ain't we ought to be, when we've got no children to keep, and get nigh as much as them as has."

"Eight shillings a week now, ain't it?"

Mrs. Haden nodded. Jack looked round.

"Holloa!" he said, "the clock's gone, and the new carpet!"

"Well, you see, my boy," Mrs. Haden said, hesitatingly, "Bill is down-hearted sometimes, and he wants a drop of comfort."

"I understand," Jack said significantly.

"Jack,"—and she again spoke hesitatingly—"I wish ee'd carry off all they books out o' thy little room. There's scores of 'em, and the smallest would fetch a glass o' beer. I've kept the door locked, but it might tempt him, my boy—not when he's in his right senses, you know, he'd scorn to do such a thing; but when he gets half on, and has no more money, and credit stopped, the craving's too much for him, and he'd sell the bed from under him—anything he's got, I do believe, except his pups;" and she pointed to some of Juno's great grandchildren, which were, as usual, lying before the fire, a mere handful of coal now, in comparison with past times.

Facing death

"I'll pick out a parcel of them that will be useful to me," Jack said, "and take them away. The rest may go. And now look here, mother. After paying you for my board, I have had for a long time now some eight shillings a week over. I have spent some in books, but second-hand books are very cheap—as dad will find when he tries to sell them. So I've got some money put by. It don't matter how much, but plenty to keep the wolf away while the strike lasts. But I don't mean, mother, to have my savings drunk away. I'm getting sixteen bob a week, and I can live on ten or eleven, so I'll send you five shillings a week. But dad mustn't know it. I'll be home in a month again, and I'll leave you a pound, so that you can get food in. If he thinks about it at all, which ain't likely, you can make out you get it on tick. Well, dad, how are you?" he asked, as Bill Haden entered the cottage.

"Ah, Jack, lad, how be it with 'ee?"

"All right, dad; getting on well. And how are things here?"

"Bad, Jack. Those scoundrels, the masters, they won't give in; but we're bound to beat 'em—bound to. If they don't come to our terms we mean to call the engine-men, and the hands they've got to keep the ways clear, out of the pits. That'll bring 'em to their senses quick enough. I've been for it all along."

"Call off the engine-hands!" Jack said, in tones of alarm; "you ain't going to do such a mad thing as that! Why, if the water gains, and the mines get flooded, it'll be weeks, and maybe months, before the mines can be cleared and put in working order; and what will you all be doing while that's being done?"

"It'll bring 'em to their senses, lad," Bill Haden said, bringing his hand down on the table with a thump. "They mean to starve us; we'll ruin them. There, let's have the price of a quart, Jack; I'm dry."

Jack saw that argument against this mad scheme would be of no use, for his foster-father was already half-drunk, so he handed him a shilling, and with a shrug of his shoulders walked off to Mr. Merton's.

He had long since written to his master, saying that he preferred working his way up slowly in mining, to entering upon a new life, in which, however successful he might be at college, the after course was not clear to him; and his teacher had answered in a tone of approval of his choice.

On his way he stopped at the houses of many of his boy friends, and was shocked at the misery which already prevailed in some of them. Harry Shepherd's home was no better than the others.

Facing death

"Why, Harry, I should scarce have known you," he said, as the lad came to the door when he opened it and called him. "You look bad, surely."

"We're a big family, Jack; and the extra children's allowance was dropped last week. There's eight of us, and food's scarce. Little Annie's going fast, I think. The doctor came this morning, and said she wanted strengthening food. He might as well ha' ordered her a coach-and-four. Baby died last week, and mother's ailing. You were right, Jack; what fools we were to strike! I've been miles round looking for a job, but it's no use; there's fifty asking for every place open."

The tears came into Jack's eyes as he looked at the pinched face of his friend.

"Why did you not write to me?" he asked, almost angrily. "I told you where a letter would find me; and here are you all clemming, and me know nought of it. It's too bad. Now look here, Harry, I must lend you some money—you know I've got some put by, and you and your father can pay me when good times come again. Your dad gets his eight shillings from the union, I suppose?"

"Yes," the lad answered.

"Well, with fifteen shillings a week you could make a shift to get on. So I'll send you ten shillings a week for a bit; that'll be seven shillings to add to the eight, and the other three will get meat to make broth for Annie. The strike can't last much over another month, and that won't hurt me one way or the other. Here's the first ten shillings; put it in your pocket, and then come round with me to the butcher and I'll get a few pounds of meat just to start you all. There, don't cry, and don't say anything, else I'll lick you."

But when Jack himself entered the schoolmaster's house, and was alone with Mr. Merton, he threw himself in a chair and burst into tears.

"It is awful, sir, awful. To see those little children, who were so noisy and bright when I went away, so pale, and thin, and quiet now. Poor little things! poor little things! As to the men, they are starving because they don't choose to work, and if they like it, let them; even the women I don't pity so much, for if they did right they would take broomsticks and drive the men to work; but the children, it's dreadful!"

"It is dreadful, Jack, and it makes me feel sick and ill when I go into the infant-school. The clergyman's wife has opened a sort of soup-kitchen, and a hundred children get a bowl of soup and a piece of bread at dinner-time every day, and they sell soup under cost price to the women. Mr. Brook has given fifty pounds towards it."

Facing death

"Look here, sir," Jack said; "you know I've over fifty pounds laid by—and money can't be better spent than for the children. The strike can't last over a month, or six weeks at the outside, and maybe not that. I'll give you three pounds a week, if you will kindly hand it over to Mrs. Street, and say it's been sent you. But it's to go to feeding children. Let me see; the soup don't cost above a penny a bowl, and say a halfpenny for a hunch of bread. So that will give a good many of 'em a dinner every day. Will you do that for me, sir?"

"I will, my boy," Mr. Merton said heartily. "You may save many a young life."

"Well, sir, and what do you think of things?"

"I fear we shall have trouble, Jack. Last night there was rioting over at Crawfurd; a manager's house was burnt down, and some policemen badly hurt. There is angry talk all over the district, and I fear we shall have it here."

When Jack started on Sunday evening for Birmingham, his last words to his mother were:

"Mind, mother, the very first word you hear about violence or assault, you post this envelope I have directed, to me. I will come straight back. I'll keep father out of it somehow; and I'll do all I can to save Mr. Brook's property. He's a good master, and he's been specially kind to me, and I won't have him or his property injured."

"Why, lauk a' mercy, Jack, you ain't going to fight the whole place all by yourself, are you?"

"I don't know what I am going to do yet," Jack said; "but you may be quite sure I shall do something."

And as his mother looked at the set bull-dog expression of his mouth and jaw, she felt that Jack was thoroughly in earnest.

CHAPTER X.

HARD TIMES.

It was when the pinch came, the subscriptions fell off, and the weekly payments by the union dwindled to a few shillings for the support of a whole family, that the rough virtues of the people of the mining districts came strongly into prominence. Starvation was doing its work, and told first upon the women and children. Little faces, awhile since so rosy and bright, grew thin and pinched, chubby arms shrank until the bone could almost be seen through the skin, and low fever, a sure accompaniment of want, made its appearance.

No more tender and devoted nurses could be found than the rough women, who hushed their voices, and stole with quiet feet around the little beds, letting fall many a silent tear when the sufferer asked for little things, for tea or lemonade, which there were no means to purchase, or when the doctor shook his head and said that good food and not medicine was needed.

The pitmen themselves would saunter aimlessly in and out of the houses, so changed from the cottages well stocked with furniture, with gay-coloured pictures on the wall, an eight-day clock, and many another little valuable, and all gone one after another. Very many of them lived upon the scantiest allowance of dry bread which would keep life together, in order that the allowance might all go for the children, retaining as their sole luxury a penny or two a week for the purchase of a pipe or two of tobacco daily. Had it not been for the soup-kitchen scores of children would have died, but the pint of soup and the slice of bread enabled them to live.

There was no talk of surrender yet, although compromises, which would at first have been indignantly rejected, were now discussed, and a deputation had waited upon Mr. Brook, but the owner refused to enter into any compromise.

"No, never," he said; "you have chosen to join the hands of the other pits in an endeavour to force your employers into giving you a higher rate of wages than they can afford to pay. I, therefore, have joined the other employers. We know, what you cannot know, what are our expenses, and what we can afford to pay, and we will accept no dictation whatever from the men as to their rate of wages. If I prefer, as I do prefer, that the colliery should stand idle, to raising your rate of wages, it is a clear proof that I should lose money if I agreed to your demand. If needs be I would rather that the pit was closed for a year, or for ten years. We have bound ourselves together to make no advance, just as you have bound yourselves not to go to work at the old rate. When you choose to go in at that rate there are your places ready for you, but I will give way in no single point, I will not pay a halfpenny a ton more than before. You best know how long you can hold out. Don't let it be too long, lads, for the sake of your wives and children; remember that the time may come, when, thinking over some empty chair, recalling some little face you will never see again, you will curse your folly and obstinacy in ruining your homes, and destroying those dependent upon you in a struggle in which it was from the first certain that you could not win, and in which, even if you won, the amount at stake is not worth one day of the suffering which you are inflicting upon those you love."

Left to themselves the men would have much sooner given in, would indeed never have embarked on the strike, but the influence of the union being over them, they feared to be called "black sheep," and to be taunted with deserting the general cause, and so the strike went on.

The tale of the suffering over the wide district affected by the strike was told through the land, and the subscriptions of the benevolent flowed in. Public opinion was, however, strongly opposed to the strike, and for the most part the money was subscribed wholly for soup-kitchen, for children, and for relief of the sick. But the area was wide, there were scores of villages as badly off as Stokebridge, and the share of each of the general fund was very small. A local committee was formed, of which the vicar was at the head, for the management of the funds, and for organizing a body of nurses. All the women who had no children of their own were enrolled upon its lists, and many of the girls of the sewing-class volunteered their services.

No one during this sad time devoted herself more untiringly and devotedly than Nelly Hardy. The quiet manner, the steady and resolute face, rendered her an excellent nurse, and as her father and mother were, perforce, sober, she could devote her whole time to the work. A portion of the funds was devoted to the preparation of the articles of food and drink necessary for the sick, and the kitchen of the schoolroom was freely employed in making milk-puddings, barley-water, and other things which brought pleasure and alleviation to the parched little lips for which they were intended.

The distress grew daily more intense. The small traders could no longer give credit; the pawnbrokers were so overburdened with household goods that they were obliged absolutely to decline to receive more; the doctors were worn out with work; the guardians of the poor were nearly beside themselves in their efforts to face the frightful distress prevailing; and the charitable committee, aided as they were by subscriptions from without, could still do but little in comparison to the great need. Jane Haden and the other women without families, did their best to help nurse in the houses where sickness was rife. The children were mere shadows, and the men and women, although far less reduced, were yet worn and wasted by want of food. And still the strike went on, still the men held out against the reduction. Some of the masters had brought men from other parts, and these had to be guarded to and from their work by strong bodies of police, and several serious encounters had taken place. Some of the hands were wavering now, but the party of resistance grew more and more violent, and the waverers dared not raise their voices. The delegates of the union went about holding meetings, and assuring their hearers that the masters were on the point of being beaten, and must give way; but they were listened to in sullen and gloomy silence by the men. Then came muttered threats and secret gatherings; and then Jane Haden, obedient to her promise, but very doubtful as to its wisdom, posted the letter Jack had left with her.

It was three o'clock next day before he arrived, for he had not received the letter until he went out for his breakfast, and he had to go back to his work and ask to be allowed to go away for the afternoon on particular business, for which he was wanted at home.

"Well, mother, what is it?" was his first question on entering.

"I oughtn't to tell 'ee, Jack; and I do believe Bill would kill me if he knew."

"He won't know, mother, and you must tell me," Jack said quietly.

"Well, my boy, yesterday afternoon Bill came in here with eight or ten others. I were upstairs, but I suppose they thought I were out, and as I did not want to disturb 'em, and was pretty nigh worn out—I had been up three nights with Betsy Mullin's girl—I sat down and nigh dozed off. The door was open, and I could hear what they said downstairs when they spoke loud. At first they talked low, and I didn't heed what they were saying; then I heard a word or two which frighted me, and then I got up and went quiet to my door and listened. Jack, they are going to wreck the engines, so as to stop the pumping and drown the mines. They are going to do for the 'Vaughan,' and the 'Hill Side,' and 'Thorns,' and the 'Little Shaft,' and 'Vale.' It's to be done to-night, and they begin with the 'Vaughan' at ten o'clock, 'cause it's closest, I suppose."

"They are mad," Jack said sternly. "How are they to earn bread if they flood the mines? and it will end by a lot of them being sent to jail for years.

But I'll stop it if it costs me my life."

"Oh, Jack! don't 'ee do anything rash," Mrs. Haden said piteously. "What can one lad do against two or three hundred men?"

"Now, mother," Jack said promptly, not heeding her appeal, "what police are there within reach?"

"The police were all sent away yesterday to Bampton. There were riots there, I heard say. That's why they chose to-night."

"Now the first thing, mother, is to prevent dad from going out to-night. He must be kept out of it, whatever others do. I've brought a bottle of gin from Birmingham. Tell him I've come over for an hour or two to see schoolmaster, and I'm going back again afterwards, but I've brought him this as a present. Get the cork out; he's sure to drink a glass or two anyhow, perhaps more, but it will send him off to sleep, sure enough. It's the strongest I could get, and he's out of the way of drink now. I don't suppose they'll miss him when they start; but if any one comes round for him, you tell 'em I brought him some Old Tom over, and that he's so dead sleepy he can't move. Later on, if you can, get some woman or child to come in, and let them see him, so that there'll be a witness he was at home when the thing came off, that'll make him safe. I've thought it all over."

"But what be'est thou going to do, Jack?"

"Don't mind me, mother. I'm going to save the Vaughan colliery. Don't you fret about me; all you've got to do is to make dad drink, which ain't a difficult job, and to stick to the story that I have been over for an hour to see schoolmaster. Good-bye, mother. Don't fret; it will all come out right."

As Jack went down the street he tapped at the door of his friend's house.

"Is Harry in?"

Harry was in, and came out at once.

"How's Annie?" was Jack's first question.

"Better, much better, Jack; the doctor thinks she'll do now. The broth put fresh life into her; we're all better, Jack, thanks to you."

"That's all right, Harry. Put on your cap and walk with me to the schoolroom. Now," he went on, as his friend rejoined him, and they turned up the street, "will you do a job for me?"

Facing death

"Anything in the world, Jack—leastways, anything I can."

"You may risk your life, Harry."

"All right, Jack, I'll risk it willing for you. You risked yours for me at the old shaft."

"Dost know what's going to be done to-night Harry?"

"I've heard summat about it."

"It must be stopped, Harry, if it costs you and me our lives. What's that when the whole district depends upon it? If they wreck the engines and flood the mines there will be no work for months; and what's to become of the women and children then? I'm going to Mr. Merton to tell him, and to get him to write a letter to Sir John Butler—Brook's place would be watched—he's the nearest magistrate, and the most active about here, and won't let the grass grow under his feet by all accounts. The letter must tell him of the attack that is to be made to-night, and ask him to send for the soldiers, if no police can be had. I want you to take the letter, Harry. Go out the other side of the village and make a long sweep round. Don't get into the road till you get a full mile out of the place. Then go as hard as you can till you get to Butler's. Insist on seeing him yourself; say it's a question of life and death. If he's out, you must go on to Hooper—he's the next magistrate. When you have delivered the letter, slip off home and go to bed, and never let out all your life that you took that letter."

"All right, Jack; but what be'est thou going to do?"

"I'm going another way, lad; I've got my work too. You'd best stop here, Harry; I will bring the letter to you. It may get out some day that Merton wrote it, and it's as well you shouldn't be seen near his place."

CHAPTER XI.

THE ATTACK ON THE ENGINE-HOUSE.

No sooner did Mr. Merton hear of the resolution of the miners to destroy the engines, than he sat down and wrote an urgent letter to Sir John Butler.

"Is there anything else, Jack?"

"I don't know, sir. If the masters could be warned of the attack they might get a few viewers and firemen and make a sort of defence; but if the men's blood's up it might go hard with them; and it would go hard with you if you were known to have taken the news of it."

"I will take the risk of that," Mr. Merton said. "Directly it is dark I will set out. What are you going to do, Jack?"

"I've got my work marked out," Jack said. "I'd rather not tell you till it's all over. Good-bye, sir; Harry is waiting for the letter."

Mr. Merton did not carry out his plans. As soon as it was dark he left the village, but a hundred yards out he came upon a party of men, evidently posted as sentries. These roughly told him that if he didn't want to be chucked into the canal he'd best go home to bed; and this, after trying another road with the same result, he did.

Jack walked with Harry as far as the railway-station, mentioning to several friends he met that he was off again. The lads crossed the line, went out of the opposite booking-office, and set off—for it was now past five, and already dark—at the top of their speed in different directions. Jack did not stop till he reached the engine-house of the Vaughan mine. The pumps were still clanking inside, and the water streaming down the shoot. Peeping carefully in, to see that his friend, John Ratcliffe, was alone, Jack entered.

"Well, John," he said, "the engine's still going."

"Ay, Jack; but if what's more nor one has told me to-day be true, it be for the last time."

"Look here, John; Mr. Brook has been a good master, will you do him a good turn?"

"Ay, lad, if I can; I've held on here, though they've threatened to chuck me down the shaft; but I'm a married man, and can't throw away my life."

"I don't ask you to, John. I want you to work hard here with me till six o'clock strikes, and then go home as usual."

"What dost want done, lad?"

"What steam is there in the boiler?"

"Only about fifteen pounds. I'm just knocking off, and have banked the fire up."

"All right, John. I want you to help me fix the fire hose, the short length, to that blow-off cock at the bottom of the boiler. We can unscrew the pipe down to the drain, and can fasten the hose to it with a union, I expect. You've got some unions, haven't you?"

"Yes, lad; and what then?"

"That's my business, John. I'm going to hold this place till the soldiers come; and I think that with twenty pounds of steam in the boiler, and the hose, I can keep all the miners of Stokebridge out. At any rate, I'll try. Now, John, set to work. I want thee to go straight home, and then no one will suspect thee of having a hand in the matter. I'll go out when thou dost, and thou canst swear, if thou art asked, that there was not a soul in the house when thou camest away."

"Thou wilt lose thy life, Jack."

"That be my business," Jack said. "I think not. Now set to work, John; give me a spanner, and let's get the pipe off the cock at once."

John Ratcliffe set to work with a will, and in twenty minutes the unions were screwed on and the hose attached, a length of thirty feet, which was quite sufficient to reach to the window, some eight feet above the ground. Along by this window ran a platform. There was another, and a smaller window, on the other side.

While they were working, John Ratcliffe tried to dissuade Jack from carrying out his plan.

71

Facing death

"It's no use, John. I mean to save the engines, and so the pit. They'll never get in; and no one knows I am here, and no one will suspect me. None of 'em will know my voice, for they won't bring boys with them, and dad won't be here. There, it's striking six. Let me just drop a rope out of the window to climb in again with. Now we'll go out together; do thou lock the door, take the key, and go off home. Like enough they'll ask thee for the key, or they may bring their sledges to break it in. Anyhow it will make no difference, for there are a couple of bolts inside, and I shall make it fast with bars. There, that's right. Good-night, John. Remember, whatever comes of it, thou knowest nought of it. Thou camest away and left the place empty, as usual, and no one there."

"Good-bye, lad, I'd stop with 'ee and share thy risk, but they'd know I was here, and my life wouldn't be worth the price of a pot o' beer. Don't forget, lad, if thou lowerst the water, to damp down the fire, and open the valves."

Jack, left to himself, clambered up to the window and entered the engine-house again, threw some fresh coal on the fire, heaped a quantity of coal against the door, and jammed several long iron bars against it. Then he lighted his pipe and sat listening, occasionally getting up to hold a lantern to the steam-gauge, as it crept gradually up.

"Twenty-five pounds," he said; "that will be enough to throw the water fifty or sixty yards on a level, and the door of the winding-engine's not more than thirty, so I can hold them both if they try to break in there."

He again banked up the fires, and sat thinking. Harry would be at the magistrate's by a quarter to six. By six o'clock Sir John could be on his way to Birmingham for troops; fifteen miles to drive—say an hour and a half. Another hour for the soldiers to start, and three hours to do the nineteen miles to the Vaughan, half-past eleven—perhaps half an hour earlier, perhaps half an hour later. There was no fear but there was plenty of water. The boiler was a large one, and was built partly into, partly out of the engine-house. That is to say, while the furnace-door, the gauges, and the safety-valve were inside, the main portion of the boiler was outside the walls. The blow-off cock was two inches in diameter, and the nozzle of the hose an inch and a half. It would take some minutes then, even with the steam at a pressure of twenty-five pounds to the inch, to blow the water out, and a minute would, he was certain, do all that was needed.

Not even when, upon the first day of his life in the pit, Jack sat hour after hour alone in the darkness, did the time seem to go so slowly as it did that evening. Once or twice he thought he heard footsteps, and crept cautiously up to the window to listen; but each time, convinced of his error, he returned to his place on a bench near the furnace. He heard the hours strike, one after another, on the Stokebridge church clock—eight, nine, ten —and then he took his post by the window and listened. A quarter of an hour passed, and then there was a faint, confused sound. Nearer it came, and nearer, until it swelled into the trampling of a crowd of many hundreds of men. They came along with laughter and rough jests, for they had no thought of opposition—no thought that anyone was near them. The crowd moved forward until they were within a few yards of the engine-house, and then one, who seemed to be in command, said, "Smash the door in with your sledges, lads."

Jack had, as they approached, gone down to the boiler, and had turned the blow-off cock, and the boiling water swelled the strong leathern hose almost to bursting. Then he went back to the window, threw it open, and stood with the nozzle in his hand.

"Hold!" he shouted out in loud, clear tones. "Let no man move a step nearer for his life."

The mob stood silent, paralyzed with surprise. Jack had spoken without a tinge of the local accent, and as none of the boys were there, his voice was quite unrecognized. "Who be he?" "It's a stranger!" and other sentences, were muttered through the throng.

"Who be you?" the leader asked, recovering from his surprise.

"Never mind who I am," Jack said, standing well back from the window, lest the light from the lanterns which some of the men carried might fall on his face. "I am here in the name of the law. I warn you to desist from your evil design. Go to your homes; the soldiers are on their way, and may be here any minute. Moreover, I have means here of destroying any man who attempts to enter."

There was a movement in the crowd. "The soldiers be coming" ran from mouth to mouth, and the more timid began to move towards the outside of the crowd.

"Stand firm, lads, it be a lie," shouted the leader. "Thee baint to be frighted by one man, be'est 'ee? What! five hundred Staffordshire miners afeard o' one? Why, ye'll be the laughing-stock of the country! Now, lads, break in the door; we'll soon see who be yon chap that talks so big."

There was a rush to the door, and a thundering clatter as the heavy blows of the sledge-hammers fell on the wood; while another party began an assault upon the door of the winding-engine house.

Then Jack, with closely pressed lips and set face, turned the cock of the nozzle.

Facing death

With a hiss the scalding water leaped out in a stream. Jack stood well forward now and with the hose swept the crowd, as a fireman might sweep a burning building. Driven by the tremendous force of the internal steam, the boiling water knocked the men in front headlong over; then, as he raised the nozzle and scattered the water broadcast over the crowd, wild yells, screams, and curses broke on the night air. Another move, and the column of boiling fluid fell on those engaged on the other engine-house door, and smote them down.

Then Jack turned the cock again, and the stream of water ceased.

It was but a minute since he had turned it on, but it had done its terrible work. A score of men lay on the ground, rolling in agony; others danced, screamed, and yelled in pain; others, less severely scalded, filled the air with curses; while all able to move made a wild rush back from the terrible building.

When the wild cries had a little subsided, Jack called out,—

"Now, lads, you can come back safely. I have plenty more hot water, and I could have scalded the whole of you as badly as those in front had I wanted to. Now I promise, on my oath, not to turn it on again if you will come and carry off your mates who are here. Take them off home as quick as you can, before the soldiers come. I don't want to do you harm. You'd all best be in bed as soon as you can."

The men hesitated, but it was clear to them all that it had been in the power of their unknown foe to have inflicted a far heavier punishment upon them than he had done, and there was a ring of truth and honesty in his voice which they could not doubt. So after a little hesitation a number of them came forward, and lifting the men who had fallen near the engine-house, carried them off; and in a few minutes there was a deep silence where, just before, a very pandemonium had seemed let loose.

Then Jack, the strain over, sat down, and cried like a child.

Half an hour later, listening intently, he heard a deep sound in the distance. "Here come the soldiers," he muttered, "it is time for me to be off." He glanced at the steam-gauge, and saw that the steam was falling, while the water-gauge showed that there was still sufficient water for safety, and he then opened the window at the back of the building, and dropped to the ground. In an instant he was seized in a powerful grasp.

"I thought ye'd be coming out here, and now I've got ye," growled a deep voice, which Jack recognized as that of Roger Hawking, the terror of Stokebridge.

Facing death

For an instant his heart seemed to stand still at the extent of his peril; then, with a sudden wrench, he swung round and faced his captor, twisted his hands in his handkerchief, and drove his knuckles into his throat. Then came a crashing blow in his face—another, and another. With head bent down, Jack held on his grip with the gameness and tenacity of a bull-dog, while the blows rained on his head, and his assailant, in his desperate effort to free himself, swung his body hither and thither in the air, as a bull might swing a dog which had pinned him. Jack felt his senses going—a dull dazed feeling came over him. Then he felt a crash, as his adversary reeled and fell —and then all was dark.

A LIFE OR DEATH STRUGGLE.

It could have been but a few minutes that he lay thus, for he awoke with the sound of a thunder of horses' hoofs, and a clatter of swords in the yard on the other side of the engine-house. Rousing himself, he found that he still grasped the throat of the man beneath him. With a vague sense of wonder whether his foe was dead, he rose to his feet and staggered off, the desire to avoid the troops dispersing all other ideas in his brain. For a few hundred yards he staggered along, swaying like a drunken man, and knowing nothing of where he was going; then he stumbled, and fell again, and lay for hours insensible.

It was just the faint break of day when he came to, the cold air of the morning having brought him to himself. It took him a few minutes to recall what had happened and his whereabouts. Then he made his way to the canal, which was close by, washed the blood from his face, and set out to walk to Birmingham. He was too shaken and bruised to make much progress, and after walking for a while crept into the shelter of a haystack, and went off to sleep for many hours. After it was dusk in the evening he started again, and made his way to his lodgings at ten o'clock that night. It was a fortnight before he could leave his room, so bruised and cut was his face, and a month before the last sign of the struggle was obliterated, and he felt that he could return to Stokebridge without his appearance being noticed.

There, great changes had taken place. The military had found the splintered door, the hose, and the still steaming water in the yard, and the particulars of the occurrence which had taken place had been pretty accurately judged. They were indeed soon made public by the stories of the scalded men, a great number of whom were forced to place themselves in the hands of the doctor, many of them having had very narrow escapes of their lives, but none of them had actually succumbed. In searching round the engine-house the soldiers had found a man, apparently dead, his tongue projecting from his mouth. A surgeon had accompanied them, and a vein having been opened and water dashed in his face, he gave signs of recovery. He had been taken off to jail as being concerned in the attack on the engine-house; but no evidence could be obtained against him, and he would have been released had he not been recognized as a man who had, five years before, effected a daring escape from Portland, where he was undergoing a life sentence for a brutal manslaughter.

The defeat of the attempt to destroy the Vaughan engines was the death-blow of the strike. Among the foremost in the attack, and therefore so terribly scalded that they were disabled for weeks, were most of the leaders of the strike in the pits of the district, and their voices silenced, and their counsel discredited, the men two days after the attack had a great meeting, at which it was resolved almost unanimously to go to work on the masters' terms.

Great excitement was caused throughout the district by the publication of the details of the defence of the engine-house, and the most strenuous efforts were made by Mr. Brook to discover the person to whom he was so indebted. The miners were unanimous in describing him as a stranger, and as speaking like a gentleman; and there was great wonder why any one who had done so great a service to the mine-owners should conceal his identity. Jack's secret was, however, well kept by the three or four who alone knew it, and who knew too that his life would not be safe for a day did the colliers, groaning and smarting over their terrible injuries, discover to whom they were indebted for them.

CHAPTER XII.

AFTER THE STRIKE.

" Well, Jack, so you're back again," Nelly Hardy said as she met Jack Simpson on his way home from work on the first day after his return.

"Ay, Nelly, and glad to see you. How have things gone on?" and he nodded towards her home.

"Better than I ever knew them," the girl said. "When father could not afford to buy drink we had better times than I have ever known. It was a thousand times better to starve than as 'twas before. He's laid up still; you nigh scalded him to death, Jack, and I doubt he'll never be fit for work again."

"I," Jack exclaimed, astounded, for he believed that the secret was known only to his mother, Harry, John Ratcliffe, Mr. Merton and perhaps the schoolmaster's daughter.

"Has Harry—"

"No, Harry has not said a word. Oh, Jack, I didn't think it of you. You call me a friend and keep this a secret, you let Harry know it and say nowt to me. I did not think it of you," and the dark eyes filled with tears.

"But if Harry did not tell you, how—"

"As if I wanted telling," she said indignantly. "Who would have dared do it but you? Didn't I know you were here an hour or two before, and you think I needed telling who it was as faced all the pitmen? and to think you hid it from me! Didn't you think I could be trusted? couldn't I have gone to fetch the redcoats for you? couldn't I have sat by you in the engine-house, and waited and held your hand when you stood against them all? oh, Jack!" and for the first time since their friendship had been pledged, nearly four years before, Jack saw Nelly burst into tears.

"I didn't mean unkind, Nell, I didn't, indeed, and if I had wanted another messenger I would have come to you. Don't I know you are as true as steel? Come, lass, don't take on. I would have sent thee instead o' Harry only I thought he could run fastest. Girls' wind ain't as good as lads'."

"And you didn't doubt I'd do it, Jack?"

"Not for a moment," Jack said. "I would have trusted thee as much as Harry."

"Well then, I forgive you, Jack, but if ever you get in danger again, and doant let me know, I'll never speak a word to you again."

In the years which had passed since this friendship began Nelly Hardy had greatly changed. The companionship of two quiet lads like Jack and Harry had tamed her down, and her love of reading and her study of all the books on history and travel on Jack's book-shelves had softened her speech. When alone the three spoke with but little of the dialect of the place, Jack having insisted on improvement in this respect. With Nelly his task had been easy, for she was an apt pupil, but Harry still retained some of his roughness of speech.

Nelly was fifteen now, and was nearly as tall as Jack, who was square and somewhat stout for his age. With these two friends Jack would talk sometimes of his hopes of rising and making a way for himself. Harry, who believed devoutly in his friend, entered most warmly into his hopes, but Nelly on this subject alone was not sympathetic.

"You don't say anything," Jack remarked one day; "do you think my castles in the air will never come true?"

"I know they will come true, Jack," she said earnestly; "but don't ask me to be glad. I can't; I try to but I can't. It's selfish, but, but—" and her voice quivered. "Every step thou takest will carry you farther up from me, and I can't be glad on it, Jack!"

"Nonsense, Nelly," Jack said angrily, "dos't think so little of me as to think that I shall not be as true to my two friends, Harry and you, as I am now?"

The girl shook her head.

"You will try, Jack, you will try. Don't think I doubt you, but—" and turning round she fled away at full speed.

"I believe she ran away because she was going to cry," Harry said. "Lasses are strange things, and though in some things Nell's half a lad, yet she's soft you see on some points. Curious, isn't it, Jack?"

"Very curious," Jack said; "I thought I understood Nell as well as I did you or myself, but I begin to think I doant understand her as much as I thought. It comes of her being a lass, of course, but it's queer too," and Jack shook his head over the mysterious nature of lasses. "You can't understand 'em," he went on again, thoughtfully. "Now, if you wanted some clothes, Harry, and you were out of work, I should just buy you a set as a matter of course, and you'd take 'em the same. It would be only natural like friends, wouldn't it?"

Harry assented.

"Now, I've been wanting to give Nelly a gown, and a jacket, and hat for the last two years. I want her to look nice, and hold her own with the other lasses of the place—she's as good looking as any—but I daren't do it. No, I daren't, downright. I know, as well as if I see it, how she'd flash up, and how angry she'd be."

"Why should she?" Harry asked.

"That's what I doan't know, lad, but I know she would be. I suppose it comes of her being a lass, but it beats me altogether. Why shouldn't she take it? other lasses take presents from their lads, why shouldn't Nell take one from her friend? But she wouldn't, I'd bet my life she wouldn't, and she wouldn't say, 'No, and thank you,' but she'd treat it as if I'd insulted her. No, it can't be done, lad; but it's a pity, for I should ha' liked to see her look nice for once."

Not satisfied with his inability to solve the question Jack took his mother into his confidence.

Jane Haden smiled.

"Noa, Jack, I don't think as how thou canst give Nell Hardy a dress. She is a good quiet girl and keeps herself respectable, which, taking into account them she comes from, is a credit to her, but I don't think thou could'st gi' her a gown."

"But why not, mother?" Jack persisted. "I might gi' her a pair o' earrings or a brooch, I suppose, which would cost as much as the gown."

"Yes, thou might'st do that, Jack."

"Then if she could take the thing which would be no manner o' use to her, why couldn't she take the thing that would?"

"I doant know as I can rightly tell you, Jack, but there's a difference."

Facing death

"But can't you tell me what is the difference?" Jack insisted.

"Noa, Jack, I can't, but there be a difference."

Jack seized his candle with a cry of despair, and ran upstairs. He had solved many a tough problem, but this was beyond him altogether. He was not, however, accustomed to be baffled, and the next day he renewed the subject, this time to Nelly herself.

"Look here, Nell," he said, "I want to ask you a question. It is a supposition, you know, only a supposition, but it bothers me."

"What is it, Jack?" she said, looking up from the ground, upon which as was her custom she was sitting with a book while Jack sat on a gate.

"If I was to offer you a pair of gold earrings."

"I wouldn't take 'em," the girl said rising, "you know I wouldn't, Jack; you know I never take presents from you."

"I know, lass, I know. We'll suppose you wouldn't take it, but you wouldn't be angered, would you?"

"I should be angered that you had spent money foolishly," the girl said after a pause, "when you knew I shouldn't take it, but I couldn't be angered any other way."

"Well, but if I were to buy you a hat and a jacket and a gown."

"You dare not," the girl said passionately, her face flushed scarlet; "you dare not, Jack."

"No," Jack said consciously, "I know I dare not, though I should like to; but why don't I dare?"

"Because it would be an insult, a gross insult, Jack, and you dare not insult me."

"No lass, I darena; but why should it be an insult? that's what I canna make out; why wouldn't it be an insult to offer you a gold brooch worth three or four pounds, and yet be an insult to offer you the other things? what's the difference?"

Nelly had calmed down now when she saw that the question was a hypothetical one, and that Jack had not, as she at first supposed, bought clothes for her.

She thought for some time. "I suppose, Jack, the difference is this. It's the duty of a girl's father and mother to buy fit clothes for her, and if they don't it's either their fault, or it's because they are too poor. So to give clothes is an interference and a sort of reproach. A brooch is not necessary; it's a pretty ornament, and so a lad may give it to his lass wi'out shame."

"Yes, I suppose it must be that," Jack said thoughtfully. "I'm glad I've got some sort of answer."

CHAPTER XIII.

A HEAVY LOSS.

" I thought, sir, that you promised to say nothing about that soup-kitchen money," Jack said rather indignantly one evening a fortnight after he had gone to work again.

"Here all the women of the place seem to know about it, and as I was coming home from work to-day, there was Mrs. Thompson run out and shook me by the hand and would ha' kissed me if I'd let her, and said I'd saved her children's lives. I ha' been thinking of going away; I can't stand this; and I thought you promised to say nowt about it."

"'Nothing,' Jack," corrected Mr. Merton. "It is a long time since I heard you say 'nowt.' No, Jack, I did not promise; you told me to say nothing about it, but I was careful not to promise. Sit down, lad, you're a little hot now, and I am not surprised, but I am sure that you will credit me for having acted for the best."

Jack sat down with a little grunt, and with the expression of dissatisfaction on his face in no way mollified.

"In the first place, Jack, you will, I know, be sorry to hear that I am going away."

"Going away!" Jack exclaimed, leaping to his feet, all thought of his grievance gone at once. "Oh! Mr. Merton."

"I told you, you will remember, Jack, when the strike first began, that for the sake of my daughter I should make an effort to obtain a superior position, and I am glad to say that I have done so. I have obtained the post of mathematical master at the Foundation School at Birmingham, with a salary of three hundred a year, and this, Jack, I partly owe to you."

"To me!" Jack exclaimed in astonishment; "how could that be, sir?"

"Well, Jack, you got me to write that letter to Sir John Butler, that was the means of bringing the troops over from Birmingham. As we know, they arrived too late, for in point of fact the hot water from the Vaughan boiler put an end to the riot and the strike together. However, Sir John Butler mentioned to Mr. Brook, and the other owners whose mines were threatened, that it was I who at some risk to myself sent the message which brought down the troops. I can assure you that I disclaimed any merit in the affair; however, they chose to consider themselves under an obligation, and when I applied for the vacant mastership, sending in, of course, my college testimonials, they were good enough to exert all their influence with the governors in my favour, and I was elected unanimously. The salary is an increasing one, and I am to be allowed to coach private pupils for the university. So, Jack, you may congratulate me."

"I do, sir, most heartily, most heartily," Jack said as he grasped the hand which Mr. Merton held out, but his voice quivered a little and tears stood in his eyes. "I am glad, indeed, although I shall miss you so terribly, you have been so good to me," and Jack fairly broke down now, and cried silently.

Mr. Merton put his hand on his shoulder: "Jack, my work is nearly done, so far as you are concerned. You have worked nearly as far as can be of any use to you in pure mathematics. For the next few months you may go on; but then you had better turn your attention to the useful application of what you have learned. You want to fit yourself to be an engineer, especially, of course, a mining engineer; still the more general your knowledge the better. You will have, therefore, to devote yourself to the various strains and stresses in iron bridges, and the calculation of the strength of the various forms of these structures. Then all calculations as to the expenditure of heat and force in steam engines will be quite material for you to master. In fact, there is work before you for another four or five years. But for much of this you will not require a master. You will find the practical part easy to you when you have a thorough knowledge of mathematics. At the same time if you will once a week send me your papers, noting all difficulties that you may meet with, I will go through them and answer you, and will also give you papers to work out."

"You are very, very kind, sir," Jack said; "but it will not be the same thing as you being here."

"No, not quite the same, Jack; still we can hardly help that."

"Oh, no, sir!" Jack said eagerly, "and please do not think that I am not glad to hear that you have got a place more worthy of you. It was a blow to me just at first, and I was selfish to think of myself even for a moment."

"Well, Jack, and now about this question of the soup dinner?"

"Oh! it does not matter, sir. I had forgot all about it."

Facing death

"It matters a little, Jack, because, although I did not promise to keep silence, I should certainly have respected your wish, had it not been that it seemed to be a far more important matter that the truth should be known."

"More important, sir?" Jack repeated in a puzzled tone.

"More important, Jack. My successor has been chosen. He is just the man for this place—earnest, well trained, a good disciplinarian. He will be no help to you, Jack. He is simply taught and trained as the master of a national school, but he is thoroughly in earnest. I have told him that his most efficient assistant here will be yourself."

"I?" Jack exclaimed in extreme astonishment.

"You, Jack, not as a teacher, but as an example. You have immense power of doing good, Jack, if you do but choose to exert it."

Jack was altogether too surprised to speak for some time.

"A power of good," he said at last. "The only good I can do, sir, and that is not much, is to thrash chaps I see bullying smaller boys, but that's nothing."

"Well, that's something, Jack; and indeed I fear you are fond of fighting."

"I am not fond of it," Jack said. "I don't care about it, one way or the other. It doesn't hurt me; I am as hard as nails, you see, so I don't think more about fighting than I do about eating my dinner."

"I don't like fighting, Jack, when it can be avoided, and I don't think that you are quarrelsome though you do get into so many fights."

"Indeed I am not quarrelsome, Mr. Merton; I never quarrel with anyone. If any of the big chaps interfere with us and want to fight, of course I am ready, or if chaps from the other pits think that they can knock our chaps about, of course I show them that the Vaughans can fight, or if I see any fellow pitching in to a young one—"

"Or, in fact, Jack, on any pretext whatever. Well, if it were anyone else but yourself I should speak very strongly against it; but in your case I avow that I am glad that you have fought, and fought until, as I know, no one anywhere near your age will fight with you, because it now makes you more useful for my purpose."

Jack looked astonished again. "You don't want me to thrash anyone, Mr. Merton?" he said; "because if you do—"

Facing death

"No, no, Jack, nothing is further from my thoughts. I want you to get the lads of your own age to join a night-school, and to become a more decent Christian set of young fellows than they are now. It is just because you can fight well, and are looked up to by the lads as their natural leader, that you can do this. Were anyone else to try it he would fail. He would be regarded as a milksop, and be called a girl, and a Molly, and all sorts of names, and no one would join him. Now with you they can't say this, and boys joining would say to those who made fun of them, 'There's Jack Simpson, he's one of us; you go and call him Molly and see what you'll get.' Now you can talk to your comrades, and point out to them the advantages of learning and decent manners. Show that not only will they become happier men, but that in a worldly point of view they will benefit, for that the mine-owners have difficulty in getting men with sufficient education to act as overmen and viewers. Get them to agree to keep from drink and from the foul language which makes the streets horrible to a decent person. You can work a revolution in the place. You won't get them to do all this at present, but the first step is to get them to attend a night-school. I have for the last year been thinking over the matter, and was intending to speak to you about it when the strike began, and everything else was put aside. Now, I have spoken to my successor, and he is willing, and indeed anxious, to open such a school if the young fellows can be induced to come."

Jack sat for some time in silence. He was always slow at coming to a conclusion, and liked to think over every side of a question.

"How often would it be held, sir?" he asked presently.

"Two or three nights a week, Jack. Those who are anxious to get on can do as you did, and work between times."

"Two nights would be enough at first," Jack said; "but I think, yes, I think I could get some of them to give that. Harry Shepherd would, I'm sure, and Bill Cummings, and Fred Wood, and I think five or six others. Yes, sir, I think we could start it, and all I can do I will. It would do a sight—I mean a great deal of good. I'll come myself at first, sir, and then if any of them make a noise or play games with the schoolmaster I'll lick 'em next day."

"No, Jack, I don't think that would do, but your presence would no doubt aid the master at first. And you'll think of the other things, Jack, the drinking, and the bad language, and so on."

"I'll do what I can, Mr. Merton," Jack said, simply, "but it must be bit by bit."

"That's right, Jack, I knew that I could rely upon you; and now come in to tea, and there was one thing I wanted to say, I want you once a month to come over to me at Birmingham on Saturday afternoon and stay till Sunday evening. It will be a great pleasure to me; I shall see how you are getting on, and shall hear all the news of Stokebridge."

"I am very very much obliged to you, sir," Jack said, colouring with pleasure, "but I am afraid I am not, not fit—"

"You are fit to associate with anyone, Jack, and it is good for you that you should occasionally have other association than that of your comrades of the pit. You will associate with people of higher rank than mine, if you live, and it is well that you should become accustomed to it. And now, Jack, I know you will not take it amiss, but clothes do go for something, and I should advise you to go to a good tailor's at Birmingham the first time you come over—I will obtain the address of such a one—and order yourself a suit of well made clothes. As you get on in life you will learn that first impressions go a long way, and that the cut of the clothes have not a little to do with first impressions. I shall introduce you to my friends there, simply as a friend; not that either you or I are ashamed of your working in a pit—indeed, that is your highest credit—but it would spare you the comments and silly questions which would be put to you. Now let us go into the next room, Alice will be expecting us."

Jack had taken tea with Mr. Merton more than once since that first evening before the strike, and was now much more at his ease with Miss Merton, who, having heard from her father that it was he who saved the Vaughan pit, viewed him with a constant feeling of astonishment. It seemed so strange to her that this quiet lad, who certainly stood in awe of her, although he was a year her senior, should have done such a daring action; equally wonderful to think that in spite of his well chosen words and the attainments her father thought so highly of, he was yet a pit boy, like the rough noisy lads of the village.

A week later Mr. Merton and his daughter left Stokebridge, and upon the following day his successor arrived, and Jack, at Mr. Merton's request, called upon him the same evening. He was a tall man of some forty years old, with a face expressive of quiet power. Jack felt at once that he should like him.

He received the lad very kindly. "I have heard so much of you from Mr. Merton," he said, "and I am sure that you will be a great help to me. Harriet," he said to his wife, a bright-looking woman of about thirty-five years old, who came into the room, "this is Mr. Simpson, of whom Mr. Merton spoke so highly to me. My wife is going to have the girls' school, have you heard?"

"No, indeed," Jack said; "Mr. Merton did not mention it."

"It was only settled yesterday; the managers heard that my wife was a trained mistress, and as they were going to pension off the present mistress they offered it to her."

"I am very glad," Jack said, "for Mrs. White has long been past her work, and the girls did pretty well as they liked."

"I expect to have some trouble with them at first," Mrs. Dodgson said cheerfully. "I often tell my husband girls are ever so much more troublesome than boys, but I daresay I shall manage; and now, Mr. Simpson, we are just going to have supper, will you join us? It will be our first regular meal in the house."

"Thank you very much," Jack said, colouring and hesitating, "but I think, perhaps, you don't know that I am only a lad in the pit."

"Stuff and nonsense," Mrs. Dodgson said, "what has that to do with it? Why, Mr. Merton says that you will be John's right hand. Besides, you will be able to tell us all about the people we shall have to do with."

In another moment Jack was seated at table, and really enjoyed the meal, lightened, as it was, by the pleasant talk of his hostess, and the grave but not less kindly conversation of her husband.

CHAPTER XIV.

THE NIGHT-SCHOOL.

Jack found that, as he expected, his friends Harry Shepherd, Bill Cummings, and Fred Wood, would be glad to attend a night-school, and to work in earnest; for the example of what Jack had done for himself, even so far as they knew, had excited a strong desire for improvement among them. They, however, were doubtful as to others, and agreed that it would not do to propose it in a straightforward manner, but that a good deal of careful management would be necessary.

Jack, it was arranged, should open the subject after leading up to it carefully. Harry should be the first to consent, Bill Cummings was to give in his adhesion when he saw signs of wavering among the others, and Fred Wood to delay his until a moment when his coming forward would be useful.

The following Saturday, when many of them were always together, should be the occasion, and Fred Wood was to lead up to the matter by asking Jack some questions as to the relative bigness of the earth and the sun.

Saturday came, the lads gathered in a field which belonged to the Vaughan, and upon which a great tip of rubbish and shale was gradually encroaching. Here choosing sides they played at rounders for a couple of hours, and then flung themselves down on the grass. Some of them lighted pipes, and all enjoyed the quiet of the fine autumn evening.

Presently Fred Wood artfully fired off the questions he had prepared, which Jack answered.

"What a sight o' things thou know'st, Jack!" Bill Cummings said.

"I don't know much yet, Bill, but I hopes to know a goodish deal some day."

"And thou really lik'st reading, Jack? I hate it," John Jordan said.

Facing death

"I didn't like it ower much at first," Jack answered, "but as I got on I liked it more and more. I wish you chaps had the chances I had. It isn't every one who would take the pains wi' a fellow as Merton took wi' me."

"What ud be t' good o't?" John Jordan asked. "I doan't see no good in knowing that t' sun be a hundred thousand times as big as t' world."

"There's use in a great deal o' what one gets to know, though," Jack said; "not so much now as some day, maybe. A chap as has some sort o' edication has chances over another o' being chosen as a viewer or an oversman."

"Oh! that's what thou be'est looking forward to, Jack, eh? Well there's summat in that, and I shouldna' wonder if we see thee that some day; but we can't all be oversmen."

"Not in the Vaughan," Jack said; "but there's plenty o' other pits, and a chap as has got his head screwed on straight, and can write well and figure a bit, and have read up his work, may always look forward to getting a step up wherever he goes. Besides, look at the difference it makes to the pleasures o' life. What has a man got to do who ain't learnt to be fond o' reading? Nowt but to go to t' public to spend his evenings and drink away his earnings. So 'ee goes on, and his woife doan't care about taking pains about a house when t' maister ain't never at home but to his meals, and his children get to look for him coming home drunk and smashing the things, and when he gets old he's just a broken-down drunkard, wi'out a penny saved, and nowt but the poorhouse before him. Now, that's the sort o' life o' a man who can't read, or can't read well enough to take pleasure in it, has before him. That is so, bean't it?"

There was a long silence; all the lads knew that the picture was a true one.

"Now look at t'other side," Jack went on; "look at Merton. He didn't get moore pay a week than a pitman does; look how he lived, how comfortable everything was! What a home that ud be for a man to go back to after his work was done! Noice furniture, a wife looking forward neat and tidy to your coming hoam for the evening. Your food all comfortable, the kids clean and neat, and delighted to see feyther home."

There was again a long silence.

"Where be the girls to make the tidy wife a' cooming from, I wonder?" John Jordan said; "not in Stokebridge, I reckon!"

"The lasses take mostly after the lads," Jack said. "If we became better they'd be ashamed to lag behind. Mrs. Dodgson, the new schoolmaister's wife, told me t'other day she thought o' opening a sort o' night class for big girls, to teach 'em sewing, and making their own clothes, and summat about cooking, and such like."

"That would be summat like," said Harry Shepherd, who saw that his opportunity had come. "I wonder whether t' maister would open a night-school for us; I'd go for one, quick enough. I doan't know as I've rightly thought it over before, but now ye puts it in that way, Jack, there be no doubt i' my moind that I should; it would be a heap better to get some larning, and to live like a decent kind o' chap."

"I doan't know," John Jordan said; "it moight be better, but look what a lot o' work one ud have to do."

"Well, John, I always finds plenty o' time for play," Jack said. "You could give an hour a day to it, and now the winter's coming on you'd be main glad sometimes as you'd got summat to do. I should ha' to talk to the schoolmaister a bit. I doan't know as he'd be willing to give up his time of an evening two or three evenings a week, say two, when he's been at work all day. It be a good deal to ask a man, that is."

"It be, surely," Harry said; "but what a sight o' good it would do, and if his woife be willing to give oop her time to the girls, maybe he would do as much for us." There was a pause again. Several of the lads looked irresolute.

"Well," Bill Cummings said, "I be ready for another if some more of 'ee will join't." The example was contagious. Four others agreed to join.

"Come," Harry Shepherd said, "it bean't no use if Jack can't tell schoolmaister that a dozen o' us will come in ef he will open a school two nights a week. You'll join, woan't you, Fred Wood?"

"Oi allers hated my books," Fred said, "and used to be bottom o' class. It ain't as I doan't believe what Jack Simpson says; there be no doubt as it would be a sight better look-out if one got to be fond o' books, and such loike. I doan't believe as ever I shall be, but I doan't mind giving it a trial for six months, and if at the end o' that time I doan't like it, why I jacks it oop."

The adhesion of this seemingly reluctant recruit settled the matter. Even John Jordan yielded upon the same terms, and the whole party, fifteen in number, put down their names, and Jack Simpson undertook to speak to Mr Dodgson.

"See how we shall get laughed at," John Jordan said. "Why, we shall get made fun o' by the whole place."

Facing death

"Let 'em laugh," Jack said, "they won't laugh long. I never was laughed at, and why should you be? They canna call us Jennies, for we sixteen will play any sixteen wi'in five miles round, at any game they like, or fight 'em if it comes to that. We has only got to stick together. I sha'n't be one of the night-school, but I am one wi' you, and we'll just stick together. Don't let us mind if they do laugh; if they go on at it, and I doubt they will, just offer to fight anyone your own size, and if he be bigger than you like I'll take him in hand."

"That's it," Harry Shepherd said enthusiastically; "we'll stick together, and you see how we'll get on; and look here, I vote we each pay threepence a week, that will get us a room at two bob, and candles. Then we can work a' night wi'out being disturbed."

"This be a good idea o' thine, Harry. I'll give my threepence a week as well as the rest, and I'll come in on the nights when you don't go to school and help any that wants it."

"Yes," Bill Cummings said, "and we'll send round challenges to the other pits to play football and rounders. I vote we call ourselves the 'Bull-dogs,' and Jack shall be our captain."

The proposition was carried with unanimity, and the "Bull-dogs" became a body from that time. Harry was appointed treasurer, and the first week's subscriptions were paid forthwith, and an hour later a room was hired.

"Hullo!" Fred Wood said, as they poured in and took possession; "we forgot furniture. We must have a table and some benches."

"It is the captain's duty to provide furniture," Jack said. "I will get a big table and some benches on Monday, and then we'll draw up rules and get 'em framed and hung over the fireplace, then we shall be all in order."

Nothing could have been more happy than this plan of starting a club; it gave all the members a lively interest in the matter, and united them by a bond which would keep the lazy and careless from hanging back, and it was quite with a sense of excitement that they met on the Monday evening.

Jack had got a large table and some benches. Inkstands, slates, paper, and pencils were on the table, and four candles were burning. He took the place of honour at the head of the table, and the others, much pleased with the appearance of the room, took their seats round the table.

"In the first place," Jack said, striking the table with his fist to call for order, "I have to report to you that I ha' seen the schoolmaister, and he says that he will willingly give two hours two nights a week to teaching the 'Bull-dogs.'"

This announcement was received with great applause, for the lads had all become deeply interested in the matter.

"He says Tuesdays and Fridays will suit him, from seven till nine; and I have, in your name, accepted with very many thanks his offer; for, lads, it be no light thing that a man who has been all day teaching, should give up two evenings a week to help us on, and that wi'out charge or payment."

"That's so, Jack!" Fred Wood said. "I voate we pass a vote o' thanks to Mr. Dodgson."

There was a chorus of approval.

"Someone ha' got to second that proposal," Jack said; "we must do things in the proper form."

"I second it," John Jordan said.

"Very well," Jack said, "are you all agreed?" "All." "Very well, then, I'll write that out neatly in this book I ha' bought to keep the records o' the club, and I'll send a copy to Mr. Dodgson; I'm sure he will be pleased. I had best act as secretary as well as captain at present, till one o' you gets on wi' his writing and can take it off my hands. Now we must draw out our rules. First, we must put down that the following are the original members of the Bull-dog Club. Then, that the objects of the club are to improve ourselves, and to make decent men o' ourselves. Next, to stick together in a body and to play all sorts o' games against any other set. All that's been agreed, ain't it?"

There were cries of "Ay, ay," and Jack wrote down the items on the sheet o' paper before him.

"Now about new members. Do we mean to keep it to ourselves, or to let in other chaps?"

"Keep it to ourselves," shouted several.

"Well, I dunno," Harry Shepherd said; "if this is going to do us as much good as we hopes, and think it is, would it be right to keep the chaps o' the place out? O' course we wouldn't go beyond Stokebridge, but we might keep it to that."

The point was hotly debated, the majority being in favour of confining the club to its present members; some saying that if it were opened the original members would be swamped by numbers, and that their bond of union would be broken.

When all had spoken Jack Simpson said:

"I think we might go between both opinions. If we were to limit the club to twenty-four members, this room would just about hold 'em. We would only elect one each week, so as to have time to make a good choice. Any member who broke the rules or made himself unpleasant would be expelled, and so we should see in a while all the young chaps o' t' village wanting to join, and it would get to be looked upon as a feather in a chap's cap to belong to it."

This proposal was agreed to unanimously.

"Now the next rule I propose," Jack said, "is that this room is to be used from seven to nine for work. No talking to be allowed. Arter nine, books to be put away and pipes to be lit by them as smoke, and to talk till ten. I ha' been talking to the woman o' the house, and she will supply cups o' coffee or tea at a penny a piece between nine and ten."

This rule was agreed to without a dissentient voice.

"Now," Jack said, "I doan't know as you'll all like the next rule I ha' to propose, but I do think it is a needful one. That is that no swearing or bad language be used in this room. A fine of a penny being inflicted for each time the rule be broken."

There was a dead silence.

"You see," Jack said, "you will all be fined a few times at first, but this money will go to the club fund, and will help up to get fires i' winter. You'll soon break yourselves of it, it be only a trick. I did. Mr. Merton told me that it was a bad habit and horrible to decent people. I said I could never break myself o't. He said if I fined myself a penny every time I did it, and put it in the poor box o' Sunday, I should soon get out o' t'way. Well, the first day cost me thirteen pence, the next fourpence, and afterwards it was only a penny now and then. First and last it didn't cost me half a crown, and you never hear me swear or use bad language now. Come, Bull-dogs, this will be the first step toward improving yourselves, and when you find how easy it be to do wi'out it here, you will soon do wi'out it outside."

The rule was finally agreed to, but during the first week it carried a good deal of heart-burning in the club. One of the members left altogether, but the rest soon found that the fines, which had been so alarming for the first day or two, dwindled down.

Facing death

It cost the Bull-dogs collectively over three pounds to cure themselves of using bad language, and the fines kept them in firing, paper, pens, and ink all the winter.

On the evening after the opening of the club-room the whole party accompanied by Jack went to the night-school. They looked rather shamefaced as they tramped in, but Jack introduced them one by one to the master, who with a few cordial words put them at their ease. For the first night he contented himself by finding out how much each knew, how much he remembered of what he had formerly heard. For the last half hour he gave them a short lecture on geography, drawing a map on the black-board, taking a traveller from place to place, and telling them what he saw there. Then he set them each a task to be learned and a few sums to be done by the following Friday, and they returned to the club-room greatly pleased with the first night's lessons.

It was not always so light, but the lads were in earnest and really worked hard. Jack visited the room on the off nights, explained questions they did not understand, and after nine o'clock generally read aloud for half an hour while they smoked; that is to say, he read short sentences and then one or other read them after him, Jack correcting mistakes in dialect and pronunciation.

Mr. Merton had indeed been a friend to Jack Simpson, but there was another friend to whom, according to his promise, Jack reported his doings, not telling everything, perhaps, for Jack was not very apt to talk or write about himself; but once a year he sent a letter in reply to a long and wise one which he received from his friend the artist, according to their agreement, for Jack had not "given up."

Before the end of a month Mr. Dodgson wrote to Mr. Merton, saying that, thanks to Jack, the night-school was a great success, that the lads all behaved extremely well, and were making really surprising efforts to improve themselves. He augured great things for the village from the movement.

CHAPTER XV.

THE SEWING CLASS.

Stokebridge contained altogether a population of some three thousand souls, of whom more than half consisted of the men and boys of the Vaughan mine, and the families dependent upon them. It was a place where, except as to accidents at one or other of the pits, news was scarce, and a small thing therefore created much interest. Thus the news that the new schoolmaster had opened a night school, and that some sixteen or eighteen of the lads belonging to the Vaughan had joined it, created quite an excitement. At first the statement was received with positive disbelief. There was no precedent for such a thing, and in its ways at least Stokebridge was strictly conservative.

When the tale was confirmed wonder took the place of unbelief. The women were unanimous in the opinion that if the school only kept the lads from drink it would be a blessing to the place. Drink was indeed the grand test by which they viewed all things. To anything which led lads to avoid this curse of their homes their approval was certain and complete. Whether the acquisition of learning was likely to improve their prospects in life, or to make them better men, was not considered, the great point about the new organization was that it would keep them from the public-houses, the curses of the working men, and still more of the working men's wives and families, of this country.

Among the men, who were, however, disposed to view the matter as a boys' fancy which would soon die away, the movement met with slight approval. Newfangled notions were held in but low estimation among the miners of Stokebridge. They had got on wi'out larning, and saw no reason why t' lads could not do as they had done. "They'll be a cocking they noses oop aboove their feythers, joost acause they know moore reading and writing, but what good ul it do they I wonder?" an elderly pitman asked a circle of workmen at the "Chequers;" and a general affirmatory grunt betokened assent with the spirit of his words.

Among the young men, those of from eighteen to three or four and twenty, the opposition was still stronger, for here a strong feeling of jealousy was aroused at the thought that their juniors were, as they considered, stealing a march upon them. Gibes and jeers were showered upon the "Bull-dogs," and two of them were ducked in the canal by a party of five or six of their elders. On scrambling out, however, they ran back to the village, and the rest of the party, headed by Jack, at once started on the war-path. Coming up to the band who had assaulted their comrades they fell upon them with fury, and in spite of the latter's superior individual strength, thrashed them soundly, and then gave them a ducking in the canal, similar to that which they had inflicted. After that it came to be understood in Stokebridge that it was best to leave the bull-dogs alone, or at least to be content with verbal assaults, at which indeed the lads were able to hold their own.

But it was among the girls of Stokebridge, those of from fourteen to seventeen years old, that this movement upon the part of the boys excited the greatest discussion and the widest divergence of opinion. Up to the time of the strike Jack Simpson had been by no means popular among their class. It was an anomaly in Stokebridge that a lad should have no avowed favourite of his own age among the lasses. These adhesions were not often of a permanent character, although later on sometimes marriages came of them, but for a time, and until the almost inevitable quarrel came, they were regarded as binding. The lad would sometimes buy a ribbon or neckerchief for the lass, and she and two or three others would accompany him as with some of his comrades he strolled in the lanes on Sunday, or would sit by him on a wall or a balk of timber as he smoked and talked with his friends.

Jack's rigid seclusion after his hour of play was over, his apparent indifference to the lasses of the place, was felt as a general slight, and resented accordingly; although the girls were not insensible to his prowess in battle and in sports, to his quiet steadiness of character, or to the frankness and good temper of his face. The general opinion, therefore, among the young girls of Stokebridge was that he was "stuck up," although in fact few boys in the place had less of conceit and self-glorification than he had.

"Did 'ee ever hear of such a tale," asked one of a group of girls sitting together on a bank, while the little ones, of whom they were supposed to be in charge, played and rolled on the grass, "as for a lot o' boys to go to school again o' their own free-will."

"I don't see no good in it," another said, "not for the schooling they'll get. But if it teaches them to keep out o' the publics, it will be good for their wives some day."

"It will that," put in another earnestly; "my! how feyther did beat mother last night; he were as drunk as could be, and he went on awful."

Facing death

"I think sometimes men are worse nor beasts," another said.

"Do 'ee know I've heard," Sarah Shepherd said, "that the new schoolmistress be a-going to open a night-school for girls, to teach sewing, and cutting out, and summat o' cooking." There was a general exclamation of astonishment, and so strange was the news that it was some time before any one ventured a comment on it.

"What dost think o't?" Sarah questioned at last.

"Only sewing and cutting out and cooking and such like, and not lessons?" Bess Thompson asked doubtfully.

"Not reg'lar lessons I mean. She'll read out while the girls work, and perhaps they will read out by turns; not lessons, you know, but stories and tales, and travels, and that kind o' book. What dost think o't?"

"'Twould be a good thing to know how to make dresses," Fanny Jones, who was fond of finery, remarked.

"And other things too," put in Peggy Martin, "and to cook too. Mother ain't a good hand at cooking and it puts feyther in such tempers, and sometimes I hardly wonder. I shall go if some others go. But be'est sure it be true, Sally?"

"Harry told me," she said, "and I think Jack Simpson told him as the schoolmaster said so."

The news was too important to be kept to themselves, and there was soon a general move homewards.

There Sally Shepherd's story received confirmation. The schoolmistress had been going from house to house, asking all the women who had daughters between the ages of fifteen and eighteen, to let them attend a working class in the schoolroom two evenings a week, and the answer she almost always received was, "Well, I ha' no objection to my lass going if she be willing; and I think it would be very good for her to know how to make her clothes; I can hardly do a stitch myself."

Mrs. Dodgson had also informed the women that any of them who liked to supply the material for undergarments or for children's dresses, could have them for the present made up without charge by the class.

"But suppose they spiles 'em?"

"They wont spoil them. The work may not be very neat at first, but the things will be well cut out and strongly put together. I will see to that."

Facing death

In a short time the class was opened, and forty girls at once attended. So pleased were these with their teacher, and with the pleasant books that Mr. Dodgson read to them—for his wife was far too much occupied to read, and too wise to give the girls a distaste for the class by asking them to do so —that the number of applicants for admission soon far exceeded the number who could be received.

Mr. Brook heard shortly afterwards from Mr. Dodgson of the success of the scheme and the great benefit which was likely to accrue from it, and at once offered to contribute twenty pounds a year to secure the services of a young woman capable of assisting in the girls' school by day and of teaching needlework.

Thenceforth the number of class evenings was raised to three a week, and sixty girls in all were admitted. The books chosen for reading were not always tales, but for a portion of each evening books treating on domestic matters, the care of a house, the management of illness, cottage gardening, &c., were read; and these were found greatly to interest the hearers. The book on gardening was a special favourite, and soon the pitmen were astonished to see changes in the tiny plots of ground behind their houses. The men in charge of the pit horses were coaxed for baskets of manure, pennies were saved and devoted to the purchase of seed, and the boys found that the most acceptable present was no longer a gay handkerchief or ribbon, but a pot of flowers.

Revolutions are not made in a day, but as month passed after month the change in Stokebridge became marked. The place assumed a smarter and brighter aspect; it was rare to hear bad language from lads or girls in the streets, for the young ones naturally followed the fashion set by their elder brothers and sisters, and as a foul expression not unfrequently cost its utterer a cuff on the head, they soon became rare.

The girls became more quiet in demeanour, neater in dress, the boys less noisy and aggressive.

The boys' night-school had increased greatly in number. The Bull-dogs, after much deliberation, had declined to increase their numbers, but at Jack Simpson's suggestion it had been agreed that any of them might join other similar associations, in order that these might be conducted on the same lines as their own, and the benefits of which they were conscious be thus distributed more widely. Four other "clubs" were in consequence established, all looking upon the Bull-dogs as their central association.

The vicar of the parish aided the efforts of the school master and mistress for the improvement of the rising generation of Stokebridge. Hitherto all efforts that way had failed, but he now got over a magic lantern from Birmingham, hiring sets of slides of scenery in foreign countries, astronomical subjects, &c., and gave lectures once a fortnight. These were well attended, and the quiet attention with which he was listened to by the younger portion of his audience, contrasted so strongly with the indifference or uproar with which a similar attempt had been met some two years before, that he told Mr. Brook something like a miracle was being wrought in the parish.

Mr. Brook warmly congratulated Mr. and Mrs. Dodgson on the change, but these frankly said that although they had done their best, the change was in no slight degree due to the influence of one of the pit lads, with whom Mr. Merton had taken great pains, and who was certainly a remarkable lad.

"Ah, indeed," Mr. Brook said. "I have a faint recollection of his speaking to me some years ago of one of the boys; and, now I think of it, he is the same boy who behaved so bravely in going down that old shaft to save another boy's life. The men gave him a gold watch; of course, I remember all about it now. I am glad to hear that he is turning out so well. In a few years I must see what I can do for him."

Mr. Dodgson would have said much more, but Mr. Merton had impressed upon him that Jack would object, above all things, to be brought forward, and that it was better to let him work his way steadily and bide his time.

It was not for some months after the sewing classes had been instituted that those for cooking were established. The difficulty was not as to the necessary outlay for stoves and utensils, for these Mr. Brook at once offered to provide, but as to the food to be cooked.

The experiments began on a small scale. At first Mrs. Dodgson sent round to say that in all cases of illness, she would have broths, puddings, and cooling drinks prepared at the schools free of charge, upon the necessary materials being sent to her. This was followed by the plan of buying the materials for food for invalids, which was to be supplied at a price that just paid the cost. Then little steak puddings and pies were made, and these commanded a ready sale; excellent soups from cheap materials were also provided, and for this in winter the demand was greater than they could supply; and so the work was extended until the two stoves were fully occupied for three days a week.

Eight girls at a time were instructed in cookery, doing the whole work under the supervision of the mistress. Two fresh hands came as two left each week; thus each received a month's teaching. On the first week the new-comers simply cleaned and washed the utensils, stoves, &c., during the remaining three weeks they learned to make simple soups, puddings, and pies, to cook meat and vegetables. The time was short for the purpose, but the girls were delighted with their lessons, and took the greatest pride in keeping up the reputation of the school kitchens, and learned at any rate sufficient to enable them to assist their mothers at home with such effect, that the pitmen of Stokebridge were astonished at the variety and improvement of their fare.

CHAPTER XVI.

A NEW LIFE.

Jack Simpson did not forget the advice Mr. Merton had given him about clothes, and a fortnight after his master had gone to Birmingham Jack went over on Saturday afternoon, and his kind friend accompanied him to one of the leading tailors there, and he was measured for two suits of clothes. He went to other shops and bought such articles as Mr. Merton recommended—hats, gloves, boots, &c. Mr. Merton smiled to himself at the grave attention which Jack paid to all he said upon the subject; but Jack was always earnest in all he undertook, and he had quite appreciated what his friend had told him as to the advantage of being dressed so as to excite no attention upon the part of those whom he would meet at Mr. Merton's.

The following Saturday he went over again, and went again to the tailor's to try his things on.

"Do you want a dress suit, sir?" the foreman asked with suppressed merriment.

"What is a dress suit?" Jack said simply. "I am ignorant about these matters."

"A dress suit," the foreman said, struck with the young fellow's freedom from all sort of pretence or assumption, "is the dress gentlemen wear of an evening at dinner parties or other gatherings. This is it," and he showed Jack an engraving.

Jack looked at it—he had never seen anyone so attired.

"He looks very affected," he said.

"Oh, that is the fault of the artist," the foreman answered. "Gentlemen look just as natural in these clothes as in any other. They are quite simple, you see—all black, with open vest, white shirt, white tie and gloves, and patent leather boots."

A quiet smile stole over Jack's face. Humour was by no means a strong point in his character, but he was not altogether deficient in it.

"I had better have them," he said; "it would look strange, I suppose, not to be dressed so when others are?"

"It would be a little marked in the event of a dinner or evening party," the foreman answered, and so Jack gave the order.

It was two weeks later before he paid his first visit to Mr. Merton; for the pretty little house which the latter had taken a mile out of the town had been in the hands of the workmen and furnishers, Mr. Merton having drawn on his little capital to decorate and fit up the house, so as to be a pretty home for his daughter.

It was, indeed, a larger house than, from the mere salary attached to his post, he could be able to afford, but he reckoned upon considerably increasing this by preparing young men for the university, and he was wise enough to know that a good establishment and a liberal table go very far in establishing and widening a connection, and in rendering people sensible to a man's merits, either in business or otherwise.

As Mr. Merton, M.A., late of St. John's, Cambridge, and third wrangler of his year, he had already been received with great cordiality by his colleagues, and at their houses had made the acquaintance of many of the best, if not the wealthiest men in Birmingham, for at Birmingham the terms were by no means more synonymous than they are elsewhere.

Jack had ordered his clothes to be sent to a small hotel near the railway station, and had arranged with the landlord that his portmanteau should be kept there, and a room be placed at his service on Saturday afternoon and Monday morning once a month for him to change his things. He had walked with Mr. Merton and seen the house, and had determined that he would always change before going there on a Saturday, in order to avoid comments by servants and others who might be visiting them.

In thus acting Jack had no personal thoughts in the matter; much as he always shrank from being put forward as being in any way different from others, he had otherwise no self-consciousness whatever. No lad on the pits thought less of his personal appearance or attire, and his friend Nelly had many times taken him to task for his indifference in this respect. Mr. Merton perceived advantages in Jack's position in life not being generally known, and Jack at once fell into the arrangement, and carried it out, as described, to the best of his ability. But even he could not help seeing, when he had attired himself for his first visit to Mr. Merton's house, how complete had been the change in his appearance.

"Who would have thought that just a little difference in the make of a coat would have made such an alteration in one's look?" he said to himself.

"I feel different altogether; but that is nonsense, except that these boots are so much lighter than mine, that it seems as if I were in my stockings. Well, I suppose I shall soon be accustomed to it."

Packing a black coat and a few other articles in a hand-bag, and locking up the clothes he had taken off in his portmanteau, Jack started for Mr. Merton's. He was dressed in a well-fitting suit of dark tweed, with a claret-coloured neckerchief with plain gold scarf-ring. Jack's life of exercise had given him the free use of his limbs—he walked erect, and his head was well set back on his shoulders; altogether, with his crisp short waving hair, his good-humoured but resolute face, and his steadfast look, he was, although not handsome, yet a very pleasant-looking young fellow.

He soon forgot the fact of his new clothes, except that he was conscious of walking with a lightness and elasticity strange to him, and in half an hour rang at the visitors' bell of Mr. Merton's villa.

"A visitor, papa," said Alice, who was sitting near the window of the drawing-room. "How tiresome, just as we were expecting Jack Simpson. It is a gentleman. Why, papa!" and she clapped her hands, "it is Jack himself. I did not know him at first, he looks like a gentleman."

"He is a gentleman," Mr. Merton said; "a true gentleman in thought, feeling, and speech, and will soon adapt himself to the society he will meet here. Do not remark upon his dress unless he says something about it himself."

"Oh, papa, I should not think of such a thing. I am not so thoughtless as that."

The door was opened and Jack was shown in.

"How are you, Jack? I am glad to see you."

"Thank you, sir, I am always well," Jack said. Then turning to Miss Merton he asked her how she liked Birmingham. He had seen her often since the time when he first met her at the commencement of the strike, as he had helped them in their preparations for removing from Stokebridge, and had entirely got over the embarrassment which he had felt on the first evening spent there.

After talking for a few minutes, Jack said gravely to Mr. Merton, "I hope that these clothes will do, Mr. Merton?"

"Excellently well, Jack," he answered smiling; "they have made just the difference I expected; my daughter hardly knew you when you rang at the bell."

Facing death

"I hardly knew myself when I saw myself in a glass," Jack said. "Now, on what principle do you explain the fact that a slight alteration in the cutting and sewing together of pieces of cloth should make such a difference?"

"I do not know that I ever gave the philosophy of the question a moment's thought, Jack," said Mr. Merton smiling. "I can only explain it by the remark that the better cut clothes set off the natural curve of the neck, shoulders, and figure generally, and in the second place, being associated in our minds with the peculiar garb worn by gentlemen, they give what, for want of a better word, I may call style. A high black hat is the ugliest, most shapeless, and most unnatural article ever invented, but still a high hat, good and of the shape in vogue, certainly has a more gentlemanly effect, to use a word I hate, than any other. And now, my boy, you I know dined early, so did we. We shall have tea at seven, so we have three hours for work, and there are nearly six weeks' arrears, so do not let us waste any more time."

After this first visit Jack went out regularly once every four weeks. He fell very naturally into the ways of the house, and although his manner often amused Alice Merton greatly, and caused even her father to smile, he was never awkward or boorish.

As Alice came to know him more thoroughly, and their conversations ceased to be of a formal character, she surprised and sometimes quite puzzled him. The girl was full of fun and had a keen sense of humour, and her playful attacks upon his earnestness, her light way of parrying the problems which Jack, ever on the alert for information, was constantly putting, and the cheerful tone which her talk imparted to the general conversation when she was present, were all wholly new to the lad. Often he did not know whether she was in earnest or not, and was sometimes so overwhelmed by her light attacks as to be unable to answer.

Mr. Merton looked on, amused at their wordy conflicts; he knew that nothing does a boy so much good and so softens his manner as friendly intercourse with a well-read girl of about his own age, and undoubtedly Alice did almost as much towards preparing Jack's manner for his future career as her father had done towards preparing his mind.

As time went on Jack often met Mr. Merton's colleagues, and other gentlemen who came in in the evening. He was always introduced as "my young friend Simpson," with the aside, "a remarkably clever young fellow," and most of those who met him supposed him to be a pupil of the professor's.

Mr. Merton had, within a few months of his arrival at Birmingham, five or six young men to prepare for Cambridge. None of them resided in the house, but after Jack had become thoroughly accustomed to the position, Mr. Merton invited them, as well as a party of ladies and gentlemen, to the house on one of Jack's Saturday evenings.

Jack, upon hearing that a number of friends were coming in the evening, made an excuse to go into the town, and took his black bag with him.

Alice had already wondered over the matter.

"They will all be in dress, papa. Jack will feel awkward among them."

"He is only eighteen, my dear, and it will not matter his not being in evening dress. Jack will not feel awkward."

Alice, was, however, very pleased as well as surprised when, upon coming down dressed into the drawing-room, she found him in full evening dress chatting quietly with her father and two newly arrived guests. Jack would not have been awkward, but he would certainly have been uncomfortable had he not been dressed as were the others, for of all things he hated being different to other people.

He looked at Alice in a pretty pink muslin dress of fashionable make with a surprise as great as that with which she had glanced at him, for he had never before seen a lady in full evening dress.

Presently he said to her quietly, "I know I never say the right thing, Miss Merton, and I daresay it is quite wrong for me to express any personal opinions, but you do look—"

"No, Jack; that is quite the wrong thing to say. You may say, Miss Merton, your dress is a most becoming one, although even that you could not be allowed to say except to some one with whom you are very intimate. There are as many various shades of compliment as there are of intimacy. A brother may say to a sister, You look stunning to-night—that is a very slang word, Jack—and she will like it. A stranger or a new acquaintance may not say a word which would show that he observes a lady is not attired in a black walking dress."

"And what is the exact degree of intimacy in which one may say as you denoted, 'Miss Merton, your dress is a most becoming one?'"

"I should say," the girl said gravely, "it might be used by a cousin or by an old gentleman, a friend of the family."

Then with a laugh she went off to receive the guests, now beginning to arrive in earnest.

Facing death

After this Mr. Merton made a point of having an "at home" every fourth Saturday, and these soon became known as among the most pleasant and sociable gatherings in the literary and scientific world of Birmingham.

So young Jack Simpson led a dual life, spending twenty-six days of each month as a pit lad, speaking a dialect nearly as broad as that of his fellows, and two as a quiet and unobtrusive young student in the pleasant home of Mr. Merton.

Before a year had passed the one life seemed as natural to him as the other. Even with his friends he kept them separate, seldom speaking of Stokebridge when at Birmingham, save to answer Mr. Merton's questions as to old pupils; and giving accounts, which to Nelly Hardy appeared ridiculously meagre, of his Birmingham experience to his friends at home.

This was not from any desire to be reticent, but simply because the details appeared to him to be altogether uninteresting to his friends.

"You need not trouble to tell me any more, Jack," Nelly Hardy said indignantly. "I know it all by heart. You worked three hours with Mr. Merton; dinner at six; some people came at eight, no one in particular; they talked, and there was some playing on the piano; they went away at twelve. Next morning after breakfast you went to church, had dinner at two, took a walk afterwards, had tea at half-past six, supper at nine, then to bed. I won't ask you any more questions, Jack; if anything out of the way takes place you will tell me, no doubt."

CHAPTER XVII.

THE DOG FIGHT.

Saturday afternoon walks, when there were no special games on hand, became an institution among what may be called Jack Simpson's set at Stokebridge. The young fellows had followed his lead with all seriousness, and a stranger passing would have been astonished at the talk, so grave and serious was it. In colliery villages, as at school, the lad who is alike the head of the school and the champion at all games, is looked up to and admired and imitated, and his power for good or for evil is almost unlimited among his fellows. Thus the Saturday afternoon walks became supplements to the evening classes, and questions of all kinds were propounded to Jack, whose attainments they regarded as prodigious.

On such an afternoon, as Jack was giving his friends a brief sketch of the sun and its satellites, and of the wonders of the telescope, they heard bursts of applause by many voices, and a low, deep growling of dogs.

"It is a dog fight," one of the lads exclaimed.

"It is a brutal sport," Jack said. "Let us go another way."

One of the young fellows had, however, climbed a gate to see what was going on beyond the hedge.

"Jack," he exclaimed, "there is Bill Haden fighting his old bitch Flora against Tom Walker's Jess, and I think the pup is a-killing the old dorg."

With a bound Jack Simpson sprang into the field, where some twenty or thirty men were standing looking at a dog fight. One dog had got the other down and was evidently killing it.

"Throw up the sponge, Bill," the miners shouted. "The old dorg's no good agin the purp."

Jack dashed into the ring, with a kick he sent the young dog flying across the ring, and picked up Flora, who, game to the last, struggled to get at her foe.

Facing death

A burst of indignation and anger broke from the men.

"Let un be." "Put her down." "Dang thee, how dare'st meddle here?" "I'll knock thee head off," and other shouts sounded loudly and threateningly.

"For shame!" Jack said indignantly. "Be ye men! For shame, Bill Haden, to match thy old dog, twelve year old, wi' a young un. She's been a good dorg, and hast brought thee many a ten-pun note. If be'est tired of her, gi' her poison, but I woant stand by and see her mangled."

"How dare 'ee kick my dorg?" a miner said coming angrily forward; "how dare 'ee come here and hinder sport?"

"Sport!" Jack said indignantly, "there be no sport in it. It is brutal cruelty."

"The match be got to be fought out," another said, "unless Bill Haden throws up the sponge for his dog."

"Come," Tom Walker said putting his hand on Jack's shoulder, "get out o' this; if it warn't for Bill Haden I'd knock thee head off. We be coom to see spoort, and we mean to see it."

"Spoort!" Jack said passionately. "If it's spoort thee want'st I'll give it thee. Flora sha'n't go into the ring agin, but oi ull. I'll fight the best man among ye, be he which he will."

A chorus of wonder broke from the colliers.

"Then thou'st get to fight me," Tom Walker said. "I b'liev'," he went on looking round, "there bean't no man here ull question that. Thou'st wanted a leathering for soom time, Jack Simpson, wi' thy larning and thy ways, and I'm not sorry to be the man to gi' it thee."

"No, no," Bill Haden said, and the men round for the most part echoed his words. "'Taint fair for thee to take t' lad at his word. He be roight. I hadn't ought to ha' matched Flora no more. She ha' been a good bitch in her time, but she be past it, and I'll own up that thy pup ha' beaten her, and pay thee the two pounds I lay on her, if ee'll let this matter be."

"Noa," Tom Walker said, "the young 'un ha' challenged the best man here, and I be a-goaing to lick him if he doant draw back."

"I shall not draw back," Jack said divesting himself of his coat, waistcoat, and shirt. "Flora got licked a'cause she was too old, maybe I'll be licked a'cause I be too young; but she made a good foight, and so'll oi. No, dad, I won't ha' you to back me. Harry here shall do that."

The ring was formed again. The lads stood on one side, the men on the other. It was understood now that there was to be a fight, and no one had another word to say.

"I'll lay a fi'-pound note to a shilling on the old un," a miner said.

"I'll take 'ee," Bill Haden answered. "It hain't a great risk to run, and Jack is as game as Flora."

Several other bets were made at similar odds, the lads, although they deemed the conflict hopeless, yet supporting their champion.

Tom Walker stood but little taller than Jack, who was about five feet six, and would probably grow two inches more; but he was three stone heavier, Jack being a pound or two only over ten while the pitman reached thirteen. The latter was the acknowledged champion of the Vaughan pits, as Jack was incontestably the leader among the lads. The disproportion in weight and muscle was enormous; but Jack had not a spare ounce of flesh on his bones, while the pitman was fleshy and out of condition.

It is not necessary to give the details of the fight, which lasted over an hour. In the earlier portion Jack was knocked down again and again, and was several times barely able to come up to the call of time; but his bull-dog strain, as he called it, gradually told, while intemperate habits and want of condition did so as surely upon his opponent.

The derisive shouts with which the men had hailed every knock-down blow early in the fight soon subsided, and exclamations of admiration at the pluck with which Jack, reeling and confused, came up time after time took their place.

"It be a foight arter all," one of them said at the end of the first ten minutes. "I wouldn't lay more nor ten to one now."

"I'll take as many tens to one as any o' ye like to lay," Bill Haden said, but no one cared to lay even these odds.

At the end of half an hour the betting was only two to one. Jack, who had always "given his head," that is, had always ducked so as to receive the blows on the top of his head, where they were supposed to do less harm, was as strong as he was after the first five minutes. Tom Walker was panting with fatigue, wild and furious at his want of success over an adversary he had despised.

Facing death

The cheers of the lads, silent at first, rose louder with each round, and culminated in a yell of triumph when, at the end of fifty-five minutes, Tom Walker, having for the third time in succession been knocked down, was absolutely unable to rise at the call of "time" to renew the fight.

161

JACK IS VICTORIOUS.

Never had an event created such a sensation in Stokebridge. At first the news was received with absolute incredulity, but when it became thoroughly understood that Bill Haden's boy, Jack Simpson, had licked Tom Walker, the wonder knew no bounds. So struck were some of the men with Jack's courage and endurance, that the offer was made to him that, if he liked to go to Birmingham and put himself under that noted pugilist the "Chicken," his expenses would be paid, and £50 be forthcoming for his first match. Jack, knowing that this offer was made in good faith and with good intentions, and was in accordance with the custom of mining villages, declined it courteously and thankfully, but firmly, to the surprise and disappointment of his would-be backers, who had flattered themselves that Stokebridge was going to produce a champion middle-weight.

He had not come unscathed from the fight, for it proved that one of his ribs had been broken by a heavy body hit; and he was for some weeks in the hands of the doctor, and was longer still before he could again take his place in the pit.

Bill Haden's pride in him was unbounded, and during his illness poor old Flora, who seemed to recognize in him her champion, lay on his bed with her black muzzle in the hand not occupied with a book.

The victory which Jack had won gave the finishing stroke to his popularity and influence among his companions, and silenced definitely and for ever the sneers of the minority who had held out against the change which he had brought about. He himself felt no elation at his victory, and objected to the subject even being alluded to.

"It was just a question of wind and last," he said. "I was nigh being done for at the end o' the first three rounds. I just managed to hold on, and then it was a certainty. If Tom Walker had been in condition he would have finished me in ten minutes. If he had come on working as a getter, I should ha' been nowhere; he's a weigher now and makes fat, and his muscles are flabby. The best dorg can't fight when he's out o' condition."

But in spite of that, the lads knew that it was only bull-dog courage that had enabled Jack to hold out over these bad ten minutes.

As for Jane Haden, her reproaches to her husband for in the first place matching Flora against a young dog, and in the second for allowing Jack to fight so noted a man as Tom Walker, were so fierce and vehement, that until Jack was able to leave his bed and take his place by the fire, Bill was but little at home; spending all his time, even at meals, in that place of refuge from his wife's tongue,—"the Chequers."

CHAPTER XVIII.

STOKEBRIDGE FEAST.

Even among the mining villages of the Black Country Stokebridge had a reputation for roughness; and hardened topers of the place would boast that in no village in the county was there so much beer drunk per head. Stokebridge feast was frequented by the dwellers of the mining villages for miles round, and the place was for the day a scene of disgraceful drunkenness and riot. Crowds of young men and women came in, the public-houses were crowded, there was a shouting of songs and a scraping of fiddles from each tap-room, and dancing went on in temporary booths.

One of these feasts had taken place just after the establishment of the night classes, and had been marked by even greater drunkenness and more riotous scenes than usual. For years the vicar in the church and the dissenting ministers in their meeting-houses had preached in vain against the evil. Their congregations were small, and in this respect their words fell upon ears closed to exhortation. During the year which had elapsed, however, there was a perceptible change in Stokebridge, a change from which those interested in it hoped for great results.

The Bull-dogs and their kindred societies had set the fashion, and the demeanour and bearing of the young men and boys was quiet and orderly. In every match which they had played at rounders, football, and quoits, with the surrounding villages Stokebridge had won easily, and never were the games entered into with more zest than now.

The absence of bad language in the streets was surprising. The habit of restraint upon the tongue acquired in the club-rooms had spread, and two months after Jack's first proposal had been so coldly received, the proposition to extend the fines to swearing outside the walls as well as in was unanimously agreed to. The change in the demeanour of the girls was even greater. Besides the influence of Mrs. Dodgson and her assistant, aided perhaps by the desire to stand well in the eyes of lads of the place, their boisterous habits had been toned down, dark neatly made dresses took the place of bright-coloured and flimsy ones; hair, faces, and hands showed more care and self-respect.

Facing death

The example of the young people had not been without its influence upon the elders. Not indeed upon the regular drinking set, but upon those who only occasionally gave way. The tidier and more comfortable homes, the better cooked meals, all had their effect; and all but brutalized men shrank from becoming objects of shame to their children. As to the women of Stokebridge they were for the most part delighted with the change. Some indeed grumbled at the new-fangled ways, and complained that their daughters were getting above them, but as the lesson taught in the night-classes was that the first duty of a girl or woman was to make her home bright and happy, to bear patiently the tempers of others, to be a peacemaker and a help, to bear with children, and to respect elders, even the grumblers gave way at last.

The very appearance of the village was changing. Pots of bright flowers stood in the windows, creepers and roses climbed over the walls, patches full of straggling weeds were now well-kept gardens; in fact, as Mr. Brook said one day to the vicar, one would hardly know the place.

"There has indeed been a strange movement for good," the clergyman said, "and I cannot take any share of it to myself. It has been going on for some time invisibly, and the night schools and classes for girls have given it an extraordinary impulse. It is a changed place altogether. I am sorry that the feast is at hand. It always does an immense deal of mischief, and is a time of quarrel, drunkenness, and license. I wish that something could be done to counteract its influence."

"So do I," Mr. Brook said. "Can you advise anything?"

"I cannot," the vicar said; "but I will put on my hat and walk with you down to the schoolhouse. To Dodgson and his wife is due the real credit of the change; they are indefatigable, and their influence is very great. Let us put the question to them."

The schoolmaster had his evening class in; Mrs. Dodgson had ten girls working and reading in her parlour, as she invited that number of the neatest and most quiet of her pupils to tea on each evening that her husband was engaged with his night-school. These evenings were greatly enjoyed by the girls, and the hope of being included among the list of invited had done much towards producing a change of manners.

It was a fine evening, and the schoolmaster and his wife joined Mr. Brook out of doors, and apologizing for the room being full asked them to sit down in the rose-covered arbour at the end of the garden. The vicar explained the object of the visit.

"My wife and I have been talking the matter over, Mr. Brook," the schoolmaster said, "and we deplore these feasts, which are the bane of the place. They demoralize the village; all sorts of good resolutions give way under temptation, and then those who have given way are ashamed to rejoin their better companions. It cannot be put down, I suppose?"

"No," Mr. Brook said. "It is held in a field belonging to "The Chequers," and even did I succeed in getting it closed—which of course would be out of the question—they would find some other site for the booths."

"Would you be prepared to go to some expense to neutralize the bad effects of this feast, Mr. Brook?"

"Certainly; any expense in reason."

"What I was thinking, sir, is that if upon the afternoon of the feast you could give a fête in your grounds, beginning with say a cricket-match, followed by a tea, with conjuring or some such amusement afterwards—for I do not think that they would care for dancing—winding up with sandwiches and cakes, and would invite the girls of my wife's sewing-classes with any other girls they may choose to bring with them, and the lads of my evening class, with similar permission to bring friends, we should keep all those who are really the moving spirits of the improvement which has taken place here out of reach of temptation."

"Your idea is excellent," Mr. Brook said. "I will get the band of the regiment at Birmingham over, and we will wind up with a display of fireworks, and any other attraction which, after thinking the matter over, you can suggest, shall be adopted. I have greatly at heart the interests of my pitmen, and the fact that last year they were led away to play me a scurvy trick is all forgotten now. A good work has been set on foot here, and if we can foster it and keep it going, Stokebridge will in future years be a very different place to what it has been."

Mr. Dodgson consulted Jack Simpson the next day as to the amusements likely to be most popular; but Jack suggested that Fred Wood and Bill Cummings should be called into consultation, for, as he said, he knew nothing of girls' ways, and his opinions were worth nothing. His two friends were sent for and soon arrived. They agreed that a cricket-match would be the greatest attraction, and that the band of the soldiers would delight the girls. It was arranged that a challenge should be sent to Batterbury, which lay thirteen miles off, and would therefore know nothing of the feast. The Stokebridge team had visited them the summer before and beaten them, therefore they would no doubt come to Stokebridge. They thought that a good conjuror would be an immense attraction, as such a thing had never been seen in Stokebridge, and that the fireworks would be a splendid wind up. Mr. Brook had proposed that a dinner for the contending cricket teams should be served in a marquee, but to this the lads objected, as not only would the girls be left out, but also the lads not engaged in the match. It would be better, they thought, for there to be a table with sandwiches, buns, lemonade, and tea, from which all could help themselves.

The arrangements were all made privately, as it was possible that the publicans might, were they aware of the intended counter attraction, change the day of the feast, although this was unlikely, seeing that it had from time immemorial taken place on the 3rd of September except only when that day fell on a Sunday; still it was better to run no risk. A meeting of the "Bull-dogs" was called for the 27th of August, and at this Jack announced the invitation which had been received from Mr. Brook. A few were inclined to demur at giving up the jollity of the feast, but by this time the majority of the lads had gone heart and soul into the movement for improvement. The progress made had already been so great, the difficulties at first met had been so easily overcome, that they were eager to carry on the work. One or two of those most doubtful as to their own resolution were the most ready to accept the invitation of their employer, for it was morally certain that everyone would be drunk on the night of the feast, and it was an inexorable law of the "Bull-dogs" that any of the members getting drunk were expelled from that body. The invitation was at last accepted without a dissenting voice, the challenge to Batterbury written, and then the members went off to the associated clubs of which they were members to obtain the adhesion of these also to the fête at Mr. Brook's. Mrs. Dodgson had harder work with the sewing-class. The attraction of the dancing and display of finery at the feast was greater to many of the girls than to the boys. Many eagerly accepted the invitation; but it was not until Mr. Dodgson came in late in the evening and announced in an audible tone to his wife that he was glad to say that the whole of the young fellows of the night-school had accepted the invitation, that the girls all gave way and agreed to go to the fête.

Accordingly on the 3rd of September, just as the people from the pit villages round were flocking in to Stokebridge, a hundred and fifty of the young people of that place, with a score or two of young married couples and steady men and women, set out in their Sunday suits for Mr. Brook's.

It was a glorious day. The cricket-match was a great success, the military band was delightful, and Mr. Brook had placed it on the lawn, so that those of the young people who chose could dance to the inspiring strains. Piles of sandwiches disappeared during the afternoon, and the tea, coffee, and lemonade were pronounced excellent. There was, too, a plentiful supply of beer for such of the lads as preferred it; as Mr. Brook thought that it would look like a want of confidence in his visitors did he not provide them with beer.

Batterbury was beaten soundly; and when it was dark the party assembled in a large marquee. There a conjuror first performed, and after giving all the usual wonders, produced from an inexhaustible box such pretty presents in the way of well-furnished work-bags and other useful articles for the girls that these were delighted. But the surprise of the evening was yet to come. It was not nine o'clock when the conjuror finished, and Mr. Dodgson was thinking anxiously that the party would be back in Stokebridge long before the feast was over. Suddenly a great pair of curtains across the end of the tent drew aside and a regular stage was seen. Mr. Brook had obtained the services of five or six actors and actresses from the Birmingham theatre, together with scenery and all accessories; and for two hours and a half the audience was kept in a roar of laughter by some well-acted farces.

When the curtain fell at last, Mr. Brook himself came in front of it. So long and hearty was the cheering that it was a long time before he could obtain a hearing. At last silence was restored.

"I am very glad, my friends," he said, "that you have had a happy afternoon and evening, and I hope that another year I shall see you all here again. I should like to say a few words before we separate. You young men, lads and lasses, will in a few years have a paramount influence in Stokebridge; upon you it depends whether that place is to be, as it used to be, like other colliery villages in Staffordshire, or to be a place inhabited by decent and civilized people. I am delighted to observe that a great change has lately come over it, due in a great measure to your good and kind friends Mr. and Mrs. Dodgson, who have devoted their whole time and efforts to your welfare." The cheering at this point was as great as that which had greeted Mr. Brook himself, but was even surpassed by that which burst out when a young fellow shouted out, "and Jack Simpson." During this Jack Simpson savagely made his way out of the tent, and remained outside, muttering threats about punching heads, till the proceedings were over. "And Jack Simpson," Mr. Brook went on, smiling, after the cheering had subsided. "I feel sure that the improvement will be maintained. When you see the comfort of homes in which the wives are cleanly, tidy, and intelligent, able to make the dresses of themselves and their children, and to serve their husbands with decently cooked food; and in which the husbands spend their evenings and their wages at home, treating their wives as rational beings, reading aloud, or engaged in cheerful conversation, and compare their homes with those of the drunkard and the slattern, it would seem impossible for any reasonable human being to hesitate in his or her choice between them. It is in your power, my friends, each and all, which of these homes shall be yours. I have thought that some active amusement is necessary, and have arranged, after consultation with your vicar and with Mr. and Mrs. Dodgson, that a choir-master from Birmingham shall come over twice a week, to train such of you as may wish and may have voices, in choir-singing. As the lads of Stokebridge can beat those of any of the surrounding villages at cricket, so I hope in time the choir of the lads and lasses of this place will be able to hold its own against any other." Again the speaker had to pause, for the cheering was enthusiastic. "And now, good-night; and may I say that I hope and trust that when the fireworks, which will now be displayed, are over, you will all go home and straight to bed, without being tempted to join in the doings at the feast. If so, it will be a satisfaction to me to think that for the first time since the feast was first inaugurated, neither lad nor lass of Stokebridge will have cause to look back upon the feast-day with regret or shame."

CHAPTER XIX.

THE GREAT RIOT.

Stokebridge feast had not gone off with its usual spirit. The number of young pitmen and lads from the surrounding villages were as large as ever, and there was no lack of lasses in gay bonnets and bright dresses. The fact, however, that almost the whole of the lads and girls of Stokebridge between the ages of fifteen and eighteen had left the village and gone to a rival fête elsewhere, cast a damper on the proceedings. There were plenty of young women and young men in Stokebridge who were as ready as ever to dance and to drink, and who were, perhaps, even gaudier in attire and more boisterous in manner than usual, as a protest against the recession of their juniors; for Stokebridge was divided into two very hostile camps, and, as was perhaps not unnatural, those over the age of the girls and lads at the night-schools resented the changes which had been made, and rebelled against the, as they asserted, airs of superiority of younger sisters and brothers.

In some cases no doubt there was ground for the feeling. The girls and lads, eager to introduce the new lessons of order and neatness which they had learned, may have gone too fast and acted with too much zeal, although their teacher had specially warned them against so doing. Hence the feeling of hostility to the movement was strong among a small section of Stokebridge, and the feeling was heightened by the secession in a body of the young people from the feast.

As the day went on the public-houses were as full as ever, indeed it was said that never before had so much liquor been consumed; the fiddles played and the dancing and boisterous romping went on as usual, but there was less real fun and enjoyment. As evening came on the young fellows talked together in angry groups. Whether the proposal emanated from some of the Stokebridge men or from the visitors from other villages was afterwards a matter of much dispute, but it gradually became whispered about among the dancing booths and public-houses that there was an intention to give the party from Brook's a warm reception when they arrived. Volleys of mud and earth were prepared, and some of the overdressed young women tossed their heads, and said that a spattering with mud would do the stuck-up girls no harm.

Facing death

The older pitmen, who would have certainly opposed any such design being carried out, were kept in ignorance of what was intended; the greater portion were indeed drunk long before the time came when the party would be returning from the fête.

At a quarter before twelve Jane Haden, who had been sitting quietly at home, went up to the "Chequers" to look after her husband, and to see about his being brought home should he be incapable of walking. The music was still playing in the dancing booths, but the dancing was kept up without spirit, for a number of young men and lads were gathered outside. As she passed she caught a few words which were sufficient to inform her of what was going on. "Get some sticks oot o' hedges." "Fill your pockets oop wi' stones." "We'll larn 'em to spoil the feast."

Jane saw that an attack was going to be made upon the party, and hesitated for a moment what to do. The rockets were going up in Mr. Brook's grounds, and she knew she had a few minutes yet. First she ran to the house of James Shepherd. The pitman, who was a sturdy man, had been asleep for the last three hours. She knocked at the door, unlocked it, and went in.

"Jim," she called in a loud voice.

"Aye, what be't?" said a sleepy voice upstairs; "be't thou, Harry and Sally?"

"No, it be I, Jane Haden; get up quickly, Jim; quick, man, there be bad doings, and thy lad and lass are like to have their heads broke if no worse."

Alarmed by the words and the urgent manner of his neighbour, Jim and his wife slipped on a few clothes and came down. Jane at once told them what she had heard.

"There be between two and three hundred of 'em," she said, "as far as I could see the wust lot out o' Stokebridge, and a lot o' roughs from t' other villages. Quick, Jim, do you and Ann go round quick to the houses o' all the old hands who ha' kept away from the feast or who went home drunk early, they may ha' slept 't off by this, and get 'un together. Let 'em take pick-helves, and if there's only twenty of ye and ye fall upon this crowd ye'll drive 'em. If ye doan't it will go bad wi' all our lads and lasses. I'll go an' warn 'em, and tell 'em to stop a few minutes on t' road to give 'ee time to coom up. My Jack and the lads will foight, no fear o' that, but they can't make head agin so many armed wi' sticks and stones too; but if ye come up behind and fall on 'em when it begins ye'll do, even though they be stronger."

Facing death

Fully awake now to the danger which threatened the young people, for the pitman and his wife knew that when blows were exchanged and blood heated things would go much further than was at first intended, they hurried off to get a few men together, while Jane Haden started for the hall.

Already the riotous crowd had gone on and she had to make a detour, but she regained the road, and burst breathless and panting into the midst of the throng of young people coming along the lane chatting gaily of the scenes of the evening.

"Stop, stop!" she cried; "don't go a foot further—where be my Jack?"

"It's Mrs. Haden," Nelly Hardy said. "Jack, it's your mother."

"What is it?" Jack said in astonishment. "Anything wrong wi' dad?"

"Stop!" Mrs. Haden gasped again; "there's three hundred and more young chaps and boys wi' sticks and stones joost awaiting on this side t'village, awaiting to pay you all oot."

Ejaculations of alarm were heard all round, and several of the girls began to whimper.

"Hush!" Mr. Dodgson said, coming forward. "Let all keep silence, there may be no occasion for alarm; let us hear all about it, Mrs. Haden."

Mrs. Haden repeated her story, and said that Harry's father and mother were getting a body of pitmen to help them.

"I think, Mr. Dodgson," said Jack, "the girls had best go back to Mr. Brook's as quickly as possible; we will come and fetch them when it's all over."

"I think so too," said Mr. Dodgson, "they might be injured by stones. My dear, do you lead the girls back to Mr. Brook's. The house will hardly be shut up yet, and even if it is, Mr. Brook will gladly receive you. There is no chance of any of the ruffians pursuing them, do you think, Jack, when they find they have only us to deal with?"

"I don't know, sir. If three or four of us were to put on their cloaks, something light to show in the dark, they will think the girls are among us."

"Quick! here they come," Mr. Dodgson said, "go back silently, girls, not a word."

Two or three cloaks and shawls were hastily borrowed and the lads then turned up the road, where the sound of suppressed laughter and coarse oaths could be heard, while the young women went off at a rapid pace towards the hall.

"There are four of the clubs, nigh twenty in each," Jack said; "let each club keep together and go right at 'em. Stick together whatever ye do."

"I'll take my place by you, Jack," Mr. Dodgson said; "you are our captain now."

Talking in a careless voice the party went forward. The road here was only divided from the fields on either side by a newly planted hedge of a foot or so in height. Jack had arranged that he, with the few married pitmen, Mr. Dodgson, and the eight Bull-dogs who did not belong to the other associations, should hold the road; that two of the other clubs should go on each side, fight their way as far as they could, and then close in on the road to take the assailants there on both flanks.

The spirit of association did wonders; many of the lads were but fourteen or fifteen, yet all gathered under their respective leaders and prepared for what they felt would be a desperate struggle. Presently they saw a dark mass gathered in the road.

As soon as the light shawls were seen there was a cry of "Here they be, give it 'em well, lads;" and a volley of what were, in the majority of cases, clods of earth, but among which were many stones, was poured in. Without an instant's pause the party attacked separated, two bands leapt into the field on either side, and then the whole rushed at the assailants. No such charge as this had been anticipated. The cowardly ruffians had expected to give a complete surprise, to hear the shrieks of the girls, and perhaps some slight resistance from a few of the older lads; the suddenness of this attack astonished them.

In an instant Jack and his supporters were in their midst, and the fury which animated them at this cowardly attack, and the unity of their action, bore all before them; and in spite of their sticks the leaders of the assailants were beaten to the ground. Then the sheer weight of the mass behind stopped the advance and the conflict became a general one. In the crowd and confusion it was difficult to distinguish friend from foe, and this prevented the assailants from making full use of their stakes, rails, and other implements with which they were armed. They were, however, getting the best of it, Mr. Dodgson had been knocked down with a heavy stake and several others were badly hurt, when the strong bands in the field who had driven back the scattered assailants there, fell upon the flanks of the main body in the road.

Facing death

For five minutes the fight was a desperate one, and then, just as numbers and weapons were telling, there was a shout in the rear, and fifteen pitmen, headed by Jim Shepherd and armed with pick handles, as formidable weapons as could be desired in the hands of strong men, fell upon the rear of the assailants. Yells, shouts, and heavy crashing blows told the tale to those engaged in front; and at once the assailants broke and scattered in flight.

"Catch 'em and bring 'em down," Jack shouted; "they shall pay for this night's work."

Such of the lads as were not disabled started off, and being fleet of foot, those of the assailants nearest to them had little chance of escape. Two or three lads together sprung upon one and pulled him down, and so when the pursuit ended twenty-nine of the assailants had fallen into their hands. In addition to this a score of them lay or sat by the road with broken heads and bones, the work of the pitmen's weapons.

Of the lads the greater part had been badly knocked about, and some lay insensible in the road. The prisoners were brought together, five of the pitmen with twenty of the lads marched with those able to walk, to the village, where they shut them up in the school-room. The other pitmen remained in charge of the wounded of both sides, and the rest of the party were sent back to Mr. Brook's to fetch the women and girls. Near the house they met Mr. Brook, accompanied by his two men-servants and gardener, armed with spades, hurrying forward; and he expressed his delight at the issue of the conflict, but shook his head at the number of serious injuries on both sides.

In a shed near the house were a number of hurdles, and twenty of these were at once sent forward with the men to carry those unable to walk into the village.

Mrs. Dodgson turned pale as her husband, his face covered with blood, entered the dining-room, where, huddled together, the frightened girls were standing; Mrs. Dodgson, aided by Nelly Hardy, having done her utmost to allay their fears.

"I am not hurt," Mr. Dodgson said heartily, "at least not seriously; but I fear that some are. It is all over now, and those ruffians have fled. Jack Simpson and a party are outside to escort you home. We don't know who are hurt yet, but they will be carried to the girls' school-room and attended there. Harry Shepherd has gone on to get the doctor up, and Mr. Brook is sending off a man on horseback to Birmingham for some more medical aid and a body of police to take charge of the fellows we have captured; they will be in by the early train."

Facing death

Everything was quiet in Stokebridge when the party with the prisoners arrived. The pitmen, before starting, had gone into the public-house to get any sober enough to walk to join them; and the few who had kept up the dancing, alarmed at the serious nature of the affair, of which they had tacitly approved, scattered to their homes.

The news of the conflict, however, quickly circulated, lights appeared in windows, and the women who had sons or daughters at the fête flocked out into the streets to hear the news. Many other pitmen, whom there had not been time enough to summon, soon joined them, and deep indeed was the wrath with which the news of the assault was received. Most of the men at once hurried away to the scene of conflict to see who were hurt, and to assist to carry them in; and the sole ground for satisfaction was that the women and girls had all escaped injury.

CHAPTER XX.

THE ARM OF THE LAW.

That was a sad night at Stokebridge. Seven of the lads were terribly injured, and in two cases the doctors gave no hope of recovery. Thirteen of the other party were also grievously hurt by the blows of the pitmen's helves, some had limbs broken, and three lay unconscious all night. Most of the boys had scalp wounds, inflicted by stones or sticks, which required dressing. Worst of all was the news that among the twenty-five uninjured prisoners were eight who belonged to Stokebridge, besides five among the wounded.

Very few in the village closed an eye that night. Mothers went down and implored the pitmen on guard to release their sons, but the pitmen were firm; moreover Mr. Brook as a magistrate had placed the two constables of the place at the door, with the strictest order to allow none of the prisoners to escape. The six o'clock train brought twenty policemen from Birmingham, and these at once took charge of the schoolhouse, and relieved the pitmen of their charge. The working of the mine was suspended for the day, and large numbers of visitors poured into the place. So desperate a riot had never occurred in that neighbourhood before, for even the attack upon the machinery of the mine was considered a less serious affair than this.

Not only did curiosity to learn the facts of the case attract a crowd of visitors, but there were many people who came from the pit villages near to inquire after missing husbands and sons, and loud were the wailings of women when it was found that these were either prisoners or were lying injured in the temporary hospital.

Strangers entering the village would have supposed that a great explosion had taken place in some neighbouring pit. Blinds were down, women stood at the doors with their aprons to their eyes, children went about in an awed and silent way, as if afraid of the sound of their own voice, many of the young men and lads had their heads enveloped in surgical bandages, and a strange and unnatural calm pervaded the village. The "Chequers" and other public-houses, however, did a roaring trade, for the sight-seer in the black country is the thirstiest of men.

Facing death

It was soon known that the magistrates would sit at Mr. Brook's at one o'clock, and a policeman went round the village with a list of names given him by Mr. Dodgson, to summon witnesses to attend. Jack Simpson had strongly urged that his name might not be included, in the first place because above all things he hated being put forward, and in the second, as he pointed out to the schoolmaster, it might excite a feeling against him, and hinder his power for good, if he, the leader of the young men, was to appear as a witness against the elders, especially as among the prisoners was Tom Walker, with whom he had fought. As Jack could give no more testimony than his companions, and as generally it was considered an important and responsible privilege to appear as witness, Mr. Dodgson omitted Jack's name from the list.

There was some groaning in the crowd when the uninjured prisoners were marched out under escort of the police, for the attack upon young women was so contrary to all the traditions of the country that the liveliest indignation prevailed against all concerned in it. The marquee used the night before for the theatricals had been hastily converted into a justice room. At a table sat Mr. Brook with four other magistrates, with a clerk to take notes; the prisoners were ranged in a space railed off for the purpose, and the general public filled the rest of the space.

Jane Haden was the first witness called. She gave her evidence clearly, but with an evident wish to screen some of the accused, and was once or twice sharply reproved by the bench. She could not say who were among the men she saw gathered, nor recognize any of those who had used the threatening expressions which had so alarmed her that she went round to arouse the elder men, and then ran off to warn the returning party.

"Mrs. Haden," Sir John Butler, who was the chairman of the magistrates, said, "very great praise is due to you for your quickness and decision; had it not been for this there can be no doubt that the riot would have led to results even more disastrous than those which have taken place. At the same time it is the feeling of the court that you are now trying to screen the accused, for it can hardly be, that passing so close you could fail to recognize some of those whom you heard speak."

Mr. Dodgson then gave his evidence, as did several of the lads, who proved the share that the accused had taken in the fray, and that they were captured on the spot; while two of the pitmen proved that when they arrived upon the spot a desperate riot was going on, and that they joined in the fray to assist the party attacked.

The examination lasted for four hours, at the end of which the whole of the prisoners were remanded to prison, the case being adjourned for two days.

Facing death

Before these were passed, both the lads whose cases had been thought hopeless from the first, died, and the matter assumed even a more serious appearance. Before the next hearing several of the prisoners offered to turn king's evidence, and stated that they had been incited by the young women at the feast.

Great excitement was caused in the village when ten or twelve young women were served with warrants to appear on the following day. They were placed in the dock with the other prisoners, but no direct evidence was taken against them. The number of the accused were further swelled by two men belonging to other villages, who had been arrested on the sworn evidence of some of the lads that they had been active in the fray.

At the conclusion of the case the whole of the male prisoners were committed for trial on the charges of manslaughter and riot. After these had been removed in custody, Sir John Butler addressed a severe admonition to the women.

It had, he said, been decided not to press the charge against them of inciting to riot, but that they had used expressions calculated to stir the men up to their foul and dastardly attack upon a number of young women and girls there could be no doubt. The magistrates, however, had decided to discharge them, and hoped that the inward reproach which they could not but feel at having a hand in this disgraceful and fatal outrage would be a lesson to them through life.

Trembling and abashed, the women made their way home, many of the crowd hissing them as they passed along.

When, six weeks later, the assizes were held, four of the prisoners, including Tom Walker, who was proved to be the leader, were sentenced to seven years penal servitude. Ten men had terms of imprisonment varying from two to five years, and the rest were let off with sentences of from six to eighteen months.

Very long did the remembrance of "The Black Feast," as it came to be called, linger in the memories of the people of Stokebridge and the surrounding district. Great as was the grief and suffering caused alike to the friends of those injured and of those upon whom fell punishment and disgrace, the ultimate effect of the riot was, however, most beneficial to Stokebridge. Many of the young men who had most strongly opposed and derided the efforts of their juniors to improve themselves, were now removed, for in addition to those captured and sentenced, several of those who had taken part in the riot hastily left the place upon the following day, fearing arrest and punishment for their share in the night's proceedings. Few of them returned after the conclusion of the trial, nor did the prisoners after the termination of their sentences, for the feeling against them in the district was so strong that they preferred obtaining work in distant parts of the country.

A similar effect was produced upon the young women. The narrow escape which they had had of being sent to prison, the disgrace of being arrested and publicly censured, the averted looks of their neighbours, and the removal from the place of the young men with whom they had been used to associate, combined to produce a great effect upon them.

Some profited by the lesson and adapted themselves to the altered ways of the place; others, after trying to brave it out, left Stokebridge and obtained employment in the factories of Birmingham; while others again, previously engaged to some of the young men who had left the village, were sooner or later married to them, and were heard of no more in Stokebridge.

This removal by one means or another of some forty or fifty of the young men and women of the place most opposed to the spirit of improvement, produced an excellent effect. Other miners came of course to the village to take the places of those who had left, but as Mr. Brook instructed his manager to fill up the vacant stalls as far as possible with middle-aged men with families, and not with young men, the new-comers were not an element of disturbance.

The price of coal was at this time high, and Mr. Brook informed the clergyman that, as he was drawing a larger income than usual from the mines, he was willing to give a sum for any purpose which he might recommend as generally useful to the families of his work-people. The vicar as usual consulted his valued assistants the Dodgsons, and after much deliberation it was agreed that if a building were to be erected the lower story of which should be fitted up as a laundry and wash-house upon the plan which was then being introduced in some large towns, it would be an immense boon to the place. The upper story was to be furnished as a reading-room with a few papers and a small library of useful and entertaining books for reading upon the spot or lending. Plans were obtained and estimates given, and Mr. Brook expressed his willingness to contribute the sum of eighteen hundred pounds for which a contractor offered to complete the work.

CHAPTER XXI.

A KNOTTY QUESTION.

It has not been mentioned that at the fête at Mr. Brook's on the memorable occasion of the Black Feast, Mr. Merton and his daughter were staying as guests with Mr. Brook. Mr. Merton was much struck with the extraordinary improvement which had taken place in the bearing and appearance of the young people.

"Yes," Mr. Dodgson, whom he congratulated upon the change, said; "it is entirely due to the suggestion which you made upon my arrival here. The night-schools for lads and the sewing and cooking classes for the girls have done wonders, and I have found in the lad you recommended to my attention, Jack Simpson, an invaluable ally. Without him, indeed, I think that our plan would have been a failure. He is a singular young fellow, so quiet yet so determined; the influence he has over the lads of his own age is immense."

"He is more than singular," Mr. Merton said warmly; "he is extraordinary. You only see one side of his character, I see both. As a scholar he is altogether remarkable. He could carry off any open scholarship at Cambridge, and could take away the highest honours; he could pass high up among the wranglers even now, and has a broad and solid knowledge of other subjects."

"Indeed!" Mr. Dodgson said, surprised; "this is quite new to me. I know that he studies hard privately, and that he went over to see you once a month, but I had no idea that his acquirements were anything exceptional, and, indeed, although his speech is often superior to that of the other young fellows, he often makes mistakes in grammar and pronunciation."

Mr. Merton laughed. "That is one of his peculiarities; he does not wish to be thought above his fellows: look at his dress, now! But if you saw him with me, and heard him talking with the first men of education and science in Birmingham you would share the astonishment they often express to me, and would take him not only for a young gentleman, but for one of singular and exceptionally cultured mind."

Facing death

Jack's attire, indeed—it was after the conclusion of the cricket-match, and he had changed his clothes—was that of the ordinary pitman in his Sunday suit. A black cutaway coat, badly fitting, and made by the village tailor, a black waistcoat and trousers, with thick high-low shoes. His appearance had attracted the attention of Miss Merton, who, as he approached her, held out her hand.

"How are you, Jack? What on earth have you been doing to yourself? You look a complete guy in these clothes. I was half tempted to cut you downright."

Jack laughed.

"This is my Sunday suit, Miss Merton, it is just the same as other people's."

"Perhaps it is," the girl said, laughing, and looking round with just a little curl of her lip; "but you know better, Jack: why should you make such a figure of yourself?"

"I dress here like what I am," Jack said simply, "a pitman. At your house I dress as one of your father's guests."

"I suppose you please yourself, and that you always do, Mr. Jack Simpson; you are the most obstinate, incorrigible—"

"Ruffian," Jack put in laughing.

"Well, I don't know about ruffian," the girl said, laughing too; "but, Jack, who is that girl watching us, the quiet-looking girl in a dark brown dress and straw bonnet?"

"That is my friend Nelly Hardy," Jack said seriously.

"Yes, you have often spoken to me about her and I have wanted to see her; what a nice face she has, and handsome too, with her great dark eyes! Jack, you must introduce me to her, I should like to know her."

"Certainly," Jack said with a pleased look; and accompanied by Alice he walked across the lawn towards her.

Nelly turned the instant that they moved, and walking away joined some other girls. Jack, however, followed.

"Nelly," he said, when he reached her, "this is Miss Merton, who wants to know you. Miss Merton, this is my friend Nelly Hardy."

Nelly bent her head silently, but Alice held out her hand frankly.

"Jack has told me so much about you," she said, "that I wanted, above all things, to see you."

Nelly looked steadily up into her face. It was a face any one might look at with pleasure, frank, joyous, and kindly. It was an earnest face too, less marked and earnest than that now looking at her, but with lines of character and firmness.

Nelly's expression softened as she gazed.

"You are very good, Miss Merton; I have often heard of you too, and wanted to see you as much as you could have done to see me."

"I hope you like me now you do see me," Miss Merton laughed; "you won't be angry when I say that I like you, though you did turn away when you saw us coming.

"You are accustomed to meet people and be introduced," Nelly said quietly; "I am not, you see."

"I don't think you are shy," Miss Merton said smiling, "but you had a reason; perhaps some day when we know each other better you will tell me. I have been scolding Jack for making such a figure of himself. You are his friend and should not let him do it."

Jack laughed, while Nelly looked in surprise at him.

"What is the matter with him?" she asked; "I don't see that there is anything wrong."

"Not wrong," Miss Merton said, "only singular to me. He has got on clothes just like all the rest, which don't fit him at all, and look as if they had been made to put on to a wooden figure in a shop window, while when we see him he is always properly dressed."

Nelly flashed a quiet look of inquiry at Jack.

"You never told me, Jack," she said, with an aggrieved ring in her voice, "that you dressed differently at Birmingham to what you do here."

"There was nothing to tell really," he said quietly. "I told you that I had had some clothes made there, and always wore them at Mr. Merton's; but I don't know," and he smiled, "that I did enter into any particulars about their cut, indeed I never thought of this myself."

Facing death

"I don't suppose you did, Jack," the girl said gently, for she knew how absolutely truthful he was; "but you ought to have told me. But see, they are getting ready to go into the tent, and I must help look after the young ones."

"What a fine face she has!" Alice said; "but I don't think she quite likes me, Jack."

"Not like you!" Jack said astonished, "what makes you think that? she was sure to like you; why, even if nobody else liked you Nelly would, because you have been so kind to me."

For the next few days the serious events of the night absorbed all thought; indeed, it was not until the following Sunday afternoon that Jack and Nelly Hardy met. Harry Shepherd, who generally accompanied them in their walks upon this day, was still suffering from the effects of the injuries he had received in the riot. Jack and his companion talked over that event until they turned to come back.

Then after a pause the girl asked suddenly, "How do you like Alice Merton, Jack?"

Jack was in no way taken by surprise, but, ignorant that the black eyes were keenly watching him, he replied:

"Oh, I like her very much, I have often told you so, Nelly."

"Do you like her better than me, Jack?"

Jack looked surprised this time.

"What should put such a thought in your head, lass? You know I like you and Harry better than any one in the world. We are like three brothers. It is not likely I should like Alice Merton, whom I only see once a month, better than you. She is very kind, very pleasant, very bright. She treats me as an equal and I would do anything for her, but she couldn't be the same as you are, no one can. Perhaps," he said, "years on—for you know that I have always said that I should not marry till I'm thirty, that's what my good friend told me more than ten years ago—I shall find some one I shall like as well as you, but that will be in a different way, and you will be married years and years before that. Let me think, you are nearly seventeen, Nelly?" The girl nodded, her face was turned the other way. "Yes, you are above a year younger than I am. Some girls marry by seventeen; I wonder no one has been after you already, Nelly; there is no girl in the village to compare with you."

But Nelly, without a word, darted away at full speed up the lane towards home, leaving Jack speechless with astonishment. "She hasn't done that for years," he said; "it's just the way she used to do when we were first friends. If she got in a temper about anything she would rush away and hide herself and cry for hours. What could I have said to vex her, about her marrying, or having some one courting her; there couldn't be anything in that to vex her." Jack thought for some time, sitting upon a stile the better to give his mind to it. Finally he gave up the problem in despair, grumbling to himself, "One never gets to understand girls; here I've known Nelly for the last seven years like a sister, and there she flies away crying—I am sure she was crying, because she always used to cry when she ran away—and what it is about I have not the least idea. Now I mustn't say anything about it when I meet her next, I know that of old, unless she does first, but as likely as not she will never allude to it."

In fact no allusion ever was made to the circumstance, for before the following Sunday came round John Hardy had died. He had been sinking for months, and his death had been looked for for some time. It was not a blow to his daughter, and could hardly be a great grief, for he had been a drunken, worthless man, caring nothing for his child, and frequently brutally assaulting her in his drunken fits. She had attended him patiently and assiduously for months, but no word of thanks had ever issued from his lip. His character was so well known that no one regarded his death as an event for which his daughter should be pitied. It would, however, effect a change in her circumstances. Hardy had, ever since the attack upon the Vaughan, received an allowance from the union, as well as from the sick club to which he belonged, but this would now cease; and it was conjectured by the neighbours that "th' old ooman would have to go into the house, and Nelly would go into a factory at Birmingham or Wolverhampton, or would go into service." Nelly's mother was a broken woman; years of intemperance had prematurely aged her, and her enforced temperance during the last few months had apparently broken her spirit altogether, and the coarse, violent woman had almost sunk into quiet imbecility.

CHAPTER XXII.

THE SOLUTION.

Among others who talked over Nelly Hardy's future were Mr. and Mrs. Dodgson. They were very fond of her, for from the first she had been the steadiest and most industrious of the young girls of the place, and by diligent study had raised herself far in advance of the rest. She had too been always so willing and ready to oblige and help that she was a great favourite with both.

"I have been thinking," Mrs. Dodgson said to her husband on the evening of the day of John Hardy's death, "whether, as Miss Bolton, the assistant mistress, is going to leave at the end of the month, to be married, Nelly Hardy would not make an excellent successor for her. There is no doubt she is fully capable of filling the situation; her manners are all that could be wished, and she has great influence with the younger children. The only drawback was her disreputable old father. It would hardly have done for my assistant to appear in school in the morning with a black eye, and for all the children to know that her drunken father had been beating her. Now he is gone that objection is at an end. She and her mother, who has been as bad as the father, but is now, I believe, almost imbecile, could live in the little cottage Miss Bolton occupies."

"I think it would be an excellent plan, my dear, excellent; we could have no one we should like better, or who could be a more trustworthy and helpful assistant to you. By all means let it be Nelly Hardy. I will go up and speak to Mr. Brook to-morrow. As he is our patron I must consult him, but he will agree to anything we propose. Let us say nothing about it until you tell her yourself after the funeral."

Mrs. Dodgson saw Nelly Hardy several times in the next few days, and went in and sat with her as she worked at her mourning; but it was not until John Hardy was laid in the churchyard that she opened the subject.

"Come up in the morning, my dear," she had said that day; "I want to have a talk with you."

136

Facing death

On the following morning Nelly, in her neatly-fitting black mourning dress, made her appearance at the school-house, after breakfast, a quarter of an hour before school began.

"Sit down, my dear," Mrs. Dodgson said, "I have some news to give you which will, I think, please you. Of course you have been thinking what to do?"

"Yes, 'm; I have made up my mind to try and get work in a factory."

"Indeed! Nelly," Mrs. Dodgson said, surprised; "I should have thought that was the last thing that you would like."

"It is not what I like," Nelly said quietly, "but what is best. I would rather go into service, and as I am fond of children and used to them, I might, with your kind recommendation, get a comfortable situation; but in that case mother must go to the house, and I could not bear to think of her there. She is very helpless, and of late she has come to look to me, and would be miserable among strangers. I could earn enough at a factory to keep us both, living very closely."

"Well, Nelly, your decision does you honour, but I think my plan is better. Have you heard that Miss Bolton is going to leave us?"

"I have heard she was engaged to be married some day, 'm, but I did not know the time was fixed."

"She leaves at the end of this month, that is in a fortnight, and her place has already been filled up. Upon the recommendation of myself and Mr. Dodgson, Mr. Brook has appointed Miss Nelly Hardy as her successor."

"Me!" exclaimed Nelly, rising with a bewildered air. "Oh, Mrs. Dodgson, you cannot mean it?"

"I do, indeed, Nelly. Your conduct here has been most satisfactory in every way, you have a great influence with the children, and your attainments and knowledge are amply sufficient for the post of my assistant. You will, of course, have Miss Bolton's cottage, and can watch over your mother. You will have opportunities for studying to fit yourself to take another step upwards, and become a head-mistress some day."

Mrs. Dodgson had continued talking, for she saw that Nelly was too much agitated and overcome to speak.

"Oh, Mrs. Dodgson," she sobbed, "how can I thank you enough?"

Facing death

"There are no thanks due, my dear. Of course I want the best assistant I can get, and I know of no one upon whom I can rely more thoroughly than yourself. You have no one but yourself to thank, for it is your good conduct and industry alone which have made you what you are, and that under circumstances of the most unfavourable kind. But there is the bell ringing for school. I suppose I may tell Mr. Brook that you accept the situation; the pay, thirty pounds a year and the cottage, is not larger, perhaps, than you might earn at a factory, but I think—"

"Oh, Mrs. Dodgson," Nelly said, smiling through her tears, "I accept, I accept. I would rather live on a crust of bread here than work in a factory, and if I had had the choice of everything I should prefer this."

Mr. Dodgson here came in, shook Nelly's hand and congratulated her, and with a happy heart the girl took her way home.

Jack, upon his return from the pit, found Nelly awaiting him at the corner where for years she had stood. He had seen her once since her father's death, and had pressed her hand warmly to express his sympathy, but he was too honest to condole with her on a loss which was, he knew, a relief. He and Harry had in the intervening time talked much of Nelly's prospects. Jack was averse in the extreme to her going into service, still more averse to her going into a factory, but could suggest no alternative plan.

"If she were a boy," he said, "it would be easy enough. I am getting eighteen shillings a week now, and could let her have five easily, and she might take in dressmaking. There are plenty of people in the villages round would be glad to get their dresses made; but she would have to live till she got known a bit, and you know she wouldn't take my five shillings. I wouldn't dare offer it to her. Now if it was you there would be no trouble at all; you would take it, of course, just as I should take it of you, but she wouldn't, because she's a lass—it beats me altogether. I might get mother to offer her the money, but Nelly would know it was me sharp enough, and it would be all the same."

"I really think that Nelly might do well wi' dressmaking," Harry said after a pause. "Here all the lasses ha' learnt to work, but, as you say, in the other villages they know no more than we did here three years back; if we got some bills printed and sent 'em round, I should say she might do. There are other things you don't seem to ha' thought on, Jack," he said hesitatingly. "You're only eighteen yet, but you are earning near a pound a week, and in another two or three years will be getting man's pay, and you are sure to rise. Have you never thought of marrying Nelly?"

Jack jumped as if he had trodden on a snake.

"I marry Nelly!" he said in astonishment. "What! I marry Nelly! are you mad, Harry? You know I have made up my mind not to marry for years, not till I'm thirty and have made my way; and as to Nelly, why I never thought of her, nor of any other lass in that way; her least of all; why, she is like my sister. What ever put such a ridiculous idea in your head? Why, at eighteen boys haven't left school and are looking forward to going to college; those boy and girl marriages among our class are the cause of half our troubles. Thirty is quite time enough to marry. How Nelly would laugh if she knew what you'd said!"

"I should advise you not to tell her," Harry said dryly; "I greatly mistake if she would regard it as a laughing matter at all."

"No, lasses are strange things," Jack meditated again. "But, Harry, you are as old as I am, and are earning the same wage; why don't you marry her?"

"I would," Harry said earnestly, "to-morrow if she'd have me."

"You would!" Jack exclaimed, as much astonished as by his friend's first proposition. "To think of that now! Why, you have always been with her just as I have. You have never shown that you cared for her, never given her presents, nor walked with her, nor anything. And do you really care for her, Harry?"

"Aye," Harry said shortly, "I have cared for her for years."

"And to think that I have never seen that!" Jack said. "Why didn't you tell me? Why, you are as difficult to understand as she is, and I thought I knew you so well!"

"What would have been the use?" Harry said. "Nelly likes me as a friend, that's all."

"That's it," Jack said. "Of course when people are friends they don't think of each other in any other way. Still, Harry, she may get to in time. Nelly's pretty well a woman, she's seventeen now, but she has no one else after her that I know of."

"Well, Jack, I fancy she could have plenty after her, for she's the prettiest and best girl o' the place; but you see, you are always about wi' her, and I think that most people think it will be a match some day."

"People are fools," Jack burst out wrathfully. "Who says so? just tell me who says so?"

Facing death

"People say so, Jack. When a young chap and a lass walk together people suppose there is something in it, and you and Nelly ha' been walking together for the last five years."

"Walking together!" Jack repeated angrily; "we have been going about together of course, and you have generally been with us, and often enough half-a-dozen others; that is not like walking together. Nelly knew, and every one knew, that we agreed to be friends from the day we stood on the edge of the old shaft when you were in the water below, and we have never changed since."

"I know you have never changed, Jack, never thought of Nelly but as a true friend. I did not know whether now you might think differently. I wanted to hear from your own lips. Now I know you don't, that you have no thought of ever being more than a true friend to her, I shall try if I cannot win her."

"Do," Jack said, shaking his friend's hand. "I am sure I wish you success. Nothing in the world would please me so much as to see my two friends marry, and though I do think, yes, I really do, Harry, that young marriages are bad, yet I am quite sure that you and Nelly would be happy together anyhow. And when do you mean to ask her?"

"What an impatient fellow you are, Jack!" Harry said smiling. "Nelly has no more idea that I care for her than you had, and I am not going to tell her so all at once. I don't think," he said gravely, "mark me, Jack, I don't think Nelly will ever have me, but if patience and love can win her I shall succeed in the end."

Jack looked greatly surprised again.

"Don't say any more about it, Jack," Harry went on. "It 'ull be a long job o' work, but I can bide my time; but above all, if you wish me well, do not even breathe a word to Nelly of what I have said."

From this interview Jack departed much mystified.

"It seems to me," he muttered to himself, "lads when they're in love get to be like lasses, there's no understanding them. I know nowt of love myself, and what I've read in books didn't seem natural, but I suppose it must be true, for even Harry, who I thought I knew as well as myself, turned as mysterious as—well as a ghost. What does he mean by he's got to be patient, and to wait, and it will be a long job. If he likes Nelly and Nelly likes him—and why shouldn't she?—I don't know why they shouldn't marry in a year or two, though I do hate young marriages. Anyhow I'll talk to her about the dressmaking idea. If Harry's got to make love to her, it will be far better for him to do it here than to have to go walking her out o' Sundays at Birmingham. If she would but let me help her a bit till she's got into business it would be as easy as possible."

Jack, however, soon had the opportunity of laying his scheme fully before Nelly Hardy, and when she had turned off from the road with him she broke out:

"Oh, Jack, I have such a piece of news; but perhaps you know it, do you?" she asked jealously.

"No, I don't know any particular piece of news."

"Not anything likely to interest me, Jack?"

"No," Jack said puzzled.

"Honour, you haven't the least idea what it is?"

"Honour, I haven't," Jack said.

"I'm going to be a schoolmistress in place of Miss Bolton."

161

THE NEW SCHOOLMISTRESS.

"No!" Jack shouted delightedly; "I am glad, Nelly, I am glad. Why, it is just the thing for you; Harry and I have been puzzling our heads all the week as to what you should do!"

"And what did your united wisdom arrive at?" Nelly laughed.

"We thought you might do here at dressmaking," Jack said, "after a bit, you know."

"The thought was not a bad one," she said; "it never occurred to me, and had this great good fortune not have come to me I might perhaps have tried. It was good of you to think of it. And so you never heard a whisper about the schoolmistress? I thought you might perhaps have suggested it somehow, you know you always do suggest things here."

"No, indeed, Nelly, I did not hear Miss Bolton was going."

"I am glad," the girl said.

"Are you?" Jack replied in surprise. "Why, Nelly, wouldn't you have liked me to have helped you?"

"Yes and no, Jack; but no more than yes. I do owe everything to you. It was you who made me your friend, you who taught me, you who urged me on, you who have made me what I am. No, Jack, dear," she said, seeing that Jack looked pained at her thanks; "I have never thanked you before, and I must do it now. I owe everything to you, and in one way I should have been pleased to owe this to you also, but in another way I am pleased not to do so because my gaining it by, if I may say so, my own merits, show that I have done my best to prove worthy of your kindness and friendship."

Tears of earnestness stood in her eyes, and Jack felt that disclaimer would be ungracious.

"I am glad," he said again after a pause. "And now, Miss Hardy," and he touched his hat laughing, "that you have risen in the world, I hope you are not going to take airs upon yourself."

Nelly laughed. "It is strange," she said, "that I should be the first to take a step upwards, for Mrs. Dodgson is going to help me to go in and qualify for a head-schoolmistress-ship some day; but, Jack, it is only for a little time. You laugh and call me Miss Hardy to-day, but the time will come when I shall say 'sir' to you; you are longer beginning, but you will rise far higher; but we shall always be friends; shall we not, Jack?"

"Always, Nelly," Jack said earnestly. "Wherever or whatever Jack Simpson may be, he will ever be your true and faithful friend, and nothing which may ever happen to me, no rise I may ever make, will give me the pleasure which this good fortune which has befallen you has done. If I ever rise it will make me happy to help Harry, but I know you would never have let me help you, and this thought would have marred my life. Now that I see you in a position in which I am sure you will be successful, and which is an honourable and pleasant one, I shall the more enjoy my rise when it comes. —Does any one else know of it?" he asked as they went on their way.

"No one," she said. "Who should know it before you?"

"Harry will be as glad as I am," he said, remembering his friend's late assertion.

"Yes, Harry will be very glad too," Nelly said; but Jack felt that Harry's opinion was of comparatively little importance in her eyes. "He is a good honest fellow is Harry, and I am sure he will be pleased, and so I hope will everyone."

Jack felt that the present moment was not a propitious one for putting in a word for his friend.

Harry Shepherd carried out his purpose. For two years he waited, and then told his love to Nelly Hardy, one bright Sunday afternoon when they were walking in the lane.

"No, Harry, no," she said humbly and sadly; "it can never be, do not ask me, I am so, so sorry."

"Can it never be?" Harry asked.

"Never," the girl said; "you know yourself, Harry, it can never be. I have seen this coming on for two years now, and it has grieved me so; but you know, I am sure you know, why it cannot be."

"I know," the young fellow said. "I have always known that you cared for Jack a thousand times more than for me, and it's quite natural, for he is worth a thousand of me; but then, then—" and he hesitated.

"But then," she went on. "Jack does not love me, and you do. That is so, Harry; but since I was a child I have loved him. I know, none better, that he never thought of me except as a friend, that he scarcely considered me as a girl. I have never thought that it would be otherwise. I could hardly wish that it were. Jack will rise to be a great man, and must marry a lady, but," she said steadfastly, "I can go on loving him till I die."

"I have not hoped much, Nelly, but remember always, that I have always cared for you. Since you first became Jack's friend I have cared for you. If he had loved you I could even stand aside and be glad to see you both happy, but I have known always that this could never be. Jack's mind was ever so much given up to study, he is not like us, and does not dream of a house and love till he has made his mark in the world. Remember only that I love you as you love Jack, and shall love as faithfully. Some day, perhaps, long hence," he added as Nelly shook her head, "you may not think differently, but may come to see that it is better to make one man's life happy than to cling for ever to the remembrance of another. At any rate you will always think of me as your true friend, Nelly, always trust me?"

"Always, Harry, in the future more than lately, for I have seen this coming. Now that we understand each other we can be quite friends again."

CHAPTER XXIII.

THE EXPLOSION AT THE VAUGHAN.

At twelve o'clock on a bright summer day Mr. Brook drove up in his dog-cart, with two gentlemen, to the Vaughan mine. One was the government inspector of the district; the other, a newly-appointed deputy inspector, whom he was taking his rounds with him, to instruct in his duties.

"I am very sorry that Thompson, my manager, is away to-day," Mr. Brook said as they alighted. "Had I known you were coming I would of course have had him in readiness to go round with you. Is Williams, the underground manager, in the pit?" he asked the bankman, whose duty it was to look after the ascending and descending cage.

"No, sir; he came up about half an hour ago. Watkins, the viewer, is below."

"He must do, then," Mr. Brook said, "but I wish Mr. Thompson had been here. Perhaps you would like to look at the plan of the pit before you go down? Is Williams's office open?"

"Yes, sir," the bankman answered.

Mr. Brook led the way into the office.

"Hullo!" he said, seeing a young man at work making a copy of a mining plan; "who are you?"

The young man rose—

"Jack Simpson, sir. I work below, but when it's my night-shift Mr. Williams allows me to help him here by day."

"Ah! I remember you now," Mr. Brook said. "Let me see what you are doing. That's a creditable piece of work for a working collier, is it not?" he said, holding up a beautifully executed plan.

Mr. Hardinge looked with surprise at the draughtsman, a young man of some one or two-and-twenty, with a frank, open, pleasant face.

"Why, you don't look or talk like a miner," he said.

"Mr. Merton, the schoolmaster here, was kind enough to take a great deal of pains with me, sir."

"Have you been doing this sort of work long?" Mr. Hardinge asked, pointing to the plan.

"About three or four years," Mr. Brook said promptly.

Jack looked immensely surprised.

Mr. Brook smiled.

"I noticed an extraordinary change in Williams's reports, both in the handwriting and expression. Now I understand it. You work the same stall as Haden, do you not?"

"Yes, sir, but not the same shift; he had a mate he has worked with ever since my father was killed, so I work the other shift with Harvey."

"Now let us look at the plans of the pit," Mr. Hardinge said.

The two inspectors bent over the table and examined the plans, asking a question of Mr. Brook now and then. Jack had turned to leave when his employer ceased to speak to him, but Mr. Brook made a motion to him to stay. "What is the size of your furnace, Mr. Brook?" asked Mr. Hardinge.

"It's an eight-foot furnace," Mr. Brook replied.

"Do you know how many thousand cubic feet of air a minute you pass?"

Mr. Brook shook his head: he left the management of the mine entirely in the hands of his manager.

Mr. Hardinge had happened to look at Jack as he spoke; and the latter, thinking the question was addressed to him, answered:

"About eight thousand feet a minute, sir."

"How do you know?" Mr. Hardinge asked.

"By taking the velocity of the air, sir, and the area of the downcast shaft."

"How would you measure the velocity, theoretically?" Mr. Hardinge asked, curious to see how much the young collier knew.

"I should require to know the temperature of the shafts respectively, and the height of the upcast shaft."

"How could you do it then?"

"The formula, sir, is $M = \dfrac{h(t'-t)}{480 \mid x}$, h being the height of the upcast, t' its temperature, t the temperature of the exterior air, and $x = t'$-32 degrees."

"You are a strange young fellow," Mr. Hardinge said. "May I ask you a question or two?"

"Certainly, sir."

"Could you work out the cube-root of say 999,888,777?"

Jack closed his eyes for a minute and then gave the correct answer to five places of decimals.

The three gentlemen gave an exclamation of surprise.

"How on earth did you do that?" Mr. Hardinge exclaimed. "It would take me ten minutes to work it out on paper."

"I accustomed myself to calculate while I was in the dark, or working," Jack said quietly.

"Why, you would rival Bidder himself," Mr. Hardinge said; "and how far have you worked up in figures?"

"I did the differential calculus, sir, and then Mr. Merton said that I had better stick to the mechanical application of mathematics instead of going on any farther; that was two years ago."

The surprise of the three gentlemen at this simple avowal from a young pitman was unbounded.

Then Mr. Hardinge said:

"We must talk of this again later on. Now let us go down the pit; this young man will do excellently well for a guide. But I am afraid, Mr. Brook, that I shall have to trouble you a good deal. As far as I can see from the plan the mine is very badly laid out, and the ventilation altogether defective. What is your opinion?" he asked, turning abruptly to Jack, and wishing to see whether his practical knowledge at all corresponded with his theoretical acquirements.

"I would rather not say, sir," Jack said. "It is not for me to express an opinion as to Mr. Thompson's plan."

"Let us have your ideas," Mr. Brook said. "Just tell us frankly what you would do if you were manager of the Vaughan?"

Jack turned to the plan.

"I should widen the airways, and split the current; that would raise the number of cubic feet of air to about twelve thousand a minute. It is too far for a single current to travel, especially as the airways are not wide; the friction is altogether too great. I should put a split in here, take a current round through the old workings to keep them clear, widen these passages, split the current again here, and then make a cut through this new ground so as to take a strong current to sweep the face of the main workings, and carry it off straight to the upcast. But that current ought not to pass through the furnace, but be let in above, for the gas comes off very thick sometimes, and might not be diluted enough with air, going straight to the furnaces."

"Your ideas are very good," Mr. Hardinge said quietly. "Now we will get into our clothes and go below."

So saying, he opened a bag and took out two mining suits of clothes, which, first taking off their coats, he and his companion proceeded to put on over their other garments. Mr. Brook went into his office, and similarly prepared himself; while Jack, who was not dressed for mining, went to the closet where a few suits were hung up for the use of visitors and others, and prepared to go down. Then he went to the lamp-room and fetched four Davy-lamps. While he was away Mr. Brook joined the inspectors.

"That young pitman is as steady as he is clever," he said; "he has come several times under my attention. In the first place, the schoolmaster has spoken to me of the lad's efforts to educate himself. Then he saved another boy's life at the risk of his own, and of late years his steadiness and good conduct have given him a great influence over his comrades of the same age, and have effected great things for the place. The vicar and schoolmaster now are never tired of praising him."

"He is clearly an extraordinary young fellow," Mr Hardinge said. "Do you know his suggestions are exactly what I had intended to offer to you myself? You will have some terrible explosion here unless you make some radical changes."

That evening the inspectors stayed for the night at Mr. Brook's, and the next day that gentleman went over with them to Birmingham, where he had some business. His principal object, however, was to take them to see Mr. Merton, to question him farther with regard to Jack Simpson.

Mr. Merton related to his visitors the history of Jack's efforts to educate himself, and gave them the opinion he had given the lad himself, that he might, had he chosen, have taken a scholarship and then the highest mathematical honours. "He has been working lately at engineering, and calculating the strains and stresses of iron bridges," he said. "And now, Mr. Brook, I will tell you—and I am sure that you and these gentlemen will give me your promise of secrecy upon the subject—what I have never yet told to a soul. It was that lad who brought me word of the intended attack on the engines, and got me to write the letter to Sir John Butler. But that is not all, sir. It was that boy—for he was but seventeen then—who defended your engine-house against the mob of five hundred men!"

"Bless my heart, Merton, why did you not tell me before? Why, I've puzzled over that ever since. And to think that it was one of my own pit-boys who did that gallant action, and I have done nothing for him!"

"He would not have it told, sir. He wanted to go on as a working miner, and learn his business from the bottom. Besides, his life wouldn't have been safe in this district for a day if it had been known. But I think you ought to be told of it now. The lad is as modest as he is brave and clever, and would go to his grave without ever letting out that he saved the Vaughan, and indeed all the pits in the district. But now that he is a man, it is right you should know; but pray do not let him imagine that you are aware of it. He is very young yet, and will rise on his own merits, and would dislike nothing so much as thinking that he owed anything to what he did that night. I may tell you too that he is able to mix as a gentleman with gentlemen. Ever since I have been over here he has come once a month to stay with me from Saturday to Monday, he has mixed with what I may call the best society in the town here, and has won the liking and esteem of all my friends, not one of whom has so much as a suspicion that he is not of the same rank of life as themselves."

"What am I to do, Mr. Hardinge?" Mr. Brook asked in perplexity. "What would you advise?"

"I should give him his first lift at once," Mr. Hardinge said decidedly. "It will be many months before you have carried out the new scheme for the ventilation of the mine; and, believe me, it will not be safe, if there come a sudden influx of gas, till the alterations are made. Make this young fellow deputy viewer, with special charge to look after the ventilation. In that way he will not have to give instruction to the men as to their work, but will confine his attention to the ventilation, the state of the air, the doors, and so on. Even then his position will for a time be difficult; but the lad has plenty of self-control, and will be able to tide over it, and the men will get to see that he really understands his business. You will of course order the underground manager and viewers to give him every support. The underground manager, at any rate, must be perfectly aware of his capabilities, as he seems to have done all his paper work for some time."

Never were a body of men more astonished than were the pitmen of the Vaughan when they heard that young Jack Simpson was appointed a deputy viewer, with the special charge of the ventilation of the mine.

A deputy viewer is not a position of great honour; the pay is scarcely more than that which a getter will earn, and the rank is scarcely higher. This kind of post, indeed, is generally given to a miner of experience, getting past his work—as care, attention, and knowledge are required, rather than hard work. That a young man should be appointed was an anomaly which simply astonished the colliers of the Vaughan. The affair was first known on the surface, and as the men came up in the cages the news was told them, and the majority, instead of at once hurrying home, stopped to talk it over.

"It be the rummest start I ever heard on," one said. "Ah! here comes Bill Haden. Hast heard t' news, Bill?"

"What news?"

"Why, your Jack's made a deputy. What dost think o' that, right over heads o' us all? Did'st e'er hear tell o' such a thing?"

"No, I didn't," Bill Haden said emphatically. "It's t' first time as e'er I heard o' t' right man being picked out wi'out a question o' age. I know him, and I tell 'ee, he mayn't know t' best place for putting in a prop, or of timbering in loose ground, as well as us as is old enough to be his fathers; but he knows as much about t' book learning of a mine as one of the government inspector chaps. You mightn't think it pleasant for me, as has stood in t' place o' his father, to see him put over my head, but I know how t' boy has worked, and I know what he is, and I tell 'ee I'll work under him willing. Jack Simpson will go far; you as live will see it."

Bill Haden was an authority in the Vaughan pit, and his dictum reconciled many who might otherwise have resented the appointment of such a lad. The enthusiastic approval of Harry Shepherd and of the rest of the other young hands in the mine who had grown up with Jack Simpson, and knew something of how hard he had worked, and who had acknowledged his leadership in all things, also had its effect; and the new deputy entered upon his duties without anything like the discontent which might have been looked for, being excited.

Facing death

The most important part of Jack's duties consisted in going round the pit before the men went down in the morning, to see that there was no accumulation of gas in the night, and that the ventilation was going on properly. The deputy usually takes a helper with him, and Jack had chosen his friend Harry for the post—as in the event of finding gas, it has to be dispersed by beating it with an empty sack, so as to cause a disturbance of the air, or, if the accumulation be important, by putting up a temporary bratticing, or partition, formed of cotton cloth stretched on a framework, in such a way as to turn a strong current of air across the spot where the gas is accumulating, or from which it is issuing. The gas is visible to the eye as a sort of dull fog or smoke. If the accumulation is serious, the main body of miners are not allowed to descend into the mine until the viewer has, with assistance, succeeded in completely dispersing it.

"It's a lonesome feeling," Harry said the first morning that he entered upon his duties with Jack Simpson, "to think that we be the only two down here."

"It's no more lonesome than sitting in the dark waiting for the tubs to come along, Harry, and it's far safer. There is not the slightest risk of an explosion now, for there are only our safety-lamps down here, while in the day the men will open their lamps to light their pipes; make what regulations the master may, the men will break them to get a smoke."

Upon the receipt of Mr. Hardinge's official report, strongly condemning the arrangements in the Vaughan, Mr. Brook at once appointed a new manager in the place of Mr. Thompson, and upon his arrival he made him acquainted with the extent of Jack's knowledge and ability, and requested him to keep his eye specially upon him, and to employ him, as far as possible, as his right-hand man in carrying out his orders.

"I wish that main wind drift were through," Jack said one day, six months after his appointment, as he was sitting over his tea with Bill Haden. "The gas is coming in very bad in the new workings."

"Wuss nor I ever knew't, Jack. It's a main good job that the furnace was made bigger, and some o' th' airways widened, for it does come out sharp surely. In th' old part where I be, a' don't notice it; but when I went down yesterday where Peter Jones be working, the gas were just whistling out of a blower close by."

"Another fortnight, and the airway will be through, dad; and that will make a great change. I shall be very glad, for the pit's in a bad state now."

"Ah! thou think'st a good deal of it, Jack, because thou'st got part of the 'sponsibility of it. It don't fret me."

Facing death

"I wish the men wouldn't smoke, dad; I don't want to get a bad name for reporting them, but it's just playing with their lives."

Bill Haden was silent; he was given to indulge in a quiet smoke himself, as Jack, working with him for five years, well knew.

"Well, Jack, thou know'st there's a craving for a draw or two of bacca."

"So there is for a great many other things that we have to do without," Jack said. "If it were only a question of a man blowing himself to pieces I should say nought about it; but it is whether he is willing to make five hundred widows and two thousand orphans rather than go for a few hours without smoking. What is the use of Davy-lamps? what is the use of all our care as to the ventilation, if at any moment the gas may be fired at a lamp opened for lighting a pipe? I like my pipe, but if I thought there was ever any chance of its becoming my master I would never touch tobacco again."

Three days later, when Jack came up from his rounds at ten o'clock, to eat his breakfast and write up his journal of the state of the mine, he saw Mr. Brook and the manager draw up to the pit mouth. Jack shrank back from the little window of the office where he was writing, and did not look out again until he knew that they had descended the mine, as he did not wish to have any appearance of thrusting himself forward. For another hour he wrote; and then the window of the office flew in pieces, the chairs danced, and the walls rocked, while a dull heavy roar, like distant thunder, burst upon his ears.

He leaped to his feet and rushed to the door. Black smoke was pouring up from the pit's mouth, sticks and pieces of wood and coal were falling in a shower in the yard; and Jack saw that his worst anticipation had been realized, and that a terrible explosion had taken place in the Vaughan pit.

CHAPTER XXIV.

IN DEADLY PERIL.

For a moment Jack stood stunned by the calamity. There were, he knew, over three hundred men and boys in the pit, and he turned faint and sick as the thought of their fate came across him. Then he ran towards the top of the shaft. The bankman lay insensible at a distance of some yards from the pit, where he had been thrown by the force of the explosion. Two or three men came running up with white scared faces. The smoke had nearly ceased already; the damage was done, and a deadly stillness seemed to reign.

Jack ran into the engine-house. The engine-man was leaning against a wall, scared and almost fainting.

"Are you hurt, John?"

"No!"

"Pull yourself round, man. The first thing is to see if the lift is all right. I see one of the cages is at bank, and the force of the explosion is in the upcast shaft. Just give a turn or two to the engine and see if the winding gear's all right. Slowly."

The engineman turned on the steam; there was a slight movement, and then the engine stopped.

"A little more steam," Jack said. "The cage has caught, but it may come."

There was a jerk, and then the engine began to work.

"That is all right," Jack said, "whether the lower cage is on or not. Stop now, and wind it back, and get the cage up again. Does the bell act, I wonder?"

Jack pulled the wire which, when in order, struck a bell at the bottom of the shaft, and then looked at a bell hanging over his head for the answer. None came.

"I expect the wire's broke," Jack said, and went out to the pit's mouth again.

The surface-men were all gathered round now, the tip-men, and the yard-men, and those from the coke-ovens, all looking wild and pale.

"I am going down," Jack said; "we may find some poor fellows near the bottom, and can't wait till some headman comes on the ground. Who will go with me? I don't want any married men, for you know, lads, there may be another blow at any moment."

"I will go with you," one of the yard-men said, stepping forward; "there's no one dependent on me."

"I, too," said another; "it's no odds to any one but myself whether I come up again or not. Here's with you, whatever comes of it."

AFTER THE FIRST EXPLOSION—THE SEARCH PARTY.

Jack brought three safety-lamps from the lamp-room, and took his place in the cage with the two volunteers.

156

Facing death

"Lower away," he shouted, "but go very slow when we get near the bottom, and look out for our signal."

It was but three minutes from the moment that the cage began to sink to that when it touched the bottom of the shaft, but it seemed an age to those in it. They knew that at any moment a second explosion might come, and that they might be driven far up into the air above the top of the shaft, mere scorched fragments of flesh. Not a word was spoken during the descent, and there was a general exclamation of "Thank God!" when they felt the cage touch the bottom.

Jack, as an official of the mine, and by virtue of superior energy, at once took the lead.

"Now," he said, "let us push straight up the main road."

Just as they stepped out they came across the bodies of two men, and stooped over them with their lamps.

"Both dead," Jack said; "we can do nought for them."

A little way on, and in a heap, were some waggons, thrown together and broken up, the body of a pony, and that of the lad, his driver. Then they came to the first door—a door no longer, not a fragment of it remaining. In the door-boy's niche the lad lay in a heap. They bent over him.

"He is alive," Jack said. "Will you two carry him to the cage? I will look round and see if there is any one else about here; beyond, this way, there is no hope. Make haste! Look how the gas is catching inside the lamps, the place is full of fire-damp."

The men took up the lad, and turned to go to the bottom of the shaft. Jack looked a few yards down a cross-road, and then followed them. He was in the act of turning into the next road to glance at that also, when he felt a suck of air.

"Down on your faces!" he shouted, and, springing a couple of paces farther up the cross-road, threw himself on his face.

CHAPTER XXV.

THE IMPRISONED MINERS.

There was a mighty roar—a thundering sound, as of an express train—a blinding light, and a scorching heat. Jack felt himself lifted from the ground by the force of the blast, and dashed down again.

Then he knew it was over, and staggered to his feet. The force of the explosion had passed along the main road, and so up the shaft, and he owed his life to the fact that he had been in the road off the course. He returned into the main road, but near the bottom of the shaft he was brought to a standstill. The roof had fallen, and the passage was blocked with fragments of rock and broken waggons. He knew that the bottom of the shaft must be partly filled up, that his comrades were killed, and that there was no hope of escape in that direction. For a moment he paused to consider; then, turning up the side road to the left, he ran at full speed from the shaft. He knew that the danger now was not so much from the fire-damp—the explosive gas—as from the even more dreaded choke-damp, which surely follows after an explosion and the cessation of ventilation.

Many more miners are killed by this choke-damp, as they hasten to the bottom of the shaft after an explosion, than by the fire itself. Choke-damp, which is carbonic acid gas, is heavier than ordinary air, and thus the lowest parts of a colliery become first filled with it, as they would with water. In all coal-mines there is a slight, sometimes a considerable, inclination, or "dip" as it is called, of the otherwise flat bed of coal. The shaft is almost always sunk at the lower end of the area owned by the proprietors of the mine, as by this means the whole pit naturally drains to the "sump," or well, at the bottom of the shaft, whence it is pumped up by the engine above; the loaded waggons, too, are run down from the workings to the bottom of the shaft with comparative ease.

The explosion had, as Jack well knew, destroyed all the doors which direct the currents of the air, and the ventilation had entirely ceased. The lower part of the mine, where the explosion had been strongest, would soon be filled with choke-damp, the product of the explosion, and Jack was making for the old workings, near the upper boundary line of the pit. There the air would remain pure long after it had been vitiated elsewhere.

Facing death

It was in this quarter of the mine that Bill Haden and some twenty other colliers worked.

Presently Jack saw lights ahead, and heard a clattering of steps. It was clear that, as he had hoped, the miners working there had escaped the force of the explosion, which had, without doubt, played awful havoc in the parts of the mine where the greater part of the men were at work.

"Stop! stop!" Jack shouted, as they came up to him.

"Is it fire, Jack?" Bill Haden, who was one of the first, asked.

"Yes, Bill; didn't you feel it?"

"Some of us thought we felt a suck of air a quarter hour since, but we weren't sure; and then came another, which blew out the lights. Come along, lad; there is no time for talking."

"It's of no use going on," Jack said; "the shaft's choked up. I came down after the first blow, and I fear there's no living soul in the new workings. By this time they must be full of the choke-damp."

The men looked at each other with blank faces.

"Hast seen Brook?" Jack asked eagerly.

"Ay, he passed our stall with Johnstone ten minutes ago, just before the blast came."

"We may catch him in time to stop him yet," Jack said, "if he has gone round to look at the walling of the old goafs. There are three men at work there."

"I'll go with you, Jack," Bill Haden said. "Our best place is my stall, lads," he went on, turning to the others; "that is pretty well the highest ground in the pit, and the air will keep good there as long as anywhere—may be till help comes. You come along of us, mate," he said, turning to the man who worked with him in his stall.

As they hurried along, Jack, in a few words, told what had taken place, as far as he knew it. Five minutes' run brought them to the place where the masons were at work walling up the entrance to some old workings. They looked astonished at the new-comers.

"Have you seen the gaffers?"

159

Facing death

"Ay, they ha' just gone on. There, don't you see their lights down the heading? No; well I saw 'em a moment since."

"Come along," Jack said. "Quick! I expect they've met it."

At full speed they hurried along. Presently they all stopped short; the lights burnt low, and a choking sensation came on them.

"Back, Jack, for your life!" gasped Bill Haden; but at that moment Jack's feet struck something, which he knew was a body.

"Down at my feet; help!" he cried.

He stooped and tried to raise the body. Then the last gleam of his light went out—his lungs seemed to cease acting, and he saw no more.

When he came to himself again he was being carried on Bill Haden's shoulder.

"All right, dad," he said. "I am coming round now; put me down."

"That's a good job, Jack. I thought thou'd'st scarce come round again."

"Have you got either of the others?"

"We've got Brook; you'd your arm round him so tight that Ned and I lifted you together. He's on ahead; the masons are carrying him, and Ned's showing the way. Canst walk now?"

"Yes, I'm better now. How did you manage to breathe, dad?"

"We didn't breathe, Jack; we're too old hands for that. When we saw you fall we just drew back, took a breath, and then shut our mouths, and went down for you just the same as if we'd been a groping for you under water. We got hold of you both, lifted you up, and carried you along as far as we could before we drew a breath again. You're sharp, Jack, but you don't know everything yet." And Bill Haden chuckled to find that for once his practical experience taught him something that Jack had not learned from his books.

Jack now hurried along after Bill Haden, and in a few minutes reached the place fixed upon. Here the miners were engaged in restoring consciousness to Mr. Brook, who, under the influence of water dashed on his face and artificial respiration set up by alternately pressing upon the chest and allowing it to rise again, was just beginning to show signs of life. Their interest in their employment was so great that it was not until Mr. Brook was able to sit up that they began to talk about the future.

Facing death

Jack's account of the state of things near the shaft was listened to gravely. The fact that the whole of the system of ventilation had been deranged, and the proof given by the second explosion that the mine was somewhere on fire, needed no comment to these experienced men. It sounded their death-knell. Gallant and unceasing as would be the efforts made under any other circumstance to rescue them, the fact that the pit was on fire, and that fresh explosions might at any moment take place, would render it an act of simple madness for their friends above to endeavour to clear the shaft and headings, and to restore the ventilation. The fact was further impressed upon them by a sudden and simultaneous flicker of the lamps, and a faint shake, followed by a distant rumble.

"Another blast," Bill Haden said. "That settles us, lads. We may as well turn out all the lamps but two, so as to have light as long as we last out."

"Is there no hope?" Mr. Brook asked presently, coming forward after he had heard from Haden's mate the manner in which he had been so far saved.

"Not a scrap, master," said Bill Haden. "We are like rats in a trap; and it would ha' been kinder of us if we'd a let you lay as you was."

"Your intention was equally kind," Mr. Brook said. "But is there nothing that we can do?"

"Nowt," Bill Haden said. "We have got our dinners wi' us, and might make 'em last, a mouthful at a time, to keep life in us for a week or more. But what 'ud be th' use of it? It may be weeks—ay, or months—before they can stifle the fire and make their way here."

"Can you suggest nothing, Jack?" Mr. Brook asked. "You are the only officer of the pit left now," he added with a faint smile.

Jack had not spoken since he reached the stall, but had sat down on a block of coal, with his elbows on his knees and his chin on his hands—a favourite attitude of his when thinking deeply.

The other colliers had thrown themselves down on the ground; some sobbed occasionally as they thought of their loved ones above, some lay in silence.

Jack answered the appeal by rising to his feet.

"Yes, sir, I think we may do something."

The men raised themselves in surprise.

Facing death

"In the first place, sir, I should send men in each direction to see how near the choke-damp has got. There are four roads by which it could come up. I would shut the doors on this side of the place it has got to, roll blocks of coal and rubbish to keep 'em tight, and stop up the chinks with wet mud. That will keep the gas from coming up, and there is air enough in the stalls and headings to last us a long time."

"But that would only prolong our lives for a few hours, Jack, and I don't know that that would be any advantage. Better to be choked by the gas than to die of starvation," Mr. Brook said, and a murmur from the men showed that they agreed with him.

"I vote for lighting our pipes," one of the miners said. "If there is fiery gas here, it would be better to finish with it at once."

There was a general expression of approval.

"Wait!" Jack said authoritatively; "wait till I have done. You know, Mr. Brook, we are close to our north boundary here, in some places within a very few yards. Now the 'Logan,' which lies next to us, has been worked out years ago. Of course it is full of water, and it was from fear of tapping that water that the works were stopped here. A good deal comes in through the crevices in No. 15 stall, which I expect is nearest to it. Now if we could work into the 'Logan,' the water would rush down into our workings, and as our pit is a good deal bigger than the 'Logan' ever was it will fill the lower workings and put out the fire, but won't reach here. Then we can get up through the 'Logan,' where the air is sure to be all right, as the water will bring good air down with it. We may not do it in time, but it is a chance. What do you say, sir?"

"It is worth trying, at any rate," Mr. Brook said. "Bravo, my lad! your clear head may save us yet."

"By gum, Jack! but you're a good un!" Bill Haden said, bringing down his hand upon Jack's shoulder with a force that almost knocked him down; while the men, with revived hope, leaped to their feet, and crowding round, shook Jack's hands with exclamations of approval and delight.

"Now, lads," Mr. Brook said, "Jack Simpson is master now, and we will all work under his orders. But before we begin, boys, let us say a prayer. We are in God's hands; let us ask his protection."

Every head was bared, and the men stood reverently while, in a few words, Mr. Brook prayed for strength and protection, and rescue from their danger.

"Now, Jack," he said, when he had finished, "give your orders."

Facing death

Jack at once sent off two men along each of the roads to find how near the choke-damp had approached, and to block up and seal the doors. It was necessary to strike a light to relight some of the lamps, but this was a danger that could not be avoided.

The rest of the men were sent round to all the places where work had been going on to bring in the tools and dinners to No. 15 stall, to which Jack himself, Bill Haden, and Mr. Brook proceeded at once. No work had been done there for years. The floor was covered with a black mud, and a close examination of the face showed tiny streamlets of water trickling down in several places. An examination of the stalls, or working places, on either side, showed similar appearances, but in a less marked degree. It was therefore determined to begin work in No. 15.

"You don't mean to use powder, Jack?" Bill Haden asked.

"No, dad; without any ventilation we should be choked with the smoke, and there would be the danger from the gas. When we think we are getting near the water we will put in a big shot, so as to blow in the face."

When the men returned with the tools and the dinners, the latter done up in handkerchiefs, Jack asked Mr. Brook to take charge of the food.

"There are just twenty of us, sir, without you, and nineteen dinners. So if you divide among us four dinners a day, it will last for five days, and by that time I hope we shall be free."

Four men only could work at the face of the stall together, and Jack divided the twenty into five sets.

"We will work in quarter-of-an-hour shifts at first," he said; "that will give an hour's rest to a quarter of an hour's work, and a man can work well, we know, for a quarter of an hour. When we get done up, we will have half-hour shifts, which will give two hours for a sleep in between."

The men of the first shift, stripped as usual to the waist, set to work without an instant's delay; and the vigour and swiftness with which the blows fell upon the face of the rock would have told experienced miners that the men who struck them were working for life or death. Those unemployed, Jack took into the adjacent stalls and set them to work to clear a narrow strip of the floor next to the upper wall, then to cut a little groove in the rocky floor to intercept the water as it slowly trickled in, and lead it to small hollows which they were to make in the solid rock. The water coming through the two stalls would, thus collected, be ample for their wants. Jack then started to see how the men at work at the doors were getting on. These had already nearly finished their tasks. On the road leading to the main workings choke-damp had been met with at a distance of fifty yards from the stall; but upon the upper road it was several hundred yards before it was found. On the other two roads it was over a hundred yards. The men had torn strips off their flannel jackets and had thrust them into the crevices of the doors, and had then plastered mud from the roadway on thickly, and there was no reason to fear any irruption of choke-damp, unless, indeed, an explosion should take place so violent as to blow in the doors. This, however, was unlikely, as, with a fire burning, the gas would ignite as it came out; and although there might be many minor explosions, there would scarcely be one so serious as the first two which had taken place.

The work at the doors and the water being over, the men all gathered in the stall. Then Jack insisted on an equal division of the tobacco, of which almost all the miners possessed some—for colliers, forbidden to smoke, often chew tobacco, and the tobacco might therefore be regarded both as a luxury, and as being very valuable in assisting the men to keep down the pangs of hunger. This had to be divided only into twenty shares, as Mr. Brook said that he could not use it in that way, and that he had, moreover, a couple of cigars in his pocket, which he could suck if hard driven to it.

Now that they were together again, all the lamps were extinguished save the two required by the men employed. With work to be done, and a hope of ultimate release, the men's spirits rose, and between their spells they talked, and now and then even a laugh was heard.

Mr. Brook, although unable to do a share of the work, was very valuable in aiding to keep up their spirits, by his hopeful talk, and by anecdotes of people who had been in great danger in many ways in different parts of the world, but who had finally escaped.

Sometimes one or other of the men would propose a hymn—for among miners, as among sailors, there is at heart a deep religious feeling, consequent upon a life which may at any moment be cut short—and then their deep voices would rise together, while the blows of the sledges and picks would keep time to the swing of the tune. On the advice of Mr. Brook the men divided their portions of food, small as they were, into two parts, to be eaten twelve hours apart; for as the work would proceed without interruption night and day, it was better to eat, however little, every twelve hours, than to go twenty-four without food.

The first twenty-four hours over, the stall—or rather the heading, for it was now driven as narrow as it was possible for four men to work simultaneously—had greatly advanced; indeed it would have been difficult even for a miner to believe that so much work had been done in the time. There was, however, no change in the appearances; the water still trickled in, but they could not perceive that it came faster than before. As fast as the coal fell—for fortunately the seam was over four feet thick, so that they did not have to work upon the rock—it was removed by the set of men who were next for work, so that there was not a minute lost from this cause.

During the next twenty-four hours almost as much work was done as during the first; but upon the third there was a decided falling off. The scanty food was telling upon them now. The shifts were lengthened to an hour to allow longer time for sleep between each spell of work, and each set of men, when relieved, threw themselves down exhausted, and slept for three hours, until it was their turn to wake up and remove the coal as the set at work got it down.

At the end of seventy-two hours the water was coming through the face much faster than at first, and the old miners, accustomed to judge by sound, were of opinion that the wall in front sounded less solid, and that they were approaching the old workings of the Logan pit. In the three days and nights they had driven the heading nearly fifteen yards from the point where they had begun. Upon the fourth day they worked cautiously, driving a borer three feet ahead of them into the coal, as in case of the water bursting through suddenly they would be all drowned.

At the end of ninety hours from the time of striking the first blow the drill which, Jack holding it, Bill Haden was just driving in deeper with a sledge, suddenly went forward, and as suddenly flew out as if shot from a gun, followed by a jet of water driven with tremendous force. A plug, which had been prepared in readiness, was with difficulty driven into the hole; two men who had been knocked down by the force of the water were picked up, much bruised and hurt; and with thankful hearts that the end of their labour was at hand all prepared for the last and most critical portion of their task.

CHAPTER XXVI.

A CRITICAL MOMENT.

After an earnest thanksgiving by Mr. Brook for their success thus far, the whole party partook of what was a heartier meal than usual, consisting of the whole of the remaining food. Then choosing the largest of the drills, a hole was driven in the coal two feet in depth, and in this an unusually heavy charge was placed.

"We're done for after all," Bill Haden suddenly exclaimed. "Look at the lamp."

Every one present felt his heart sink at what he saw. A light flame seemed to fill the whole interior of the lamp. To strike a match to light the fuse would be to cause an instant explosion of the gas. The place where they were working being the highest part of the mine, the fiery gas, which made its way out of the coal at all points above the closed doors, had, being lighter than air, mounted there.

"Put the lamps out," Jack said quickly, "the gauze is nearly red hot." In a moment they were in darkness.

"What is to be done now?" Mr. Brook asked after a pause.

There was silence for a while—the case seemed desperate.

"Mr. Brook," Jack said after a time, "it is agreed, is it not, that all here will obey my orders?"

"Yes, certainly, Jack," Mr. Brook answered.

"Whatever they are?"

"Yes, whatever they are."

"Very well," Jack said, "you will all take your coats off and soak them in water, then all set to work to beat the gas out of this heading as far as possible. When that is done as far as can be done, all go into the next stall, and lie down at the upper end, you will be out of the way of the explosion there. Cover your heads with your wet coats, and, Bill, wrap something wet round those cans of powder."

"What then, Jack?"

"That's all," Jack said; "I will fire the train. If the gas explodes at the match it will light the fuse, so that the wall will blow in anyhow."

"No, no," a chorus of voices said; "you will be killed."

"I will light it, Jack," Bill Haden said; "I am getting on now, it's no great odds about me."

"No, Dad," Jack said, "I am in charge, and it is for me to do it. You have all promised to obey orders, so set about it at once. Bill, take Mr. Brook up first into the other stall; he won't be able to find his way about in the dark."

Without a word Bill did as he was told, Mr. Brook giving one hearty squeeze to the lad's hand as he was led away. The others, accustomed to the darkness from boyhood, proceeded at once to carry out Jack's instructions, wetting their flannel jackets and then beating the roof with them towards the entrance to the stall; for five minutes they continued this, and then Jack said:

"Now, lads, off to the stall as quick as you can; cover your heads well over; lie down. I will be with you in a minute, or—" or, as Jack knew well, he would be dashed to pieces by the explosion of the gas. He listened until the sound of the last footstep died away—waited a couple of minutes, to allow them to get safely in position at the other end of the next stall—and then, holding the end of the fuse in one hand and the match in the other, he murmured a prayer, and, stooping to the ground, struck the match. No explosion followed; he applied it to the fuse, and ran for his life, down the narrow heading, down the stall, along the horse road, and up the next stall. "It's alight," he said as he rushed in.

A cheer of congratulation and gladness burst from the men. "Cover your heads close," Jack said as he threw himself down; "the explosion is nigh sure to fire the gas."

For a minute a silence as of death reigned in the mine; then there was a sharp cracking explosion, followed—or rather, prolonged—by another like thunder, and, while a flash of fire seemed to surround them, filling the air, firing their clothes, and scorching their limbs, the whole mine shook with a deep continuous roaring. The men knew that the danger was at an end, threw off the covering from their heads, and struck out the fire from their garments. Some were badly burned about the legs, but any word or cry they may have uttered was drowned in the tremendous roar which continued. It was the water from the Logan pit rushing into the Vaughan. For five minutes the noise was like thunder, then, as the pressure from behind decreased, the sound gradually diminished, until, in another five minutes, all was quiet. Then the party rose to their feet. The air in the next stall was clear and fresh, for as the Logan pit had emptied of water, fresh air had of course come down from the surface to take its place.

"We can light our lamps again safely now," Bill Haden said. "We shall want our tools, lads, and the powder; there may be some heavy falls in our way, and we may have hard work yet before we get to the shaft, but the roof rock is strong, so I believe we shall win our way."

"It lies to our right," Jack said. "Like our own, it is at the lower end of the pit, so, as long as we don't mount, we are going right for it."

There were, as Haden had anticipated, many heavy falls of the roof, but the water had swept passages in them, and it was found easier to get along than the colliers had expected. Still it was hard work for men weakened by famine; and it took them five hours of labour clearing away masses of rock, and floundering through black mud, often three feet deep, before they made their way to the bottom of the Logan shaft, and saw the light far above them —the light that at one time they had never expected to see again.

"What o'clock is it now, sir?" Bill Haden asked Mr. Brook, who had from the beginning been the timekeeper of the party.

"Twelve o'clock exactly," he replied. "It is four days and an hour since the pit fired."

"What day is it, sir? for I've lost all count of time."

"Sunday," Mr. Brook said after a moment's thought.

"It could not be better," Bill Haden said; "for there will be thousands of people from all round to visit the mine."

"How much powder have you, Bill?" Jack asked.

"Four twenty-pound cans."

"Let us let off ten pounds at a time," Jack said. "Just damp it enough to prevent it from flashing off too suddenly; break up fine some of this damp wood and mix with it, it will add to the smoke."

In a few minutes the "devil" was ready, and a light applied; it blazed furiously for half a minute, sending volumes of light smoke up the shaft.

"Flash off a couple of pounds of dry powder," Bill Haden said; "there is very little draught up the shaft, and it will drive the air up."

For twenty minutes they continued letting off "devils" and flashing powder. Then they determined to stop, and allow the shaft to clear altogether of the smoke.

Presently a small stone fell among them—another—and another, and they knew that some one had noticed the smoke.

CHAPTER XXVII.

RESCUED.

A stranger arriving at Stokebridge on that Sunday morning might have thought that a fair or some similar festivity was going on, so great was the number of people who passed out of the station as each train came in. For the day Stokebridge was the great point of attraction for excursionists from all parts of Staffordshire. Not that there was anything to see. The Vaughan mine looked still and deserted; no smoke issued from its chimneys; and a strong body of police kept all, except those who had business there, from approaching within a certain distance of the shaft. Still less was there to see in Stokebridge itself. Every blind was down—for scarce a house but had lost at least one of its members; and in the darkened room women sat, silently weeping for the dead far below.

For the last four days work had been entirely suspended through the district; and the men of the other collieries, as well as those of the Vaughan who, belonging to the other shift, had escaped, hung about the pit yard, in the vague hope of being able in some way to be useful.

Within an hour of the explosion the managers of the surrounding pits had assembled; and in spite of the fact that the three volunteers who had first descended were, without doubt, killed, plenty of other brave fellows volunteered their services, and would have gone down if permitted. But the repeated explosions, and the fact that the lower part of the shaft was now blocked up, decided the experienced men who had assembled that such a course would be madness—an opinion which was thoroughly endorsed by Mr. Hardinge and other government inspectors and mining authorities, who arrived within a few hours of the accident.

It was unanimously agreed that the pit was on fire, for a light smoke curled up from the pit mouth, and some already began to whisper that it would have to be closed up. There are few things more painful than to come to the conclusion that nothing can be done, when women, half mad with sorrow and anxiety, are imploring men to make an effort to save those below.

Facing death

Jane Haden, quiet and tearless, sat gazing at the fatal shaft, when she was touched on the shoulder. She looked up, and saw Harry.

"Thou art not down with them then, Harry?"

"No; I almost wish I was," Harry said. "I came up with Jack, and hurried away to get breakfast. When I heard the blow I ran up, and found Jack had just gone down. If I had only been near I might have gone with him;" and the young man spoke in regret at not having shared his friend's fate rather than in gladness at his own escape.

"Dost think there's any hope, Harry?"

"It's no use lying, and there's no hope for Jack, mother," Harry said; "but if any one's saved it's like to be your Bill. He was up in the old workings, a long way off from the part where the strength of the blow would come."

"It's no use telling me, Harry; I ask, but I know how it is. There ain't a chance—not a chance at all. If the pit's afire they'll have to flood it, and then it will be weeks before they pump it out again; and when they bring Jack and Bill up I sha'n't know 'em. That's what I feel, I sha'n't even know 'em."

"Don't wait here, Mrs. Haden; nought can be done now; the inspectors and managers will meet this evening, and consult what is best to be done."

"Is your father down, Harry? I can't think of aught but my own, or I'd have asked afore."

"No; he is in the other shift. My brother Willy is down. Come, mother, let me take you home."

But Mrs. Haden would not move, but sat with scores of other women, watching the mouth of the pit, and the smoke curling up, till night fell.

The news spread round Stokebridge late in the evening that the managers had determined to shut up the mouth of the pit, if there was still smoke in the morning. Then, as is always the case when such a determination is arrived at, there was a cry of grief and anger throughout the village, and all who had friends below protested that it would be nothing short of murder to cut off the supply of air. Women went down to the inn where the meeting was held, and raved like wild creatures; but the miners of the district could not but own the step was necessary, for that the only chance to extinguish the fire was by cutting off the air, unless the dreadful alternative of drowning the pit was resorted to.

Facing death

In the morning the smoke still curled up, and the pit's mouth was closed. Boards were placed over both the shafts, and earth was heaped upon them, so as to cut off altogether the supply of air, and so stifle the fire. This was on Thursday morning. Nothing was done on Friday; and on Saturday afternoon the mining authorities met again in council. There were experts there now from all parts of the kingdom—for the extent of the catastrophe had sent a thrill of horror through the land. It was agreed that the earth and staging should be removed next morning early, and that if smoke still came up, water should be turned in from the canal.

At six in the morning a number of the leading authorities met at the mine. Men had during the night removed the greater part of the earth, and the rest was now taken off, and the planks withdrawn. At once a volume of smoke poured out. This was in any case expected; and it was not for another half-hour, when the accumulated smoke had cleared off, and a straight but unbroken column began to rise as before, that the conviction that the pit was still on fire seized all present.

"I fear that there is no alternative," Mr. Hardinge said; "the pit must be flooded."

There was not a dissentient voice; and the party moved towards the canal to see what would be the best method of letting in the water, when a cry from the men standing round caused them to turn, and they saw a dense white column rise from the shaft.

"Steam!" every one cried in astonishment.

A low rumbling sound came from the pit.

"What can have happened?" Mr. Hardinge exclaimed, in surprise. "This is most extraordinary!"

All crowded round the pit mouth, and could distinctly hear a distant roaring sound. Presently this died away. Gradually the steam ceased to rise, and the air above the pit mouth was clear.

"There is no smoke rising," one of the inspectors said. "What on earth can have happened? Let us lower a light down."

Hoisting gear and rope had been prepared on the first day, in case it should be necessary to lower any one, for the wire rope had snapped when the attempt had been made to draw up the cage after the second explosion, and the sudden release from the strain had caused the engine to fly round, breaking some gear, and for the time disabling it from further work. A hundred and forty fathoms of rope, the depth of the shaft being a hundred and twenty, had been prepared, and was in readiness to be passed over a

172

pulley suspended above the shaft. A lighted candle in a candlestick was placed on a sort of tray, which was fastened to the rope, and then it was lowered gradually down. Eagerly those above watched it as it descended— down—down, till it became a mere speck below. Then it suddenly disappeared.

"Stop," Mr. Hardinge, who was directing the operations, said.

"There are six more fathoms yet, sir—nigh seven—before it gets to the hundred-and-twenty fathom mark."

"Draw up carefully, lads. What can have put the light out forty feet from the bottom of the shaft? Choke-damp, I suppose; but it's very singular."

When the candle came up to the surface there was a cry of astonishment; the tray and the candle were wet! The whole of those present were astounded, and Mr. Hardinge at once determined to descend himself and verify this extraordinary occurrence. There was no fear of an explosion now. Taking a miner's lamp, he took his seat in a sling, and was lowered down. Just before the rope had run out to the point at which the light was extinguished he gave the signal to stop by jerking a thin rope which he held in his hands.

There was a pause, and in a minute or two came two jerks, the signal to haul up.

"It is so," he said, when he gained the surface; "there are forty feet of water in the shaft, but where it came from is more than I can tell."

Much astonished at this singular occurrence, the group of mining engineers walked back to breakfast at Stokebridge, where the population were greatly excited at the news that the pit was flooded. To the miners it was a subject of the greatest surprise, while the friends of those in the pit received the news as the death-blow of their last hopes. It was now impossible that any one could be alive in the pit.

At ten o'clock the mining authorities went again to discuss the curious phenomenon. All agreed that it was out of the question that so large a quantity of water had accumulated in any old workings, for the plan of the pit had been repeatedly inspected by them all. Some inclined to the belief that there must have been some immense natural cavern above the workings, and that when the fire in the pit burned away the pillars left to support the roof, this must have fallen in, and let the water in the cavern into the mine; others pointed out that there was no example whatever of a cavern of such dimensions as this must have been, being found in the coal formation, and pointed to the worked-out Logan pit, which was known to be full of water, as the probable source of supply.

During the previous four days the plan had been discussed of cutting through from the Logan, which was known to have been worked nearly up to the Vaughan boundary. This would enable them to enter the pit and rescue any miners who might be alive, but the fact that to erect pumping gear and get out the water would be an affair of many weeks, if not months, had caused the idea to be abandoned as soon as broached. To those who argued that the water had come from the Logan, it was pointed out that there were certainly several yards of solid coal between the Vaughan and the Logan still standing, and that as the force of the explosion was evidently near the Vaughan shaft it was incredible that this barrier between the pits should have been shattered. However, it was decided to solve the question one way or the other by an immediate visit to the top of the old Logan shaft.

They were just starting when they heard a movement in the street, and men setting off to run. A moment later a miner entered the room hurriedly. "There be a big smoke coming up from the old Logan shaft; it be too light for coal smoke, and I don't think it be steam either."

With exclamations of surprise the whole party seized their hats and hurried off. It was twenty minutes' sharp walking to the shaft, where, by the time they reached it, a large crowd of miners and others were already assembled. As they approached, eager men ran forward to meet them.

"It be gunpowder smoke, sir!"

There was indeed no mistaking the sulphurous smell.

"It's one of two things," Mr. Hardinge said; "either the fire has spread to the upper workings, some powder bags have exploded, and the shock has brought down the dividing wall, in which case the powder smoke might possibly find its way out when the water from the Logan drained in; or else, in some miraculous way some of the men have made their escape, and are letting off powder to call our attention. At any rate let us drop a small stone or two down. If any one be below he will know he is noticed." Then he turned to the miners standing round: "I want the pulley and rope that we were using at the Vaughan, and that small cage that was put together to work with it. I want two or three strong poles, to form a tripod over the pit here, and a few long planks to make a stage."

Fifty willing men hurried off to fetch the required materials.

"The smoke is getting thinner, a good deal," one of the managers said. "Now if you'll hold me, I will give a shout down."

Facing death

The mouth of the pit was surrounded by a wooden fencing, to prevent any one from falling down it. The speaker got over this and lay down on his face, working nearer to the edge, which sloped dangerously down, while others, following in the same way, held his legs, and were in their turn held by others. When his head and shoulders were fairly over the pit he gave a loud shout.

There was a death-like silence on the part of the crowd standing round, and all of those close could hear a faint murmur come from below.

Then arose a cheer, echoed again and again, and then half-a-dozen fleet-footed boys started for Stokebridge with the news that some of the imprisoned pitmen were still alive.

Mr. Hardinge wrote on a piece of paper, "Keep up your courage; in an hour's time the cage will come down;" wrapped it round a stone, and dropped it down. A messenger was despatched to the Vaughan, for the police force stationed there to come up at once to keep back the excited crowd, and with orders that the stretchers and blankets in readiness should be brought on; while another went into Stokebridge for a surgeon, and for a supply of wine, brandy, and food, and two or three vehicles. No sooner were the men sent off than Mr. Hardinge said, in a loud tone:

"Every moment must be of consequence; they must be starving. Will any one here who has food give it for them?"

The word was passed through the crowd, and a score of picnic baskets were at once offered. Filling one of them full with sandwiches from the rest, Mr. Hardinge tied the lid securely on, and threw it down the shaft. "There is no fear of their standing under the shaft," he said; "they will know we shall be working here, and that stones might fall."

In less than an hour, thanks to the willing work of many hands, a platform was constructed across the mouth of the Logan shaft, and a tripod of strong poles fixed in its place. The police kept the crowd, by this time very many thousands strong, back in a wide circle round the shaft, none being allowed inside save those who had near relatives in the Vaughan. These were for the most part women, who had rushed wildly up without bonnets or shawls—just as they stood when the report reached them that there were yet some survivors of the explosion. At full speed they had hurried along the road—some pale and still despairing, refusing to allow hope to rise again, but unable to stay away from the fatal pit; others crying as they ran; some even laughing in hysterical excitement. Most excited, because most hopeful, were those whose husbands had stalls in the old workings, for it had from the first been believed that while all in the main workings were probably killed at once by the first explosion, those in the old workings might have survived for days.

Jane Haden walked steadily along the road, accompanied by Harry Shepherd, who had brought her the news, and by Nelly Hardy.

"I will go," she said, "but it is of no use; they are both gone, and I shall never see them again."

Then she had put on her bonnet and shawl, deliberately and slowly, and had started at her ordinary pace, protesting all along against its being supposed that she entertained the slightest hope; but when she neared the spot, her quivering lips and twitching fingers belied her words. Nelly remained outside the crowd, but Harry made a way for Jane Haden through the outside circle of spectators.

A smaller circle, of some thirty yards in diameter, was kept round the shaft, and within this only those directing the operations were allowed to enter. Mr. Hardinge and one of the local managers took their places in the cage. The rope was held by twenty men, who at first stood at its full length from the shaft, and then advanced at a walk towards it, thus allowing the cage to descend steadily and easily, without jerks. As they came close to the shaft the signal rope was shaken; another step or two, slowly and carefully taken, and the rope was seen to sway slightly. The cage was at the bottom of the shaft. Three minutes' pause, the signal rope shook, and the men with the end of the rope, started again to walk from the shaft.

As they increased their distance, the excitement in the great crowd grew; and when the cage showed above the surface, and it was seen that it contained three miners, a hoarse cheer arose. The men were assisted from the cage, and surrounded for a moment by those in authority; and one of the head men raised his hand for silence, and then shouted:

"Mr. Brook and twenty others are saved!" An announcement which was received with another and even more hearty cheer.

SAVED!

Passing on, the rescued men moved forward to where the women stood, anxiously gazing. Blackened as they were with coal-dust, they were recognizable, and with wild screams of joy three women burst from the rest

177

and threw themselves in their arms. But only for a moment could they indulge in this burst of happiness, for the other women crowded round.

"Who is alive? For God's sake tell us! who is alive?"

Then one by one the names were told, each greeted with cries of joy, till the last name was spoken; and then came a burst of wailing and lamentation from those who had listened in vain for the names of those they loved.

Jane Haden had not risen from the seat she had taken on a block of broken brickwork.

"No, no!" she said to Harry; "I will not hope! I will not hope!" and while Harry moved closer to the group, to hear the names of the saved, she sat with her face buried in her hands.

The very first names given were those of Jack Simpson and Bill Haden, and with a shout of joy he rushed back. The step told its tale, and Jane Haden looked up, rose as if with a hidden spring, and looked at him.

"Both saved!" he exclaimed; and with a strange cry Jane Haden swayed, and fell insensible.

An hour later, and the last survivor of those who were below in the Vaughan pit stood on the surface, the last cage load being Mr. Brook, Jack Simpson, and Mr. Hardinge. By this time the mourners had left the scene, and there was nothing to check the delight felt at the recovery from the tomb, as it was considered, of so many of those deemed lost.

When Mr. Brook—who was a popular employer, and whose popularity was now increased by his having, although involuntarily, shared the dangers of his men—stepped from the cage, the enthusiasm was tremendous. The crowd broke the cordon of police and rushed forward, cheering loudly. Mr. Hardinge, after a minute or two, held up his hand for silence, and helped Mr. Brook on to a heap of stones. Although Mr. Brook, as well as the rest, had already recovered much, thanks to the basket of food thrown down to them, and to the supply of weak brandy and water, and of soup, which those who had first descended had carried with them, he was yet so weakened by his long fast that he was unable to speak. He could only wave his hand in token of his thanks, and sobs of emotion choked his words. Mr. Hardinge, however, who had, during the hour below, learned all that had taken place, and had spoken for some time apart with Mr. Brook, now stood up beside him.

"My friends," he said, in a loud clear voice, which was heard over the whole crowd, "Mr. Brook is too much shaken by what he has gone through to speak, but he desires me to thank you most heartily in his name for your kind greeting. He wishes to say that, under God, his life, and the lives of those with him, have been saved by the skill, courage, and science of his under-viewer, Jack Simpson. Mr. Brook has consulted me on the subject, and I thoroughly agree with what he intends to do, and can certify to Jack Simpson's ability, young as he is, to fill any post to which he may be appointed. In a short time I hope that the Vaughan pit will be pumped out and at work again, and when it is, Mr. Jack Simpson will be its manager!"

The story of the escape from death had already been told briefly by the miners as they came to the surface, and had passed from mouth to mouth among the crowd, and Mr. Hardinge's announcement was greeted with a storm of enthusiasm. Jack was seized by a score of sturdy pitmen, and would have been carried in triumph, were it not that the startling announcement, coming after such a long and intense strain, proved too much for him, and he fainted in the arms of his admirers.

CHAPTER XXVIII.

CHANGES.

Beyond the body of the crowd, outside the ring kept by the police, stood Nelly Hardy, watching, without a vestige of colour in her face, for the news from below. She had given a gasping sigh of relief as the names, passed from mouth to mouth by the crowd, met her ear, and had leaned for support against the wall behind her. So great was her faith in Jack's resources and in Jack's destiny that she had all along hoped, and the assertion that those who had first gone down to rescue the pitmen must have fallen victims to the second explosion had fallen dead upon her ears.

The school had been closed from the date of the accident, and had it not been so, she felt that she could not have performed her duties. Hour after hour she had sat in her cottage alone—for her mother had died a year before—except when Mrs. Dodgson, who had long suspected her secret, came to sit awhile with her, or Harry brought the latest news. During this time she had not shed a tear, and, save for her white face and hard unnatural voice, none could have told how she suffered. Harry had brought her the news of the smoke being seen from the shaft of the Logan pit before he carried it to Mrs. Haden, and she had at once thrown on her bonnet and jacket and joined them as they started from the village. When she reached the pit she had not attempted to approach, but had taken her place at a distance. Several of her pupils, with whom she was a great favourite, had come up to speak to her, but her hoarse, "Not now, dear; please go away," had sufficed to send them off. But deeply agitated as she was, she was hopeful; and deep as was her joy at the news of Jack's safety she was hardly surprised. Dropping her veil to hide the tears of joy which streamed down her cheeks, she turned to go home; but she was more shaken than she had thought, and she had to grasp at the wall for support.

So she waited until the last of the miners arrived at the surface, and heard the speech of the government inspector. Then when she heard Jack's elevation announced, the news shook her even more than that of his safety had done, and she fainted. When she recovered the crowd was gone, and Harry only stood beside her. He had felt that she would rather stand and watch alone, and had avoided going near her, but when Jack was driven off he had hastened to her side. He knew how she would object to her emotion becoming known, and had contented himself with lifting her veil, untying her bonnet strings, putting her in a sitting attitude against the wall, and waiting patiently till she came round.

"Are you better now?" he inquired anxiously when she opened her eyes.

"Yes, I am well now," she said, glancing hastily round to see if others beside himself had noticed her situation; "I am quite well."

"Don't try to get up; sit still a few minutes longer," he said. "Don't try to talk."

"He has got his rise at last," she said smiling faintly and looking up; "he has gone right away from us at a bound."

"I am glad," Harry said simply. "He has earned it. He is a grand, a glorious fellow, is Jack. Of course I shall never be to him now what I have been, but I know that he will be as true a friend as ever, though I may not see so much of him."

"You are more unselfish than I, Harry; but as he was to rise, it was better that it should be at a bound far above me. Now I am better; let me go home."

Jack Simpson's fainting fit had been but of short duration. His sturdy organization soon recovered from the shock which the fresh air and Mr. Hardinge's announcement had made upon a frame exhausted by privation, fatigue, and excitement. None the less was he astonished and indignant with himself at what he considered a girlish weakness. His thoughts were, however, speedily diverted from himself by a pitman telling him that Jane Haden was in a second faint close by. Mr. Brook's carriage had been sent for in readiness, immediately the possibility of his being found alive had appeared; and that gentleman insisted upon Mrs. Haden being lifted into it, and upon Jack taking his seat beside her to support her. He then followed, and, amidst the cheers of the crowd, started for Stokebridge.

Mrs. Haden recovered before reaching the village; and leaving her and Jack at their home, with an intimation that the carriage would come at an early hour next morning to fetch the latter up to the hall, Mr. Brook drove off alone.

That afternoon was a proud day for Bill Haden and his wife, but a trying one for Jack.

Every one in the place who had the slightest knowledge of him called to shake his hand and congratulate him on his promotion, his friends of boyhood first among them. Harry was one of the earliest comers, and tears fell down the cheeks of both as they clasped hands in silent joy at their reunion. Not a word was spoken or needed.

"Go round to Nelly," Jack said in an undertone as other visitors arrived; "tell her I will come in and see her at seven o'clock. Come again yourself before that, let us three meet together again."

So quickly did the callers press in that the little room could not hold them; and Jack had to go to the front door, there to shake hands and say a word to all who wanted to see him. It was quite a levée, and it was only the fact that the gloom of a terrible calamity hung over Stokebridge that prevented the demonstration being noisy as well as enthusiastic.

By six o'clock all his friends had seen him, and Jack sat down with Bill Haden and his wife. Then Jane Haden's feelings relieved themselves by a copious flood of tears; and Bill himself, though he reproached her for crying on such an occasion, did so in a husky voice.

"Thou art going to leave us, Jack," Jane Haden said; "and though we shall miss thee sorely, thou mustn't go to think that Bill or me be sorry at the good fortune that be come upon you. Thou hast been a son, and a good son to us, and ha' never given so much as a day's trouble. I know'd as how you'd leave us sooner or later. There was sure to be a time when all the larning thou hast worked so hard to get would bring thee to fortune, but I didn't think 'twould come so soon."

Bill Haden removed from his lips the pipe—which, in his endeavour to make up for loss of time, he had smoked without ceasing from the moment of his rescue—and grunted an acquiescence with his wife's speech.

"My dear mother and dad," Jack said, "there must be no talk of parting between us. As yet, of course, it is too soon to form plans for the future; but be assured that there will be no parting. You took me when I was a helpless baby; but for you I should have been a workhouse child, and might now be coming out of my apprenticeship to a tinker or a tailor. I owe all I have, all I am, to you; and whatever fortune befall me you will still be dad and mother. For a short time I must go to the hall, as Mr. Brook has invited me; and we shall have much to arrange and talk over. Afterwards I suppose I shall have to go to the manager's house, but, of course, arrangements will have to be made as to Mr. Fletcher's widow and children; and when I go there, of course you will come too."

"Thee'st a good un, lad," Bill Haden said, for Mrs. Haden's tears prevented her speech; "but I doubt what thou say'st can be; but we needn't talk that over now. But t' old 'ooman and I be none the less glad o' thy words, Jack; though the bit and sup that thou had'st here till you went into th' pit and began to pay your way ain't worth the speaking o'. Thou beats me a'together, Jack. When un see's a good pup un looks to his breed, and un finds it pure; but where thou get'st thy points from beats me a'together. Thy mother were a schoolmaster's daughter, but she had not the name o' being fond o' larning, and was a'ways weak and ailing; thy dad, my mate Jack Simpson, was as true a mate as ever man had; but he were in no ways uncommon. The old 'ooman and I ha' reared ye; but, arter all, pups don't follow their foster-mother, for the best bull pup ain't noways injured by having a half-bred un, or for the matter o' that one wi' no breed at all, as a foster-mother; besides the old 'ooman and me has no points at all, 'cept on my part, such as are bad uns; so it beats me fairly. It downright shakes un's faith in breeding."

Here Harry's tap was heard at the door, and Jack, leaving Bill Haden to ponder over his egregious failure in proving true to blood, joined his friend outside.

Scarce a word was spoken between the two young men as they walked across to Nelly Hardy's little cottage by the schoolhouse. The candles were already lighted, and Nelly rose as they entered.

"My dear Nelly."

"My dear Jack," she said, throwing her arms round his neck as a sister might have done, and kissing him, for the first time in her life; and crying, "My dear Jack, thank God you are restored alive to us."

"Thank God indeed," Jack said reverently; "it has been almost a miracle, Nelly, and I am indeed thankful. We prayed nearly as hard as we worked, and God was with us; otherwise assuredly we had never passed through such danger uninjured. I thought many a time of you and Harry, and what you would be doing and thinking.

"I never gave up hope, did I, Harry?" she said; "I thought that somehow such a useful life as yours would be spared."

"Many other useful lives have been lost, Nelly," Jack said sadly; "but it was not my time."

"And now," Nelly said changing her tone, "there are other things to talk of. Will you please take a chair, sir," and she dropped a curtsy. "Didn't I tell you, Jack," she said, laughing at the astonishment in Jack's face, "that when you congratulated me on getting my post here and called me Miss Hardy, that the time would come when I should say, Sir to you. It has come, Jack, sooner than we expected, but I knew it would come."

Facing death

Then changing her tone again, as they sat looking at the fire, she went on, "You know we are glad, Jack, Harry and I, more glad than we can say, that needs no telling between us, does it?"

"None," Jack said. "We are one, we three, and no need to say we are glad at each other's success."

"We have had happy days," Nelly said, "but they will never be quite the same again. We shall always be friends, Jack, always—true and dear friends, but we cannot be all in all to each other. I know, dear Jack," she said as she saw he was about to speak vehemently, "that you will be as much our friend in one way as ever, but you cannot be our companion. It is impossible, Jack. We have trod the same path together, but your path leaves ours here. We shall be within sound of each other's voices, we shall never lose sight of each other, but we are no longer together."

"I have not thought it over yet," Jack said quietly. "It is all too new and too strange to me to see yet how things will work; but it is true, Nelly, and it is the one drawback to my good fortune, that there must be some little change between us. But in the friendship which began when you stood by me at the old shaft and helped me to save Harry, there will be no change. I have risen as I always had determined to rise; I have worked for this from the day when Mr. Pastor, my artist friend, told me it was possible I might reach it, but I never dreamed it would come so soon; and I have always hoped and thought that I should keep you both with me. How things will turn out we do not know, but, dear friends," and he held out a hand to each, "believe me, that I shall always be as I am now, and that I shall care little for my good fortune unless I can retain you both as my dearest friends."

CHAPTER XXIX.

THE NEW MANAGER.

The next day preparations for pumping out the Vaughan commenced; but it took weeks to get rid of the water which had flowed in in five minutes. Then the work of clearing the mine and bringing up the bodies commenced.

This was a sad business. A number of coffins, equal to that of the men known to be below at the time of the explosion, were in readiness in a shed near the pit mouth. These were sent down, and the bodies as they were found were placed in them to be carried above. In scarcely any instances could the dead be identified by the relatives, six weeks in the water having changed them beyond all recognition; only by the clothes could a clue be obtained. Then the funerals began. A great grave a hundred feet long by twelve wide had been dug in the churchyard, and in this the coffins were laid two deep.

Some days ten, some fifteen, some twenty bodies were laid there, and at each funeral the whole village attended. Who could know whether those dearest to them were not among the shapeless forms each day consigned to their last resting-place?

At last the tale was complete; the last of the victims of the great explosion at the Vaughan was laid to rest, the blinds were drawn up, and save that the whole of the people seemed to be in mourning, Stokebridge assumed its usual aspect.

Upon the day before the renewal of regular work, Jack Simpson, accompanied by Mr. Brook appeared upon the ground, and signified that none were to descend until he had spoken to them. He had already won their respect by his indefatigable attention to the work of clearing the mine, and by the care he had evinced for the recovery of the bodies.

Few, however, of the hands had spoken to him since his accession to his new dignity; now they had time to observe him, and all wondered at the change which had been wrought in his appearance. Clothes do not make a man, but they greatly alter his appearance, and there was not one but felt

Facing death

that Jack looked every inch a gentleman. When he began to speak their wonder increased. Except to Mr. Dodgson, Harry, Nelly Hardy, and some of his young comrades, Jack had always spoken in the dialect of the place, and the surprise of the colliers when he spoke in perfect English without a trace of accent or dialect was great indeed.

Standing up in the gig in which he had driven up with Mr. Brook he spoke in a loud, clear voice heard easily throughout the yard.

"My friends," he said, "my position here is a new and difficult one, so difficult that did I not feel sure that you would help me to make it as easy as possible I should shrink from undertaking it. I am a very young man. I have grown up among you, and of you, and now in a strange way, due in a great measure to the kindness of your employers, and in a small degree to my own exertions to improve myself, I have come to be put over you. Now it is only by your helping me that I can maintain this position here. You will find in me a true friend. I know your difficulties and your wants, and I will do all in my power to render your lives comfortable. Those among you who were my friends from boyhood can believe this, the rest of you will find it to be so. Any of you who are in trouble or in difficulty will, if you come to me, obtain advice and assistance. But while I will try to be your friend, and will do all in my power for your welfare, it is absolutely necessary that you should treat me with the respect due to Mr. Brook's manager. Without proper discipline proper work is impossible. A captain must be captain of his own ship though many of his men know the work as well as he does. And I am glad to be able to tell you that Mr. Brook has given me full power to make such regulations and to carry out such improvements as may be conducive to your comfort and welfare. He wants, and I want, the Vaughan to be a model mine and Stokebridge a model village, and we will do all in our power to carry out our wishes. We hope that no dispute will ever again arise here on the question of wages. There was one occasion when the miners of the Vaughan were led away by strangers and paid dearly for it. We hope that such a thing will never occur again. Mr. Brook expects a fair return, and no more than a fair return, for the capital he has sunk in the mine. When times are good you will share his prosperity, when times are bad you, like he, must submit to sacrifices. If disputes arise elsewhere, they need not affect us here, for you may be sure that your wages will never be below those paid elsewhere. And now I have said my say. Let us conclude by trusting that we shall be as warm friends as ever although our relations towards each other are necessarily changed."

Three rousing cheers greeted the conclusion of Jack's speech, after which he drove off with Mr. Brook. As the men gathered round the top of the shaft, an old miner exclaimed: "Dang it all, I ha' it now. I was wondering all the time he was speaking where I had heard his voice before. I know now. As sure as I'm a living man it was Jack Simpson as beat us back from that there engine-house when we were going to stop the pumps in the strike."

Now that the clue was given a dozen others of those who had been present agreed with the speaker. The event was now an old one, and all bitterness had passed. Had it been known at the time, or within a few months afterwards, Jack's life would probably have paid the penalty, but now the predominant feeling was one of admiration. Those who had, during the last few weeks, wearily watched the pumping out of the Vaughan, felt how fatal would have been the delay had it occurred when the strike ended and they were penniless and without resources, and no feeling of ill-will remained.

"He be a game 'un; to think o' that boy standing alone agin' us a', and not a soul as much as suspected it! Did'st know o't, Bill Haden?"

"Noa," Bill said, "never so much as dream't o't, but now I thinks it over, it be loikely enoo'. I often thought what wonderful luck it were as he gave me that 'ere bottle o' old Tom, and made me as drunk as a loord joost at th' roight time, and I ha' thought it were curious too, seeing as never before or since has he giv'd me a bottle o' liquor, but now it all comes natural enough. Well, to be sure, and to think that lad should ha' done all that by hisself, and ne'er a soul the wiser! You may be sure the gaffer didn't know no more than we, or he'd a done summat for the lad at the time. He offered rewards, too, for the finding out who 't were as had done it, and to think 'twas my Jack! Well, well, he be a good plucked un too, they didn't ca' him Bull-dog for nowt, for it would ha' gone hard wi' him had 't been found out. I'm main proud o' that lad."

And so the discovery that Jack had so wished to avoid, when it was at last made, added much to the respect with which he was held in the Vaughan pit. If when a boy he would dare to carry out such a scheme as this, it was clear that as a man he was not to be trifled with. The reputation which he had gained by his courage in descending into the mine, in his battle with Tom Walker, and by the clear-headedness and quickness of decision which had saved the lives of the survivors of the explosion, was immensely increased; and any who had before felt sore at the thought of so young a hand being placed above them in command of the pit, felt that in all that constitutes a man, in energy, courage, and ability, Jack Simpson was worthy the post of manager of the Vaughan mine.

Bill Haden was astonished upon his return home that night to find that his wife had all along known that it was Jack who had defended the Vaughan, and was inclined to feel greatly aggrieved at having been kept in the dark.

"Did ye think as I wasn't to be trusted not to split on my own lad?" he exclaimed indignantly.

"We knew well enough that thou mightest be trusted when thou wer't sober, Bill," his wife said gently; "but as about four nights a week at that time thou wast drunk, and might ha' blabbed it out, and had known nowt in the morning o' what thou'dst said, Jack and I were of a mind that less said soonest mended."

"May be you were right," Bill Haden said after a pause; "a man has got a loose tongue when he's in drink, and I should never ha' forgiven myself had I harmed t' lad."

CHAPTER XXX.

RISEN.

It was not until the pit was cleared of water and about to go to work again, that the question of Bill Haden and his wife removing from their cottage came forward for decision. Jack had been staying with Mr. Brook, who had ordered that the house in which the late manager had lived should be put in good order and furnished from top to bottom, and had arranged for his widow and children to remove at once to friends living at a distance. Feeling as he did that he owed his life to the young man, he was eager to do everything in his power to promote his comfort and prosperity, and as he was, apart from the colliery, a wealthy man and a bachelor, he did not care to what expense he went.

The house, "the great house on the hill," as Jack had described it when speaking to his artist friend Pastor years before, was a far larger and more important building than the houses of managers of mines in general. It had, indeed, been originally the residence of a family owning a good deal of land in the neighbourhood, but they, when coal was discovered and work began, sold this property and went to live in London, and as none cared to take a house so close to the coal-pits and village of Stokebridge, it was sold for a nominal sum to the owner of the Vaughan, and was by him used as a residence for his manager.

Now, with the garden nicely laid out, redecorated and repaired outside and in, and handsomely furnished, it resumed its former appearance of a gentleman's country seat. Mr. Brook begged Jack as a favour not to go near the house until the place was put in order, and although the young man heard that a Birmingham contractor had taken it in hand, and that a large number of men were at work there, he had no idea of the extensive changes which were taking place.

A few days before work began again at the Vaughan Jack went down as usual to the Hadens', for he had looked in every day to say a few words to them on his way back from the pit-mouth. "Now, dad," he said, "we must not put the matter off any longer. I am to go into the manager's house in a fortnight's time. I hear they have been painting and cleaning it up, and Mr. Brook tells me he has put new furniture in, and that I shall only have to go in and hang up my hat. Now I want for you to arrange to come up on the same day."

"We ha' been talking the matter over in every mortal way, the old woman and me, Jack, and I'll tell 'ee what we've aboot concluded. On one side thou really wan't t' have us oop wi' 'ee."

"Yes, indeed, dad," Jack said earnestly.

"I know thou dost, lad; me and Jane both feels that. Well that's an argiment that way. Then there's the argiment that naturally thou would'st not like the man who hast brought thee oop to be working in the pit o' which thou wast manager. That's two reasons that way; on the other side there be two, and the old 'ooman and me think they are stronger than t'others. First, we should be out o' place at the house oop there. Thou wilt be getting to know all kinds o' people, and whatever thou may'st say, Jack, your mother and me would be oot o' place. That's one argiment. The next argiment is that we shouldn't like it, Jack, we should feel we were out o' place and that our ways were out o' place; and we should be joost miserable. Instead o' doing us a kindness you'd joost make our lives a burden, and I know 'ee don't want to do that. We's getting on in loife and be too old to change our ways, and nothing thou could'st say could persuade us to live a'ways dressed up in our Sunday clothes in your house."

"Well, dad, I might put you both in a comfortable cottage, without work to do."

"What should I do wi'out my work, Jack? noa, lad, I must work as long as I can, or I should die o' pure idleness. But I needn't work at a stall. I'm fifty now, and although I ha' got another fifteen years' work in me, I hope, my bones bean't as liss as they was. Thou might give me the job as underground viewer. I can put in a prop or see to the firing o' a shot wi' any man. Oi've told my mates you want to have me and the old woman oop at th' house, and they'll know that if I stop underground it be o' my own choice. I know, lad, it wouldn't be roight for me to be a getting droonk at the "Chequers" and thou manager; but I ha' told t' old 'ooman that I will swear off liquor altogether."

"No, no, dad!" Jack said, affected at this proof of Bill Haden's desire to do what he could towards maintaining his dignity. "I wouldn't think o't. If you and mother feel that you'd be more happy and comfortable here—and maybe you are right, I didn't think over the matter from thy side as well as my own, as I ought to have done—of course you shall stay here; and, of course, you shall have a berth as under-viewer. As for swearing off drink altogether, I wouldn't ask it of you, though I do wish you could resolve never to drink too much again. You ha' been used to go to the "Chequers" every night for nigh forty years, and you couldn't give it up now. You would pine away without somewhere to go to. However, this must be understood, whenever you like to come up to me I shall be glad to see you, and I shall expect you on Sundays to dinner if on no other day; and whenever the time shall come when you feel, dad, that you'd rather give up work, there will be a cottage for you and mother somewhere handy to me, and enough to live comfortably and free from care."

"That's a bargain, lad, and I'm roight glad it be off my mind, for I ha' been bothering over't ever since thee spoke to me last."

The same evening Jack had a long talk with Harry. His friend, although healthy, was by no means physically strong, and found the work of a miner almost beyond him. He had never taken to the life as Jack had done, and his friend knew that for the last year or two he had been turning his thoughts in other directions, and that of all things he would like to be a schoolmaster. He had for years read and studied a good deal, and Mr. Dodgson said that with a year in a training college he would be able to pass. He had often talked the matter over with Jack, and the latter told him now that he had entered his name in St. Mark's College, Chelsea, had paid his fees six months in advance, his savings amply sufficing for this without drawing upon his salary, and that he was to present himself there in a week's time.

The announcement took away Harry's breath, but as soon as he recovered himself he accepted Jack's offer as frankly as it was made. It had always been natural for Jack to lend him a hand, and it seemed to him, as to Jack, natural that it should be so now.

"Have you told Nelly?"

"No, I left it for you to tell, Harry. I know, of course, one reason why you want to be a schoolmaster, and she will know it too. She is a strange girl, is Nelly; I never did quite understand her, and I never shall; why on earth she should refuse you I can't make out. She's had lots o' other offers these last four years, but it's all the same. There's no one she cares for, why shouldn't she take you?"

"I can wait," Harry said quietly, "there's plenty of time; perhaps some day I shall win her, and I think—yes, I think now—that I shall."

"Well," Jack said cheerfully, "as you say there's plenty of time; I've always said thirty was the right age to marry, and you want eight years of that, and Nelly won't get old faster than you do, so if she don't fall in love with any one else it must come right; she has stood out for nearly four years, and though I don't pretend to know anything of women, I should think no woman could go on saying no for twelve years."

Facing death

Harry, although not given to loud mirth, laughed heartily at Jack's views over love-making, and the two then walked across to Nelly Hardy's cottage. Jack told her what Bill Haden and his wife had decided, and she approved their determination. Then Harry said what Jack had arranged for him.

Nelly shook her head as if in answer to her own thoughts while Harry was speaking, but when he ceased she congratulated him warmly.

"You were never fit for pit-work, Harry, and a schoolmaster's life will suit you well. It is curious that Jack's two friends should both have taken to the same life."

Jack's surprise was unbounded when, a month after the reopening of the Vaughan, Mr. Brook took him over to his new abode. His bewilderment at the size and completeness of the house and its fittings was even greater than his pleasure.

"But what am I to do alone in this great place, Mr. Brook?" he asked; "I shall be lost here. I am indeed deeply grateful to you, but it is much too big for me altogether."

"It is no bigger now than it has always been," Mr. Brook said, "and you will never be lost as long as you have your study there," and he pointed to a room snugly fitted up as a library and study. "You will be no more lonely than I or other men without wives and families; besides you know these may come some day."

"Ah! but that will be many years on," Jack said; "I always made up my mind not to marry till I was thirty, because a wife prevents you making your way."

"Yes; but now that you have made your way so far, Jack, a wife will aid rather than hinder you. But it will be time to think of that in another three or four years. You will not find it so dull as you imagine, Jack. There is your work, which will occupy the greater part of your day. There is your study for the evening. You will speedily know all the people worth knowing round here; I have already introduced you to a good many, and they will be sure to call as soon as you are settled here. In the stable, my dear boy, you will find a couple of horses, and a saddle, and a dog-cart, so that you will be able to take exercise and call about. I shall keep the horses. I consider them necessary for my manager. My men will keep the garden in order, and I think that you will find that your salary of £350 a year to begin with ample for your other expenses."

Facing death

Jack was completely overpowered by the kindness of his employer, but the latter would not hear of thanks. "Why, man, I owe you my life," he said; "what are these little things in comparison?"

Jack found fewer difficulties than he had anticipated in his new position. His speech at the opening of the mine added to the favour with which he was held for his conduct at the time of the explosion, and further heightened the respect due to him for his defence of the Vaughan. As he went through the mine he had ever a cheery "Good morning, Bob," "Good morning, Jack," for his old comrades, and the word "sir" was now universally added to the answered "Good morning," a concession not always made by colliers to their employers.

The miners soon felt the advantages of the new manager's energy, backed as he was in every respect by the owner. The work as laid down by the government inspector was carried out, and Mr. Brook having bought up for a small sum the disused Logan mine, in which several of the lower seams of coal were still unworked, the opening between the pits was made permanent, and the Logan shaft became the upcast to the Vaughan, thus greatly simplifying the work of ventilation, lessening the danger of explosion, and giving a means of escape for the miners should such a catastrophe recur in spite of all precautions.

As nearly half the old workers at the pit had perished in the explosion, an equal number of new hands had to be taken on. Jack, sharing the anxiety of the vicar and Mr. Dodgson, that all the good work should not be checked by the ingress of a fresh population, directed that all vacancies should be filled up by such colliers of good character as resided at Stokebridge, working for other pits in the neighbourhood. As the Vaughan promised to be the most comfortable and well-worked pit in the country, these were only too glad to change service, and more names were given in than vacancies could be found for. As all the inhabitants of Stokebridge had participated in the benefits of the night schools and classes, and in the improvements which had taken place, the advance of the village suffered no serious check from the catastrophe at the Vaughan.

CHAPTER XXXI.

CONCLUSION.

Three years more of progress and Stokebridge had become the model village of the Black Country. The chief employer of labour, his manager, the vicar, and schoolmaster all worked together for this end. The library had been a great success, and it was rare, indeed, for a drunken man to be seen in the streets even of a Saturday night. Many of the public-houses had closed their doors altogether; and in addition to the library a large and comfortable club-house had been built.

The men of an evening could smoke their pipes, play at bagatelle, chess, draughts, or cards, and take such beer as they required, any man getting drunk or even noisy to be expelled the club. This, however, was a rule never requiring to be called into force. The building was conducted on the principle of a regimental canteen. The beer was good and cheap but not strong, no spirits were sold, but excellent tea, coffee, and chocolate could be had at the lowest prices.

The building was closed during the day, but beer was sent out both for dinners and suppers to those who required it. There was a comfortable room where women could sew, knit, and talk as they pleased, or they could, if they liked, sit in the general room with their husbands. Entertainments and lectures were of frequent occurrence, and the establishment, supplemented by the library and wash-house, did wonders for Stokebridge.

The promise made by Mr. Brook at the fête had been carried out. A choir-master came over twice a week from Birmingham, and the young people entered into the scheme with such zest that the choir had carried away the prize three years in succession at Birmingham. The night-school was now carried on on a larger scale than ever, and the school for cooking and sewing was so well attended that Mrs. Dodgson had now a second assistant. To encourage the children and young people an annual show was held at which many prizes were given for gardening, needlework, dressmaking, carpentering, and a variety of other subjects. It was seldom, indeed, that an untidy dress was to be seen, still more uncommon that a foul word was heard in the streets of Stokebridge. Nothing could make the rows of cottages picturesque as are those of a rural village; but from tubs, placed in front, creepers and roses climbed over the houses, while the gardens behind were gay with flowers.

No young woman needed to remain single in Stokebridge longer than she chose, for so noteworthy were they for their housewifely qualities that the young pitmen of the villages round thought themselves fortunate indeed if they could get a wife from Stokebridge. Bill Cummings, Fred Wood, and several others of Jack's boy friends, were viewers or under-managers of the Vaughan, and many had left to take similar situations elsewhere.

Jack Simpson was popular with all classes. With the upper class his simple straightforwardness, his cheerfulness and good temper, made him a great favourite, although they found it hard to understand how so quiet and unassuming a young fellow could be the hero of the two rescues at the Vaughan, for, now when the fact was known, Jack no longer made a secret of his share in the attack by the rioters on the engine-house. Among the pitmen his popularity was unbounded. Of an evening he would sometimes come down to the club-room and chat as unrestrainedly and intimately as of old with the friends of his boyhood, and he never lost an opportunity of pushing their fortunes.

Once a week he spent the evening with Bill Haden and his wife, who always came up and passed Sunday with him when he was at home. At this time all ceremony was dispensed with, the servants were sent out of the room, and when the pitman and his wife became accustomed to their surroundings they were far more at their ease than they had at first thought possible.

On the evenings when he went down to his mother he always dropped in for an hour's talk with his friend Nelly. There was no shadow of change in their relations. Nelly was his friend firm and fast, to whom he told all his thoughts and plans. Harry was assistant master in a school at Birmingham, and was, as he told Jack, still waiting patiently.

Jack was now often over at Birmingham, and one night he said to Nelly:

"Nelly, I promised you long ago that I would tell you if I ever fell in love."

"And you have come to tell me now?" she asked quietly.

"Yes," he said, "if it can be called falling in love; for it has been so gradual that I don't know how it began. Perhaps three years ago, when she refused another man. I was glad of it, and of course asked myself why I was glad. There came no answer but one—I wanted her myself."

Facing death

"I suppose it is Alice Merton?" Nelly said as quietly as before.

"Of course," Jack said; "it could be no one else. I suppose I like her because she is the reverse of myself. She is gentle but lively and full of fun, she is made to be the light of a hard working man's home. I am not at all gentle, and I have very little idea of fun. Alice is made to lean on some one. I suppose I am meant to be leant upon. I suppose it is always the case that opposite natures are attracted towards one another, the one forms the complement of the other."

Nelly sat thinking. This then was the reason why she had never attracted Jack. Both their natures were strong and firm. Both had full control over themselves, although both of a passionate nature; both had the capability of making great sacrifices, even of life if necessary; both had ambition and a steady power of work. No wonder Jack had thought of her as a comrade rather than as a possible wife; while Harry, gentler and easily led, patient rather than firm, leaned upon her strong nature.

"I think, dear Jack," she said, "that Miss Merton is the very woman to make you happy. You have known each other for twelve years, and can make no mistake. I need not say how truly and sincerely I wish you every happiness." There was a quiver in her voice as she spoke, but her face was as firm and steadfast as ever; and Jack Simpson, as he walked homewards, did not dream that Nelly Hardy was weeping as if her heart would break, over this final downfall of her life's dream. It was not that she had for the last seven years ever thought that Jack would ask her to be his wife, but she would have been content to go on to the end of her life as his first and dearest friend. Then she said at last, "That's done with. Jack and I will always be great friends, but not as we have been. Perhaps it is as well. Better now than ten years on."

Then her thoughts went to Harry, to whom, indeed, during the last few years they had gone oftener than she would have admitted to herself. "He is very faithful and kind and good, and I suppose one of these days I shall have to give in. He will not expect much, but he deserves all I could give him."

In after years, however, Nelly Shepherd learned that she could give her husband very true and earnest love; and the headmaster and mistress of the largest school at Wolverhampton are regarded by all who know them, and by none less than by Jack Simpson and his wife, as a perfectly happy couple.

It is ten years since Jack married Alice Merton, who had loved him for years before he asked her to be his wife. Jack is now part proprietor of the Vaughan pit, and is still its real manager, although he has a nominal manager under him. He cannot, however, be always on the spot, as he lives near Birmingham, and is one of the greatest authorities on mining, and the first consulting engineer, in the Black Country. At Mr. Brook's death he will be sole proprietor of the Vaughan, that gentleman having at Jack's marriage settled its reversion upon his wife.

Dinner is over, and he is sitting in the garden, surrounded by those he most cares for in the world. It is the 1st of June, a day upon which a small party always assembles at his house. By his side is his wife, and next to her are Harry Shepherd and Nelly. Between the ladies a warm friendship has sprung up of late years, while that between the three friends has never diminished in the slightest. On Jack's other hand sits an artist, bearing one of the most honoured names in England, whose health Jack always proposes at this dinner as "the founder of his fortune." Next to the artist sits Mr. Brook, and beyond him Mrs. Simpson's father, a permanent resident in the house now, but some years back a professor of mathematics in Birmingham. Playing in the garden are six children, two of whom call the young Simpsons cousins, although there is no blood relationship between them; and walking with them are an old couple, who live in the pretty cottage just opposite to the entrance of the grounds, and whom Jack Simpson still affectionately calls "dad" and "mother."

The End

Made in the USA
Las Vegas, NV
09 December 2024

76d980e0-9bbe-4bdd-9e49-be1d14004099R01